A BRUSH WITH LOVE

Tara Heavey was born and raised in London, and moved to Dublin aged twelve. A qualified solicitor, she practised law in Co. Kilkenny and Co. Waterford for five years before turning to writing full time. She is currently working on her second novel. She lives in Co. Kilkenny.

TARA HEAVEY

A BRUSH WITH LOVE

PAN BOOKS

First published 2003 by Tivoli, an imprint of Gill & Macmillan Ltd

This edition published 2004 by Pan Books
an imprint of Pan Macmillan Ltd
Pan Macmillan, 20 New Wharf Road, London N1 9RR
Basingstoke and Oxford
Associated companies throughout the world
www.panmacmillan.com

ISBN 0 330 41977 3

1 3 5 7 9 8 6 4 2

A CIP catalogue record for this book is available from
the British Library.

Printed and bound in Great Britain by
Mackays of Chatham plc, Chatham, Kent

I dedicate this book with love, to the memory of my grandmother, Winifred Cranston.

That we might all live such rich and joyous lives.

Acknowledgments

To all the team at Tivoli, who helped bring this book to fruition. A very special thanks goes to my editor, Alison Walsh. Firstly, for her vital creative input. Secondly, for giving me and my little book this amazing chance. It's all the more amazing to me since the sum total of my previous literary success comprised winning third prize in the Slate Quarries Festival poetry competition in Tullahought. (I think there may have been up to seventeen entrants.) Of course, I can admit to this now that the contract is safely signed.

To my agent, Faith O'Grady. Thank you for getting me this wonderful book deal. Also, thanks for all your great advice and for being so easy to talk to.

To my parents, Maureen and Tony, my brother Neal and to all my family for their continuous love and support. A special Hi to the Canadian and American Aunties.

To all my dear friends. For your excitement and encouragement and complete lack of begrudgery. You know who you are. A special thanks must go to MC for her unbridled enthusiasm and a big hello to all the Kilkenny girls. Remember, don't lend the book to anyone. Make them buy their own copies!

To Fran and Frank. Thank you for everything. Particularly for all the lovely dinners.

To all my former colleagues and workmates in the legal profession. Thank you for sharing the good times and the bad. I promise that if I write about you, you'll be so heavily disguised that even your own mothers wouldn't recognise you. (I don't need to remind you that for something to be libellous it has to be untrue.)

To Gerry Moran. Thank you for showing an interest in this book when nobody else did and for all your helpful editing work.

To Monty. Thank you for always being there and for your invaluable contribution to the text.

To every English teacher I've ever had. To the late Mrs Robinson for loving my Paddington Bear story when I was five years old and especially to Ms Mulcahy in Greendale Community School. I don't know if you're still teaching there, but I never really thanked you properly.

To you, dear reader. I hope you enjoy reading this book as much as I enjoyed writing it. If you do, there's plenty more where that came from! I hope we meet again soon.

Last but not least, To Rory. Thank you for being the first to read this book, even though I know that to you, a Volvo manual holds more appeal. Thank God you drew my attention to a certain phrase which couldn't possibly be included. I think we both know which one I'm talking about. Thanks also for putting up with all my tantrums and hissy fits which I now intend to get away with by claiming to be an 'artist'.

Chapter One

I was born two weeks late. I'd never really managed to catch up. I was late for work that Monday morning in mid-December. It was one of those extra crisp, cold, bright mornings that catch your breath, making you feel as if you've brushed your internal organs, as well as your teeth, with extra minty toothpaste.

I must admit that I was pretty excited. Excitement wasn't my natural state while struggling into work of a Monday morning. Not that I disliked my job exactly. The law firm where I worked may not have been one of the biggest in Dublin, but it was certainly one of the most posh. I often had to answer the phone to quite famous names – who knew which fat-cat businessman or cheesy TV celeb the senior partner would be sailing with this week?

But this morning I had a particular reason to be happy. This morning James was coming in. Yes, my current reason for living would be buzzed through the Georgian door at 10.30 a.m. precisely (James was never late), and I would be waiting for him with my perfectly polished fingernails poised above my keyboard as he dictated to me in his rich, deep voice.

Perhaps he'd stand behind me like last time, hand leaning against the back of the chair, breath hot and moist against the back of my neck. He'd pretend to peer closely at the words I was typing on the screen, all the while staring

2

down the front of my blouse. I felt weak just thinking about it.

I was sure that today would be the day that he would finally ask me out. I was wearing my new red jacket (chic – directional – cost me half a week's salary) just in case he asked me to go to lunch with him. James wouldn't lunch in any old place. It would be somewhere 'nice', as my mother would say. Some place with proper professional waiters and mint toothpicks. In fact, the kind of place where the waiters would pick your teeth for you if you wanted them to.

I ran up the steps to the front door. I could have been walking into any solicitor's office in Dublin, with its old-fashioned dimly lit reception area. The only feature distinguishing the reception of Boland, Sharpe & Co. from most other firms is the array of expensive and tasteful paintings scattered around the walls. None of your usual dodgy prints of the city, or caricatures of cantankerous looking judges whose paunches and bulbous noses aren't all that far removed from reality.

My euphoria dissolved as I reached the paper bomb-site, otherwise known as my desk. I'd forgotten the appalling state I'd left it in on Friday evening at 5.29 p.m. It wasn't that the urgent pile was so big. It was just that the urgent pile, the not-so-urgent pile and the fuck-it-I'll-do-it-tomorrow-or-maybe-some-time-next-year pile had merged into a kind of paper Mount Everest. If I ever got to the bottom of it, I'd probably find Lord Lucan – or perhaps Shergar.

I decided that the only remedy for the sinking feeling that I was beginning to experience was a huge mug of steaming black coffee.

The canteen was like a grisly scene from a war film. Casualties from the weekend sat huddled miserably around the two wobbly formica-topped tables, clutching mugs of hot, dark liquid or holding fags in trembling fingers. A few pathetic forms had to be prodded to ensure that they were still alive.

It was Monday morning and it was not a pretty sight.

I identified one of the creatures as Declan. Declan was one of the few apprentice solicitors who treated me and the other secretaries with a modicum of friendliness and respect – and not

4

just when he needed an urgent tape typed up. Because of this he was treated with the contempt he truly deserved.

'I hope you enjoyed getting yourself into that state,' I said, poking him in the arm as I spoke to make sure that he was conscious. He jumped, having previously been unaware of my presence in the room.

'Fuck off, Fern,' he croaked as he attempted the fruitless task of trying to focus his bloodshot eyes and recall his whereabouts all at once. 'I was out last night.'

'No kidding. Anyway, never mind that. James is coming in today.'

'Who the fuck is James?'

'You know – James Carver – the barrister. He's working on the Murphy case with Julie.'

Julie was my boss. In my humble opinion (and they didn't come much more humble than mine), she had single-handedly invented the concept of the ruthless, neurotic, career woman. Her only other purpose in life was to put me down to make herself feel better. It seemed to work very well for her. Me? I was just glad to be of help.

'I'd watch Carver if I were you. He's not as charming as he'd like to make out. Besides, I don't think you're his type.'

He must have seen my face fall several hundred feet because, in a rare moment of altruism, he finally came to and scrambled desperately to take back what he had just said.

'I . . . I didn't mean that – I'm just knackered. He just doesn't deserve you, that's all.'

He doesn't deserve you: male-speak for you're a fat, ugly cow and he wouldn't piss on you if you were on fire. It was too late anyway. My confidence had already plummeted to its usual depth of twenty thousand leagues under sea level.

'Let's go out somewhere for lunch today – you pick the place,' he continued, in his feeble attempt to make amends. I nodded vaguely, the vision of my luncheon date with James being relegated to the junk room of my mind, along with all my other hopes and dreams. I was aware of Declan peering uncertainly into my face, realising vaguely that he might have hurt me but not comprehending that he had cut me right to the quick. Still, at least he cared.

I supposed he was quite attractive really. But he was only an apprentice and it would be another two years before he qualified. That meant that he had no money, no car and two crap suits. Even so, his prospects were quite good . . .

Back at the desk, things weren't going all that great. I had managed to shift two pieces of paper off the great EU paper mountain by the time my boss made an appearance. Not that she hadn't been working since 7.30 a.m. as per usual, but she'd been out having a power breakfast at the Gresham Hotel. It seemed that her bionic Weetabix hadn't improved her humour. She remained the grumpy old bitch that she had been on Friday evening.

'Fern – where's the latest medical report in the Murphy case?' she barked as she strode purposefully across the office. Julie never walked. She strode purposefully everywhere. I, on the other hand, gave my well-known impression of a hermit crab as I scuttled across to the 'M' section of the filing cabinet to root out the report. With her immaculately coiffed hair-do, which usually resembled a blonde cardboard box, and her shoulder-padded designer suits (I wished I had the guts to tell her that the Eighties were over), not to mention her snottier-than-thou attitude, Julie frightened the shite out of me. I longed to be just like her.

Her ambition was legendary. She had been an associate for ten years and customarily worked from 7.30 a.m. to 9 p.m. in her constant quest to be made a partner. There had never been a female partner in the one-hundred odd years of Boland, Sharpe & Co. There were seven partners, all male, one of them younger than Julie. There were two main reasons for this. One: she hadn't had the foresight to attend an all-male boarding school; and two: she didn't have the time to play golf.

She had a husband, a daughter and a nanny on weekdays. The husband was a senior partner in one of the biggest law firms in Dublin, a man rumoured to be so boring as to make people fall asleep head-first into their desserts at dinner parties – that's if he didn't fall asleep into his first. The daughter had better be a judge, politician or brain surgeon – or else.

Still, it was hard to feel sorry for Julie. I knocked tentatively at her office door, which led in from mine, and entered her lair, placing the report gingerly on the corner of her desk, reluctant to disturb the military-style precision of its layout.

'What time is James Carver coming in?' She peered up at me over her designer lenses.

'Half past ten.' I smiled uncertainly at her as I backed out of the room, awkwardly reaching out for the door-knob behind me. I watched her watching me with a strange mixture of curiosity and contempt on her face. She didn't return my smile.

'Make sure you send him in to me straight away.'

I nodded as I hastily made my retreat, breathing easier as I made it to the other side of the door. A thrill of anticipation rose through my body as I thought about James's arrival. It fell just as quickly when I remembered Declan's blunt words and gloomily came back down to earth with a bump.

I was finding it increasingly difficult to concentrate on the document that I was meant to be typing, as I glanced for the umpteenth time at the clock. 10.28 a.m. The room suddenly felt hot and cloying. I would have taken off my jacket if it hadn't cost me a small fortune. And besides, it was red – the colour of passion and confidence. I needed all the help I could get.

The phone rang and I leapt out of my seat and grabbed the receiver in one swift movement.

'James Carver to see Julie.' The receptionist's bored tones sounded more interested than usual.

'Er, thanks. Send him up.'

Oh my God, oh my God! I began jittering around the room, knocking over anything that wasn't nailed down and creating general havoc and mayhem. I ran over to the mirror as fast as my little legs could carry me and ineffectually ruffled my hair, making it look exactly the same as before, if not worse. I rooted around in my make-up bag, looking for something – anything – to make me look better – feel better – feel worthy of James Carver. I had just managed to empty the contents of my bag all over the floor when he made his entrance. He closed the door neatly and tightly behind him.

Then he smiled deep into the pit of my stomach. (Or was it somewhere lower?)

'Hello, Fern.'

'Hi!' My voice morphed into an almost inaudible whisper as I shuffled awkwardly from one foot to the other, trying to push a lipstick under the desk with my heel.

'You look wonderful today.'

Again the smile. I was transfixed. I tried to return it but my upper lip seemed to stick to the top of my teeth in a kind of grimace.

The door to the inner sanctum was flung wide open and out came Julie.

'James! Fabulous to see you!'

There was nothing more nauseating then watching Julie gush. It was so out of character. She clasped his hands greedily between her own and kissed the air on either side of his cheeks. She herded him possessively into her office, pausing only to give me a customary glare as she brushed past me. I must have wiped out the entire population of a small African village in a previous life to have deserved that woman.

For the next half-hour I had to endure the sound of Julie's intermittent, muffled cackling coming from behind the door. What were they up to in there? I had visions of Julie sitting perched on the edge of her mahogany desk, legs crossed jauntily, skirt riding up against the top of her thighs. There she was, sticking out her chest, bold as brass, throwing back her head and laughing with abandon at one of James's witticisms. I was just beginning to work myself up into a really satisfying frenzy about the injustice of it all when I was interrupted by the internal phone. It was Julie.

'Come in, please, Fern.'

I straightened my jacket and in I went, prepared for the worst. To my surprise, Julie was sitting sedately behind her desk, her clothes perfectly in order. James was seated at a respectable distance away at the far side of the desk, leaning back into a leather-bound chair, in a relaxed and comfortable fashion.

'James would like you to do some typing for him, please, Fern.'

She only ever used the word 'please' when someone else was around. Not that I cared right at that moment. I was aware only of the strange tightening sensation in my chest and throat. Nodding, I left the room, acutely aware of James's large form shadowing me. Please God, make him like me. Make him like me. Make him like me.

It was my new mantra.

'Well then. Where shall we start?' He settled down beside me, looking too big for the chair, his hands clasped loosely between his splayed knees.

'How about the top button of my blouse and you can work your way down?' Of course, I didn't actually say this – I only thought it. I had always wanted to be the kind of girl (or woman – was I a woman yet? I was twenty-six. Did I qualify?) who could come out with something like that when the moment arose – bold and sexy – not letting my gaze drop – staring at the lucky man knowingly – promising all manner of sexual delights that I could actually deliver.

Unfortunately reality had a different scenario in mind, spoiling my fun as usual. I sat crouched over my keyboard, my face as red as my jacket, barely daring to look at James, concentrating instead on preventing my fingers from trembling.

'Look at me, Fern.' His voice was soft, authoritative. Unfortunately for me, I did. And that was really it. The chocolate in his eyes melted into mine as the corners of his mouth tilted upwards, causing delicious creases to form on either side of his lips. I felt as if he were pulling me towards him with an invisible thread. To which part of my body that thread was attached, I wouldn't like to say.

'Would you like to come out with me tonight?'

I beg your pardon? What – me?! Was there someone else in the room?

He must be some kind of a pervert. Or maybe he was just playing with me. I was afraid to answer, just in case.

'What's wrong? Cat got your tongue?'

No – but I wish you had! – I thought – not said – again.

'Okay.' I was just about able to manage. I was afraid to say anything else in case I revealed the true enormity of my gratitude and amazement.

'Great,' he said grinning easily.

I couldn't help getting the strange feeling that he hadn't actually been waiting for my response but had just been going through the formalities. To be brutally honest, I didn't care if he saw me as a foregone conclusion. That's exactly what I was, after all. The mere fact that he had asked me out was such a longed-for miracle that it was more than enough.

What glory! The great James Carver wanted to go out with me. Me! Of all people. I almost (almost) willed him to leave so that I could shout my news from the rooftops – or at least out loud in the privacy of Declan's office.

God knows what gobbledy-gook I typed that morning. I never knew because he never complained.

Chapter Two

'And what did you say?'

'Are you out of your mind? I said yes, of course. When a man like James asks a girl like me out for dinner, I'm hardly going to claim to be washing my hair.'

Declan pushed his vegetarian goulash around the plate as if he were chasing it with his fork. After a long pause he looked up at me, his face serious.

'I don't think you should go.'

I laughed, almost hysterically. 'What? You think I should keep my options open, in case I get a call from Brad Pitt?! Get real, Declan.

'It's just that I've heard stuff about him.'

'What kind of stuff?'

'You know – stuff!'

'No, I don't know.'

'Just guys' talk down the rugby club. He has what you'd call a "reputation" when it comes to the ladies.'

I tried not to laugh. He could be such an old woman sometimes.

'The ladies! I should be safe then.'

'Honestly, Fern, I don't think he's suitable for you.'

'Suitable! What are you, my mother?'

'Well, don't say I didn't warn you.' Declan sounded annoyed and avoided eye contact for the next few minutes.

It was the kind of restaurant that sprinkled seed over everything that it served. Sunflower seed, caraway seed, birdseed, who knew? It was designed to give the restaurant a vegetarian, healthy-type ambience – not a burger or chip in sight. I loved the place. Declan hated it and moaned from the moment he learned of the proposed destination. He had another reason for being morose. The girl in accounts had ignored him again. And – worse still – someone had told her that he liked her.

'And she was my number one too.'

'Your what?'

'My number one – in the firm.'

'Number one what?'

'Girl.'

How sad – that some men had to treat women as if they were in the Premier League. I nastily hoped that the girl would continue to ignore him. Not to mention humiliate him in some way. Actually, the real reason I was annoyed was that I wasn't on top of his list. I doubted that I even made the top ten (and there were only nine women below the age of sixty in the office – and one of them was Julie). Anyway, James didn't appear to think that there was anything wrong with me and you would never catch him doing anything as immature and sexist as arranging women into lists in accordance with their attractiveness. James was a gentleman. I glowed inside at the thought that a barrister – and a good-looking one at that – would deign to go out with the likes of me. What a catch! He had 'good catch' written all over him in 24-carat gold lettering.

'So where's the flash git taking you, then? McDonald's?'

'Jealousy will get you nowhere. He's taking me to Pegasus if you must know.'

I could tell that Declan was seriously impressed. Pegasus was one of the hottest eateries in town – all modern, arty décor and seven-foot-tall waitresses.

'That's if they let you in.' He was never one to let his admiration show for long.

'Anyway, it looks like a space-age toilet, if you ask me.'

'No one's asking you, are they?'

The rest of the lunchtime conversation went something like this:

'So I said to Tom, "How do you expect me to work surrounded by all those women nattering and gossiping all day long . . . " Fern – are you listening to me?'

'Hmmm?' My glazed stare hovered some place over the top of Declan's right shoulder as I mentally sifted through my extensive (not) wardrobe to try to decide if I had anything decent enough to wear that night.

'Of course I'm listening to you,' I said indignantly, jolting myself back to reality, which wasn't my favourite place to be at the best of times.

'Well, it doesn't look like it. Anyway, do you know what he had the cheek to tell me? Fern . . . Fern . . . Oh, this is a waste of time. You're a million miles away. I'll leave you to it. I have to pick up Cyril's dry-cleaning, and the food here is shite anyway. I'd better buy a Mars bar or my stomach will be digesting itself all afternoon.'

I waved absent-mindedly and barely registered the scrape of his chair before turning my thoughts back to James. I was in the furry pink fantasy room of my mind – the room in which I made head-turning entrances in glamorous evening gowns, causing grown men to weep and drool in my presence. Sometimes I wore a tight, red dress and writhed on top of a grand piano, all sultry and Michelle Pfeifferesque. Other times I had to shake off the small army of hunks that clung to my Pretty-Polly encased legs.

Today I was gliding gracefully towards our table in Pegasus, sporting a sparkly little black number, smiling confidently at James who sat in open-mouthed adoration.

Yes – I was indeed the undisputed crowned queen of escapism.

I wanted to stay in the pink fantasy room of my mind forever but it was time to go back to work – and I use the term loosely. I spent what was left of the afternoon daydreaming, interrupted only by flurries of furious typing activity every time Julie came into the room. I willed her to get lost and leave me to concentrate on the more important task to hand. I even put a curse on her but by 3 p.m. she was still very much alive and all her limbs appeared to be present and correct.

I had arranged to leave work early and I was out of that door like a hot snot, to get ready for my date. My destination? The beauty salon. My mission? The works!

'What treatments are you having done?' The beautician (sorry – beauty consultant) looked me up and down.

'The one that makes you lose two stone in an hour and transforms you into a totally different person.' I laughed at my own joke, which was just as well really because she certainly didn't. I was suitably chastened.

'Half-leg and bikini wax please,' I whispered humbly. I now knew my place in the great beauty-salon scheme of things.

The waxing went fine. As soon as the beauty consultant had released herself from the death grip (her head, my knees), I paid my money and I left. Then I hit the shops. An hour later, the shops hit me, along with desperation and panic. There was nothing suitable in the shops – nothing in the whole of Dublin! I couldn't believe it. The entire membership of The Rag Trade was ganging up on me. And then I saw it – 'That dress'. A short, figure-hugging kimono-style dress – silver satin material embossed with dark grey flowers. It fit me like a dream. My happiness knew no bounds. In fact, it was about to be charged with trespassing.

I rushed home and began the great onslaught on my body. Home was a three-bedroom semi in the suburbs. Lower middle class with aspirations – diamond-leaded glass windows and hanging baskets. Fortunately, no family members were around to cramp my style.

The bathroom. My haven. Here I could escape the trials and tribulations of my humdrum existence and become myself. No one to criticise me – unless you counted myself of course, berating the imperfections of my reflection in the mirror.

Checklist:

1. Skin on body: scrub and exfoliate
2. Hair on head: wash and condition
3. Upper thighs: body-brush
4. Under-arm hair: shave
5. Skin on body (again): drench in fragrant body lotion and douse with matching talc.
6. Course, dark, wild-woman-of-Borneo hair on upper lip: bleach
7. Eyebrows: pluck
8. Eyelashes: comb and curl
   (Steps 7 and 8 to be carried out while waiting for skin on upper lip to lose red,

bloated appearance. Could have waited whole life for body to lose bloated appearance but dinner date scheduled for 8 p.m. sharp)

9. Facial skin: cleanse, tone and moisturise
10. Body: encase in lacy black underwear (not that I ever planned to sleep with anyone on the first date, you understand) and 'That Dress'
11. Feet: encase in black strappy sandals
12. Face: plaster in make-up
13. Hair: blow-dry to perfection.

I don't think I forgot anything.

I was a new woman – the desired result. Pity I was still the same old me on the inside.

I arrived at 8.04 p.m. (not so early as to appear desperate and not so late as to irritate him). James was already there when I arrived. The relief! I felt like a bride who hadn't been jilted on her wedding day. He already had several waitresses fluttering around him.

'Fern!' He was acting as if he was delighted to see me. It was a good start. He came over to greet me, taking my hands in his and bending to kiss me on my hot cheek. The imprint of his lips seemed to sizzle into my skin. I felt like a calf that had been branded. We turned to enter the main part of the restaurant, his large hand burning a hole in the small of my back.

The waitress fixed me with an icy-blue glare as she viciously whipped the two menus out of their holder.

'Table for two?' she spat. Never had so much animosity been conveyed in such a simple phrase. I was thrilled skinny (well maybe not thrilled skinny – thrilled pear-shaped perhaps). She was jealous! I wasn't used to other women being jealous of me, and it was a heady experience.

We followed her through the restaurant which was filled with couples dining in an intimate candle-lit kind of a way. The hostess sashayed ahead of us. I was afraid that her bum would swivel right off her upper body if we didn't reach our table soon. Surely there was really no need for such an elaborate hip movement. She glanced behind at James and flashed him a meaningful look, obviously checking that he was checking out her assets. She wasn't disappointed.

The table was beautifully positioned in a quiet corner, not too cramped. This was a novelty for me. I was accustomed to being seated beside the kitchen doors, downwind of the Gents. Our waitress slammed my menu down in front of me, then turned her platinum smile onto James, evidently assuming that the colour of his credit card would match her teeth.

'Wine list, sir?' Her voice was breathy and fragile. Then she reluctantly turned to me.

'Today's specials are . . . ' She spoke like a particularly unfriendly robot. Honestly, it was like Jeckyll and Hyde.

'So, Fern.' Our orders had been taken and James had managed to tear his eyes away from the waitress's ass and back to me. 'Tell me about yourself.'

Oh my God! My whole being went into total panic. I just hate that. Being pushed into the spotlight. Forced to talk about myself and reveal to the whole world what an uninteresting fool I actually am. I never know what is expected of me. Should I start from the beginning – place of birth, weight (7 pounds – it has been rising

26

alarmingly ever since), mother's post-natal depression? Or did he want a run-down of my hobbies and interests? Vital statistics perhaps? With or without roll-on and Wonderbra?

James smiled expectantly at me for what seemed like a long stretch of eternity, but was probably only a couple of seconds, as I squirmed and fidgeted in my chair and gave him my rabbit-startled-in-headlights look. But luckily James came to the rescue, as he loved to talk about himself. He proceeded to do precisely this for the rest of the evening. My hero! We were perfectly matched really. I'm such a good listener. I had years of practice of looking attentive under my belt. No better woman.

'So, I said to the judge, "Your Honour, I would ask you to take into account my client's horrific family background. He grew up with no mother, the youngest of eight siblings and had to endure poverty, hardship and cruelty all his life . . . "' James was recounting a closing speech that he had delivered a few days before. Had he won the case? Of course he had. He had succeeded admirably in getting the guilty rapist off the hook. I was a little shocked.

'You don't think that was a bit immoral, do you?' I asked him hesitantly. He laughed indulgently at me.

'Not at all. I'm just doing my job. And everybody has the right to legal representation – even rapists and serial killers.' He spoke like a teacher explaining something to a slow but well-meaning child – gentle but firm, amused at my ignorance.

When he had finally run out of breath, he fixed me with his dark-brown gaze.

'So, what do you do when you're not being a legal secretary?'

Oh no.

'Well . . . I like art,' I said eventually.

'The arty type, eh? I have some friends who are into that kind of scene. We're all going to an exhibition on Thursday evening – promising young Irish artists or something like that. Why don't you come along.'

My heart soared. He wanted to see me again!

We spent the rest of the meal discussing his main love – golf. He kindly explained to me the finer points of the game which I had previously failed to grasp. I was delighted. While he was talking, it took the pressure off me to say anything and it gave me plenty of time and opportunity to look at him.

He really was a stunning-looking man. His hair was thick and black. The cut was conservative but not unfashionable. His eyes were just beautiful – deep-set, molten-brown and fringed with long, inky-black lashes. His bone-structure was superb, giving him a vaguely aristocratic air. When he smiled, he showed off an expensive-looking set of even, white teeth. He was so sexy. Even the mole on his cheek was sexy. And he was so clever.

By the time our schizophrenic waitress arrived with the bill, it was quite late. James had so much to say. He walked me to the nearest taxi rank. When my cab arrived, James looked me deep in the eyes and brought his face down towards mine. I was afraid to breathe. The kiss landed softly on my forehead.

'I'll call you on Thursday to arrange about the exhibition.' I was torn between disappointment that he had not attempted to kiss me properly and excitement that he wanted to see me again.

The excitement won.

Chapter Three

I suppose at this point I should tell you a little bit about myself. Well, as you already know, I am a legal secretary. I was twenty-six at this time.

Looks: hair – short and dark with mahogany highlights – I blended in with the office furniture. Eyes: green. The shade and depth of the green at any particular time is dependent on the colour of my clothes and my current pupil size/ state of arousal. I am medium height, medium build. My heart tells me that I am as fat as a fool but in my rare moments of sanity, my head tells me that I am actually a normal size and weight. In other words, I am nothing to write home about but I'm not dog-sick ugly either. Six out of ten perhaps. What an eligible, good-looking barrister saw in me was anybody's guess.

Personality: under-confidence ranks high on the list of personality traits – but you've already worked that much out for yourself. On the plus side, I've been told that I can be good fun – when I forget to be shy of course. Oh yes, I forgot to mention, kind to children and old people. Basically, I'm a sap.

But there is this one thing that I like to hug into my chest and clutch like a security blanket around my heart: I love to paint. Apart from clothes, art materials are what I spend my money on. In the privacy of my room at night I used to sketch and paint myself into oblivion. One day, I thought, I might even consider showing a non-family member one of my creations. But I didn't trust anyone enough. It seemed like handing over my soul on a platter to be poked, prodded, torn asunder and ruined forever. I couldn't do it. When it came right down to it, I just didn't trust myself enough.

But back to the art exhibition. I won't bore you with the tedium of Tuesday, Wednesday and Thursday of that week. A day that didn't involve James in some shape or form was meaningless to me. Come Thursday evening and I was at home with my family. We were all in the TV room. Well, its official title is the sitting room but since the main focus is the television – TV room it is. My father was sitting in his chair, one eye on the news and one eye on the newspaper that was hiding his face. My elder sister, Sasha – twenty-nine–painful – was leafing through a glossy magazine (my magazine!) in the corner. My mother was standing at the ironing board, working her way methodically through a pile of tea-towels, pillow-cases and handkerchiefs. She was staring into space. Who knew what she was looking at?

My parents weren't getting on too well. In fact, that's an understatement. They were at the stage where they only spoke to each other out of necessity.

'Bill, do you need anything else ironed?' My father continued to stare into his newspaper, oblivious.

'Bill!' Still nothing. Angrily and noisily, my mother pulled the plug of the iron out of the wall and put up the ironing board. The scraping and clattering seemed to register to my father on some level. He put down the newspaper and looked at her.

'Any chance of a cup of tea, Helen?'

Wordlessly my mother went out to the hall. Through the crack in the door, I watched her take her coat from where it hung on the end of the stairs, put it on and exit quickly through the front door. Mother has left the building.

'Sasha, be a pet and make your old Da a cup of tea.'

'Make it yourself.' Sasha didn't even look up from her magazine.

'Fern? Your old man is parched.'

'Sorry, Dad. I'm going out and I'm running late.'

My father heaved himself up out of his chair and grumbled his way into the kitchen.

'Honest to God, you work hard for your family all your life, struggling to put food on the table and what do you get in return? Nothing. Not even a miserable cup of tea. I ask you. I never would have dared speak to my father like that.'

Sasha looked up and shouted in after him. 'Your father was a violent, misogynistic old sod and you all hated him.'

'At least we had respect.'

'That was fear, not respect. Besides, respect is something you have to earn.'

He didn't reply but continued to grumble under his breath, loud enough for us to hear.

'Three women. I put up with three women all day long and I can't even get a decent cup of tea out of any of them. Not one of them! Is it too much to ask?' And on he went.

Little scenarios like this had become all too common in the Fennelly household. When my parents were in the same room together – hold on, they were never in the same room together, unless Sasha or I were there – and when you were in the room with them, you were joined by a terrible presence – something akin to tension and oppression. Like you couldn't get comfortable no matter what seat you sat in.

The only one who seemed oblivious to it all was Sasha. I believe 'switched off' is the term I'm looking for. She was living at home temporarily while she saved enough for the deposit for a house. Her air was as detached as the house that she was planning to buy. She might as well have been a lodger. I envied her for it.

Mam and Dad sensed her indifference and left her alone. It was me they turned to as a go between:

'Fern, ask your father if he'll be home for his dinner tonight.'

'Fern, what does your mother want for Christmas? Will I just get her another bottle of that perfume she likes. What do you call it again?'

'Fern. Did your father ask you what I want for Christmas? Whatever you do, don't let him buy me another bottle of that godawful perfume. Tell him I need a new dressing-gown. But don't let him choose it himself. His taste is terrible. You pick it for him. You know what I like.'

'Fern, did your mother leave out any clean shirts for me?'

'Fern, I hope your father doesn't expect us all to go to his stuck-up sister's for Christmas drinks again this year. Has he said anything to you about it?'

And on and on.

That's why it was such a relief to go up to my room to get ready for my date. Just shut the door, turn my stereo up as loud as I dared and pretend it wasn't happening.

James was a catch.

He was a babe.

But he was more than that.

He was a distraction.

I chose black. To wear, that is. You may think I was matching my clothes to the atmosphere in the house. Actually, I was just trying to make my bum and hips look slimmer. I was pleased with the result, even though I say so myself – and I usually don't.

Sasha, on the other hand, never has any qualms about voicing her opinion.

'You're never wearing *that*?!' Her eyebrows disappeared and her upper lip curled dangerously.

'Well, obviously I am.' I braced myself for the inevitable.

'Where are you going anyway, all done up like a dog's dinner?'

'An art exhibition'

She snorted unattractively. 'What's wrong? Run out of lame chick flicks to go see?'

Sasha only ever watched films with subtitles. I knew that she was only trying to goad me but I couldn't help rising to the bait.

'What's wrong with this outfit?'

'I would have thought it would be obvious to someone with an arse the size of yours. I mean, I know black is meant to be slimming but if it's a miracle you're after, Fern, I'd start praying to St Jude pretty sharpish.'

As I left the house, I could hear her loudly humming a Divine Comedy song. You know the one about how hard it is to get by when your arse is the size of a small country . . .

'Fern!' He was waiting for me again, even though I arrived at three minutes before the agreed time. I could see that I was going to have to be a very early bird indeed to catch James Carver's worm.

I was feeling incredibly nervous. Not only did I have James to deal with, but I had to contend with his friends too. I was flattered and quite frankly amazed that he had even considered introducing me to 'his type' of people. I would have thought he'd have preferred to meet in the kind of out-of-the-way place where married men conducted sordid affairs with their mistresses. Or maybe he wanted to introduce me as a cameo role. An interesting five-minute novelty act – a filler-in. Anyway, I needed a drink.

I snatched a glass of red (the colour of passion and confidence – I needed all the help I could get) off the tray of the first waitress who passed my way. I imagined she smiled at me sympathetically, sensing that I was way out of my depth. I knocked a large mouthful down my throat where it was met by an upcoming wave of panic and nausea. I had to get out of there. Who was I trying to fool?

James turned to me, smiling, holding out a glass of wine.

'For you – oh, you already have one. That was quick work.'

Oh God! What was he implying? That I was some sort of raving alcoholic who couldn't be in a room for two minutes without having to resort to alcohol to sustain herself?

'I can see I'm going to have to be fast to keep up with you.' He snaked his arm around my waist and squeezed my hip. It felt so nice that I even forgot to pull in my stomach muscles. Was the warm feeling in my nether regions caused by the pressure of his palm or was the wine beginning to take effect?

'Hello, James.'

There she was. A vision in white and blonde. Standing blatantly in front of James as if for all the world he didn't have his sinewy arm wrapped around a raven-haired vixen (I'm talking about myself, in case you're confused. I told you the wine was beginning to take effect).

'Hi, Bronwyn.'

His smile was wasted on her. She was already busy looking me up and down. I could tell she liked what she saw. In other words, she didn't like what she saw, if you get my drift. She assumed a more confident stance as she tossed back her mane of blonde corkscrew curls (natural, I'm afraid) and turned her slanting blue gaze onto James's brown.

Then she smiled.

God – where did these people get their teeth? Harrods?

'We're all over here. Come and join us'. Her accent immediately revealed what part of the city she hailed from – not a neighbourhood anywhere near mine. She glided back across the room that she so obviously owned. She was beautiful. What a bitch! Now, I know what you're thinking – I was jealous. But no – I could tell she was definitely a bitch. James tightened his grip around my waist (it had loosened somewhat when Bronwyn had come over) and led me over to the group of people that Bronwyn had joined. I managed to gulp down two more mouthfuls of wine on the way over. I don't think anyone noticed.

Chapter Four

'Everyone, this is Fern. Fern, meet Zara, Leonard, Phil and Bronwyn – whom you've already met.'

They all looked at me. I looked at my shoes.

'So, Fern – what do you do?' This from my new friend, Bronwyn.

'I'm a legal secretary.'

'Oh – so not just a secretary then.' She smiled sweetly. Told you she was a bitch.

'Which firm?' This from Phil – a small plain-looking person. I took to him immediately.

'Boland, Sharpe & Co.'

'Oh, do you know Lydia Boland?'

Did I what? Perhaps the most painful apprentice solicitor in the office. The size of her tits was matched only by that of her ego. She was a niece of the senior partner.

'Yes, I do.'

'Lovely girl.' Phil beamed, obviously recalling the heaving bosom. I nodded weakly. Gone was my potential ally. My boobs were tiny in comparison.

Luckily they soon lost interest in me and began to chat amongst themselves. This, of course, gave me a wonderful chance to observe them all. I'm a great observer.

While Bronwyn was tall, blonde and vivacious, Zara was petite, dark and mysterious. Together they catered for all male tastes. A bit like a compact version of the Spice Girls really. I vaguely wondered if they'd let me hang around with them if I dyed my hair red. Not that I felt I was a threat to them.

Leonard – not Len – had such a huge plum in his mouth that it was an effort to understand him. He had the air of somebody who had just stepped off the shooting field. He stood with his hands thrust deep into his pockets and kept throwing back his head and laughing very loudly at everything Phil said. It was clear that Phil's role in the group was that of 'the entertainer'. They put up with his unglamorous appearance because he made them laugh. Better keep those jokes coming, Phil!

I was rescued from feeling like a spare part by the gallery owner's introductory speech. It was long, rambling and boring, which was great because I didn't have to make small talk with anyone for ages. Then we were let loose on the paintings. Or to mingle or network as we saw fit.

Mingling and networking – two concepts that I had never quite got the hang of:

'To mingle': Step 1 – introduce yourself to a complete stranger whom you consider to look socially interesting. Step 2 – make polite and scintillating conversation for not more than ten minutes, making sure not to touch on any topics that could be considered deep or meaningful. Step 3 – during conversation, keep looking over person's shoulder to locate more interesting subject to talk to. Step 4 – when allotted ten minutes are up, excuse yourself politely, even if the person is in mid-sentence, leaving them in no doubt that you've got what you wanted out of them and that you've found someone else you'd rather talk to. The aim: to have as many meaningless conversations with as many people as possible by the end of the night.

'To network': Networking is mingling's close relative. Step 1 – inveigle yourself into having a conversation with someone whom you believe could be beneficial to your career. Step 2 – completely ignore the following: losers, those on the lower rungs of their professions, non-professionals, the unemployed, people who are 'working on their music' or 'currently writing a novel'. To talk to any of the above is a major networking *faux-pas*. To be stuck with one of these people is a veritable social disaster. Step 3 – talk to 'beneficial-to-career' person for not more than twenty minutes – twenty-five if they happen to be a managing director or own a yacht, all the while skilfully picking out a more influential person in the crowd to network with next. Step 4 – when given time is up, interrupt, hand person your business card and repeat process until evening is at an end and/or all your cards have been used up, whichever is the earlier.

In either of the above practices, shallowness and insincerity are major assets.

I noticed that Bronwyn and Zara were both pretty damn proficient – Bronwyn perhaps having the edge in the networking department and Zara being the more impressive mingler. I supposed they'd both had lessons in the Swiss Finishing School they had attended. (Timetable for Monday: 9 a.m. – flower arranging; 10 a.m. – *cordon bleu* cookery class; 11 a.m. – coffee break; 11.30 a.m. – How to be the perfect hostess; 12.30 a.m. – The art of mingling; 1.30 p.m. – luncheon; 2.30 p.m. – How to set a perfect table – today's lesson: napkin folding; 3.30 p.m. – networking – on one's own and on one's husband's behalf;

4.30 p.m. – How to get out of the back seat of a Limo without showing your knickers; 5.30 p.m. – How to have sex with an elderly billionaire without getting sick.

How I envied them their finesse!

I rode pillion to James most of the evening. To his credit, he had at least a vague interest in the work. We fought our way through the hordes of long-haired, cravat-wearing men and middle-aged, over-made-up women saying things like 'progressive' and 'wonderful use of colour and form'.

We stood together in front of a particular painting. It was a beautiful landscape, less abstract then many of the other paintings. The signature was illegible. It was similar to my own style, or at least to what I aspired to.

'Do you like it?' asked James

'Yes, It's amazing'

'A bit bland if you ask me. Don't think much of the colours,' he boomed in his massive barrister's voice. I silently wished he had a volume control button. The artist was probably mingling in the crowd as we spoke.

'Mr Carver! An unexpected pleasure.'

Oh, God – no. It was the senior partner – Cyril Boland. If there was one thing worse than meeting your boss on a night out, it was meeting your boss on a night out when he didn't even recognise you. He nodded vaguely in my direction, perhaps assuming that I was some floozie of James's to whom he'd been introduced at some other highfalutin function. Perhaps he knew me, perhaps he didn't. Maybe he just didn't give a shit.

'So, are you here to buy or look?'

'Just looking, Cyril (first name terms!) And you?'

'Oh – hoping to add a few to my collection. Some interesting new artists showing here. Actually, I've just bought this one. He gestured to the landscape in front of us.

'Really! Great choice. I was just saying how much I liked it. Wonderful use of colour, don't you think?'

'Couldn't agree more, couldn't agree more . . . How's your Dad by the way?'

Cyril and James's father, Judge Carver, were bosom buddies who regularly golfed, sailed and dined together.

After what seemed like an interminable conversation – sport mainly – Cyril went off to bore some other poor unfortunate. He gave me a funny look as he left, obviously trying to place me. Try your own reception area, you baldy-headed bastard!

I was dragged around the remaining works of art in a matter of minutes.

'Let's get another drink.'

Couldn't argue with that. We were joined by the others back at the makeshift bar. I didn't mind so much now that the vino collapso had started to course its wicked way through my veins. James had been handing me glasses at a rate of knots. He was looking at me intently, his eyes serious, as if he was trying to work out the complexities of a particularly difficult case. I smiled happily back at him and squeezed his arm. I felt very content. Even Bronwyn's frosty glares couldn't phase me. He handed me another glass of wine.

I balanced unsteadily at the edge of the conversation, vaguely comprehending, taking in snippets here and there. Increasingly I had the sensation that everyone was behind one of those false windows that you see in police stations in the movies. I could see them but they couldn't see me. Voices were muffled.

'Let's go.' James's voice was hot and moist against my ear.

'Okay.'

I allowed him to guide my arms clumsily into my coat sleeves and bundle me out into the night. The air felt shockingly chill against my cheeks. It momentarily revived me and then had the effect of driving the alcohol deeper into my body.

'What would you like to do now?' James looked at me hard.

'I don't mind.' I smiled dreamily, enjoying the sensation of my hand feeling small and feminine inside his.

'Actually, I left some papers in your office the other day. We're close by now. Do you have your key with you?'

'I think so, yes.'

'Would you mind awfully if we dropped in and picked them up? I could do with them for court tomorrow.'

'No problem.' I was glad to oblige.

'Whereabouts did you leave them?' I let us both in, and deactivated the alarm.

'Julie's office.'

He followed me up the stairs. The atmosphere of the office was different by night. It seemed less like an office and more like the Georgian dwelling house that it had once been. It was eerie. Empty. I would have been scared if James hadn't been there. Come to think of it, I felt scared anyway.

The door to Julie's office creaked open. Funny how I'd never noticed the creak in the day time.

'After you, Madam.' James held the door open for me, smiling formally like some old-fashioned butler.

'Can you see them?' I gave the room a cursory glance.

Then it dawned on me – the real reason we were there. I became flustered and pretended to search around the room in earnest.

'They must be here somewhere. What's the name of the case?'

I began frantically lifting objects and pulling piles asunder – anything to avoid looking him in the eye.

'It's impossible to find anything in this place, there are so many papers. Are you sure you left it here? Maybe you left it in your office . . . ' I gabbled. Anything to avoid addressing the real topic. Finally I ran out of babble to spout and objects to search under. I looked up at him slowly from under my floppy fringe. He was standing just inside the closed door. He hadn't moved since we'd entered the room. His eyes were hooded.

'Why don't you take your coat off, Fern? Make yourself comfortable.' He was totally in control.

I took off my coat, just like he said. I was too hot anyway. I sat awkwardly at the edge of Julie's desk, folding my arms across my stomach. I hadn't felt this self-conscious since I was fourteen years old. I couldn't bring myself to look at him. He moved slowly towards me. I watched his shoes approach. Expensive and highly polished. He was standing right in front of me now. My eyes were level with his chest, my shoulders slightly hunched.

'Fern.' His voice was soft. He gently placed the back of his fingers under my chin and tilted my face upwards, forcing me to look him directly in the eye. Very dark. Very deep.

'Would you mind terribly if I kissed you?'

I couldn't answer. He took this to mean yes. His lips came down onto mine, lightly for the first few seconds, then firmer. The blood rushed inside my head and I thought for a second that I was going to pass out, so intense was the sensation. The combination of being in the empty, dark office, the large silence enveloping us and the newness of his touch and scent was overwhelming.

Besides, I hadn't been kissed for a really long time.

His hand travelled that inevitable male route down the side of my neck and onto my breast. It had been a long time since that had happened too. And it was very nice.

'Ever since the first day I saw you, I've wanted to have you on this desk,' he muttered huskily against my neck. I almost whimpered with desire and started fumbling blindly with the buttons of his shirt. He pushed my hands away and opened the buttons himself, quickly and efficiently. Then he took my hands and placed them inside his open shirt, flat against his nipples.

We kissed again, long and hard. Then he pushed me onto my back and started pulling off my trousers. Thank God for the bikini wax and nice knickers. I kept pressing myself up against him like a mad woman, deep guttural sounds that I barely recognised emerging from my throat.

Soon I was naked. His huge brown hands moved over my white body. First my nipples, kneading and sucking in turn. Then my buttocks – clasping and clutching. I kept thrusting up into his body, into his mouth, my inhibitions lost in a haze of wine and lust. Thank God he had the presence of mind to use a condom because I certainly didn't. As he came inside me, still fully clothed, all I could think of was Julie. If she could only see me now!

With a final thrust, James landed noisily, heavily and sweatily on top of me. He lay motionless until I was forced to move out from beneath him for fear of suffocation. I still wanted more but I knew from the looks of him that it would be self-gratification or none.

Eventually he drew himself up and smiled at me.

'Thank you for assisting me in living out one of my fantasies.'

'One of them. You mean you have more?' (I couldn't believe I'd said that.)

'Oh there's plenty more where that came from, my dear.' Sounded promising. 'C'mon, let's get out of here. I'll walk you to the taxi rank.'

'I just have to tidy up in here a bit first.' I was disappointed. I had thought we'd go on somewhere else. To a late-night wine bar perhaps. But I didn't say anything. What if he said he didn't want to go?

He waited restlessly beside the door while I straightened out Julie's desk as well as I could. It was my own fault. I shouldn't have had sex with him on the second date. The drunkenness was wearing off, leaving me with a vague sense of depression and a thudding head. I shuddered to think of the hangover I'd have the next morning.

Chapter Five

Friday morning and there were shock waves around the office.

Blissfully unaware of what lay ahead, I stumbled down the corridor towards the canteen, trying to convince myself that the stabbing sensation just above my left eye was a product of my imagination.

You know those films where the heroine opens the door into a crowded bar room and the music stops and everybody freezes and stares at her? Well, that's what it was like when I opened the door to the canteen that Friday morning. I immediately examined myself. What was wrong? Had I forgotten to button up my blouse before I'd left the house? Was I still wearing my fluffy slippers?

Lydia Boland (you know, Big Tits) was the first one to speak – sorry, shriek.

'Fern! How are you? Have a seat.' She patted the chair beside her in what she imagined to be a welcoming fashion. I was the only Fern in the room so she must have been talking to me. I examined the chair carefully before I sat down, expecting to see a whoopee cushion at the very least.

'So, how was the art exhibition?'

'How did you . . . ?'

'I met Phil Howard last night in Leeson Street. I believe you were there with James

Carver.' The note of triumph in her voice was unmistakable. It was the triumph of the accomplished gossip who has managed to get her hands on a particularly juicy piece of information before anyone else.

I could feel every eye upon me as I groped in the dark and dusty recesses of my mind for a suitable response. My mental cupboards were bare.

'So, how long have you being going out together, then?' Her eyes bored into me, gimlet like. Ve have vays of making you talk. Tell her to fuck off and mind her own business, I told myself. Go on – say it.

'About a week.' I couldn't help it. I was putty in her hands. She must have been head of the Gestapo in a former life.

'You're doing well. The last one only lasted for a few days.' Her dig was thinly disguised by a pretty peal of laughter.

Of course I should have just shrugged off her petty barb, putting her remarks down to jealousy. But did I choose to do this? No. Instead I chose to turn into an emotional wreck. I was already a physical wreck anyway, so what the hell.

What last one? Was I just the latest in a long line? I miserably gulped down the remainder of my coffee and shuffled dejectedly down the corridor to my office.

I passed a couple of the secretaries along the way.

'Hi, Fern!' they chorused. I smiled weakly, shrinking into the wall, conjuring up all sorts of sinister meanings for their innocent greeting. They had probably been discussing me all morning. Did you hear the latest? Fern and that good-looking barrister – James Carver. You know Fern, works for Julie, mousy one, not much to say for herself. What does she think she's at, God love her? He's obviously using her.

The roots of my hair felt as if they had caught fire. I blushed to the core just thinking about it. I imagined my vital organs turning as red as my hot cheeks. With one fleeting remark, Lydia had managed to make me feel like a bottle of 7-Up with the fizz gone out of it.

Of course my mood wasn't improved by the fact that James hadn't made an arrangement with me for the weekend. What if he didn't ring today? Now that they all knew about him, they'd be asking what my plans were. I'd have to make something up.

It was about half-past six that evening when I opened the front door to my house. My female intuition told me that there was something up as soon as I stepped indoors. Some mysterious oestrogen-driven sixth sense alerted me to strange happenings in the household. But I took off my coat and scarf as usual and hung them at the end of the stairs as if I felt nothing untoward

My first clue was the empty, silent kitchen – devoid of all steam and cooking smells. It was dinner time. What was going on?

My father was sitting in the TV room with the TV switched off. It was news time.

I knew what had happened but I didn't want to ask. My father looked up pitifully from his chair. I looked away.

'I'm going upstairs,' I said pointlessly. My steps were leaden.

Sasha was sitting at the end of my bed. Her face was ashen. I could feel her hollow eyes following my busy movements around the room. I wouldn't look at her.

'Mam's gone.'

I continued opening and closing drawers, removing and folding clothes.

'Are you deaf? Mam's gone.'

'Where's she gone?'

'To Aunt Marjorie's. That's hardly the point, Fern. She's left Dad and she's not coming back.'

Those final words did the trick. As if someone had kicked me in the gut, I sank onto the bed, like a rag doll. We remained that way for some time, the silence punctuated by the odd sigh from one or other of us. Eventually I turned and looked at my sister. Her usual over-confident expression had been replaced by a softer, more crumpled look. It was clear that she'd been crying. I hadn't seen her cry since she was twelve years old and Dad had banned her from wearing her mini ra-ra skirt to the school disco. Awkwardly, I put my arm around her shoulder and made soothing noises, as to a small child. She slumped heavily against me, emitting a strange strangled whimper. Seconds later, she was on her feet, blowing her nose, her back to me.

'Are you okay, Sash?'

She nodded.

'Can I get you anything?'

She shook her head.

'I'd better put the dinner on then.'

I left the room, managing to avoid eye contact. My sister and I had never been close.

I went downstairs.

'Do you want some tea, Dad?'

'That'd be grand, love.' He sounded tired, grateful.

I went into the kitchen and began peeling and chopping to beat the band. I still wondered if James would ring. It wasn't that late and there was always Saturday night. I felt like going out tonight though. I wanted to be drunk. I kept thinking about James – about how warm and secure I felt with his arm around my shoulder and my hand in his. Maybe if I went out tonight I'd bump into him – recreate that warm, safe feeling.

I brought my father his dinner on a tray. He seemed engrossed in a sports quiz. I made my escape. I glared at the phone as I went upstairs, hating it for the power it had over me.

Fortunately Sasha had gone out so I had some privacy. What to do? I toyed with the idea of ringing a few people to see if they were going out but I couldn't bring myself to do it.

So I went out for a walk instead.

And I walked.

And walked.

And walked.

To nowhere in particular. Not thinking about anything in particular – apart from James. Just to be out of the house, that was the thing.

To my surprise, I found myself outside Auntie Marjorie's house. Nowhere else to go, I suppose. I decided I might as well go in.

My aunt answered the door. She was a plumper, noisier version of my mother. While Marjorie radiated energy and warmth, my mother was like a light that had gone out. You've seen women like her, walking around your home town – small, shrunken appearance; short, sensible greying hair; raincoat and canvas shopping bag; careworn expression; look older than they are.

She was sitting in an armchair by the open fire, looking blank and out of place. The only part of her that moved when I came in was her eyes. But their expression didn't shift. She stared straight back into the fire.

'Hello, Mam.' I sat down opposite her.

'I've left your father.'

'I know.'

She looked mildly surprised.

'Are you coming back at all?'

'I don't think so, love.'

We sat in silence for a while, both staring into the fire, both alone with our own thoughts. Now wasn't the time for the venting of anger or recriminations. I was grateful for that. Time enough.

'Where will you stay?'

'Here with your Auntie Marjorie and Uncle John until I can sort something else out.'

I nodded.

'I'll come and see you again soon.' I felt like I should hug her or something but we had never been the most demonstrative of families. It would have felt false and unnatural. Instead I just smiled and gave her a little wave as I backed through the door and out into the cool night again.

What to do next? Go home. There was nothing else for it.

I tried to pretend to myself that I wasn't checking the telephone table for a message that James had rung. He hadn't. I went to bed and miraculously fell into a deep sleep. That was good because I was going to need the rest for my intense telephone-monitoring ritual the next day.

It was a process that became more intense the later it got. I started off the morning in quite a carefree mood. Anything could happen – the phone was my oyster. By mid-afternoon, the nerves were starting to kick in. Surely he was leaving it a bit late to ring. If I was to complete my pre-going-out routine, I'd need a little more notice than this. By tea-time an icy fear had gripped my heart. I sat curled up in an armchair like a taut spring, staring intently at a repeat of *Gladiators*, furiously gripping my coffee mug and fiercely hating Ulrika Jonsson for being blonder, thinner and altogether chirpier than I was. I bet she never had a free Saturday night in her life! Of course, I could have put myself out of my misery and rung him. But I would rather have chewed my own fingers off. Everybody knows the golden rule that you never ring a man in those early delicate stages of a relationship. Such a move reeks of desperation and panic and sends him packing in the opposite direction. Yes – you must never, under any circumstances, let your true feelings show. I knew this to my cost. Skilful gamesmanship was all that counted at this point.

At seven o'clock, I decided to ring one of my friends. Anything was better than this torture. I picked Kathleen, on the basis that she had her inner bitch reigned in most of the time – not like some of the girls I knew who sent their inner bitches out roaming, in constant search or victims.

'Kathleen – it's me, Fern.'

'He didn't ring then.'

'Who?'

She laughed (quite nastily, I thought). I decided to ignore her.

'I was wondering if you and the girls were heading out anywhere for the night.'

'We're going to the Cinebar for about nine if you're interested.'

'Yeah – I'll see you there.

The Cinebar was a trendy new bar – full of suits after work on a Friday evening and crawling with posers on a Saturday night. I could think of places that I'd rather go to but beggars can't be choosers . . .

It was close to ten by the time I arrived. It wasn't that it took me a spectacularly long time to get ready (although it did). It was also that I didn't want to be the first to arrive and risk being on my own in there. I knew that the other girls would probably arrive together. I joined the queue outside. As a lone girl, I was let in by the bouncers without a word. I was past the age where I was likely to be stopped and asked for ID. In fact, if they'd asked, I would have been flattered.

I experienced that familiar vulnerable feeling as I searched the bar for the girls. Then the enormous relief when I eventually found them.

'How's it going, Fern?'

'Great,' I lied enthusiastically, plastering a fake smile onto my face.

'How's what's-his-face, the barrister-babe?'

'James is fine.' I grinned cheesily

'How come you're not out with him tonight then?'

'He had a do pre-planned. Something he couldn't get out of.'

The girls exchanged knowing looks.

'I've only been with him for about a week. I do have my own life to lead, you know,' I almost snapped, my mask slipping.

More knowing looks.

Fortunately the thudding music put paid to any further attempts at conversation, and I was off the hook. I ordered a large, overpriced gin to get me in the mood. Then another. Then another. We fought our way onto the dance floor in a valiant attempt to strut our stuff. It felt good. Nothing existed but the blaring music and the pleasant fuzzy feeling in my head. I wanted to stay dancing forever.

Yet again, I fell into bed in a drunken stupor. I was afraid to count the alcohol units I had consumed that week.

I spent most of Sunday in bed. There didn't seem to be any point in getting up. The monotony was normally broken by my mother's mid-afternoon Sunday roast. But not today. I listened to the rain pitter-patter against the window as I lay curled in the foetal position in the cocoon of warm air I had constructed in the middle of my bed. I willed myself asleep but nothing happened. It was tough but I had no choice but to get up. I began making preparations for dinner. It suddenly seemed important to maintain some semblance of normality. Yes, mountains may crumble, mothers may leave home, but the Sunday roast is one constant that you should be able to rely upon in this ever-changing world.

Not that my father or sister had had their breakfasts yet. The Fennellys were not a family of early risers – apart from my mother of course, but she wasn't really a Fennelly.

Eventually, they arose zombie-like from their respective rooms, lured, no doubt, by the cooking smells. My father, unshaven and wearing pin-striped pyjamas (they reminded me of one of James's suits); my sister, her hair sticking up in every direction known to man, with black streaks coming from the direction of each eye. She looked like an extra from Michael Jackson's *Thriller* video. If only her boyfriend could see her now! She had committed the cardinal sin of not taking off her make-up before she went to bed. May she burn in hell! Only a very brave man would have taken bets as to which one of us had the worst hangover.

I chatted away to no one in particular as I doled out the food. No one in particular answered. I tried to be all chirpy and Ulrika-Jonnson-like. I willed them not to bring up any unpleasant topics. Let's pretend that everything is okay.

'How many spuds do you want, Dad?'

'Hmmmmm?'

'Is four enough for you?'

'That would be grand.'

I served up everybody's food and sat down to my own.

'Pass the salt please, Sash.'

My sister passed me the salt.

'Can I have the butter, please?'

I silently passed her the butter dish.

'Do you girls have any plans for today?'

Sasha and I looked at each other fleetingly.

'No, Dad.'

'No, Dad. How about you?'

'Well, the match is on. After that, I thought I might go across for a few pints.'

We nodded in unison. Dad usually went for a few pints on a Sunday with Uncle John, Marjorie's husband, but with Mam's new living arrangements, things might be a little awkward in that department. The thought occurred to each one of us at the same time. Eyes were averted.

'Where's the white sauce?' my sister whined at me. 'I only like cauliflower with white sauce.'

'Well, make it yourself then,' I barked, my chirpiness evaporating in an instant. I mentally kicked myself.

My father didn't say much throughout the meal. He just read his newspaper and played with his food. In fact, he didn't say much at all that day. None of us did. We moved around the house like planets keeping to our own orbits. Sasha and I didn't even complain when Dad insisted on watching *Songs of Praise* directly followed by *Last of the Summer Wine*. I was almost happy at the thought of having to work the next day.

But do you know the worst of it?

The relief.

It was palpable. It was an end to all the tension. The worst had happened and we had survived. The dreaded inevitable and we were still standing. All the remaining members of the Fennelly household – and probably my mother over at Aunt Marjorie's – breathed a collective sigh of relief.

Chapter Six

So, in I went to face the onslaught of yet another Monday morning, and, more particularly, the interrogation about James that I expected to suffer at the hands – and claws – of my co-workers.

I kept my head down for most of the morning. This was not a difficult task as Julie had three weeks' worth of typing waiting for me. Did the woman never sleep? I felt she was watching me like a hawk – if you can imagine a hawk wearing designer bi-focals. It was as if she was willing me to make a mistake.

At elevenish I was buzzed down to reception.

'Cyril wants coffee for six in the boardroom,' Grace the receptionist told me.

Grace – by name and not by nature – was a cliché, plastered in make-up and exuding an air of savage boredom. The only thing she was short of doing was blatantly filing her nails all day long. God help any punter who tried to give her a hard time on the phone!

I doubt if there is anything in this world more demeaning than having to serve coffee to a boardroom full of businessmen. It made me feel like a Geisha girl. I knocked gently and opened the door with my elbow. As I walked in, the men at the far side of the table craned their necks to see my legs and those nearest to me just leered over their double chins. Women wearing trouser suits were frowned upon in the office. It was a wonder Cyril didn't just get us all to wear bikinis and have done with it.

I felt suitably subservient as I poured the coffee into the bone-china cups. I had to restrain myself from offering to massage the feet of the man nearest to me.

'Is that a new painting, Cyril?' This from the 'gentleman' to my right.

'Yes, one of my latest acquisitions. Got it just the other night. Good, isn't it?'

I glanced in the direction of the painting and realised with a jolt that it was the landscape that he had bought at the exhibition. He noticed me staring at it.

'Do you like it?'

I blushed, 'Yes, very nice.'

'Guess how much it cost.'

This was terrible. They were all looking at me.

'I have no idea.'

'Try half your yearly salary.' He guffawed and the others joined in, jowls wobbling, buttons straining on their shirts. I smiled tightly and retreated with my empty tray. For some strange reason, I felt hot tears starting at the corners of my eyes, and my vision blurred slightly. Luckily I managed to collect myself before I came across anyone. I didn't know what was wrong with me.

I had lunch with Declan again. He was obviously too tired on a Monday to organise meeting anyone else.

'So. Where did he take you this weekend?'

'I didn't see James this weekend.'

Here we go again. I steeled myself for the sarcastic tirade. It didn't come. He just kept eating. He was letting me away with it. Thank you, Declan.

At four o'clock Grace buzzed me.

'James Carver on line 3.'

My heart leapt right out of my mouth and onto my desk. I put it back in again and picked up the receiver, my knuckles white.

'Fern!'

I dissolved at the sound of his voice.

'Hi, James!' I couldn't hide my delight. My resolve to be cool when he rang was forgotten. Playing hard to get has never been one of my strong points. Playing hard to get rid of – now that is my area of expertise.

'Did you have a good weekend?'

'Great, thanks. I went to the Cinebar on Saturday night.'

To my disappointment, he sounded unconcerned.

'That was nice. Sorry I wasn't in contact. I had to work all weekend.'

I wasn't sure whether to believe him or not. Still, at least he had apologised. That must mean that he thought we had something going on.

'Are you free for lunch tomorrow?'

'Er . . . I think so.' That was as hard to get as I got.

'How about meeting me at the canteen in the Courthouse at one o'clock.'

'Okay.'

'Fantastic. See you, Fern.'

'Bye.'

Yippee! I did a little dance in my seat. He still wanted to see me! Maybe I wasn't so bad after all.

I began practising my new signature on the message pad. Fern Carver. It had a lovely ring to it. Should I do a fancy 'C'? How about underlining it?

'Was that James Carver you were just talking to?'

I nearly jumped out of my skin. The dreaded Julie was standing in the doorway that adjoined our two offices. I hid my doodles under a piece of legitimate paperwork and prepared myself for a bollocking. She took measured steps towards my desk. Now she was within striking distance. I gulped. She sat down on the edge of my desk and crossed her arms and legs.

'I went to school with his older sister, you know.'

'Who . . . what . . . ?'

Her plastered-on smile was interrupted by a flash of impatience.

'James Carver's sister. We went to Kylemore together. Super girl. She was captain of the hockey team, you know.'

I nodded uncertainly. This was new territory and I wasn't sure how to respond. Was I even allowed to respond?

'I hear you've been seeing quite a lot of James lately.' She nudged me. Julie actually nudged me. All girls together. Weren't we having so much gossipy, giggly fun!

'We've been out a couple of times,' I mumbled.

'Have you met his family yet?'

'Not yet.'

Lovely family! Just lovely. Especially his father, Judge Carver. Such a pet. And such a brilliant legal mind too. They say James takes after him, you know – that he's destined for the bench himself.'

I couldn't fathom what was going on. Why wasn't she giving out to me for slacking off? And why was she still smiling so hard? And why did she remind me so much of a snake?

She nudged me again, playfully. 'Don't forget to tell James that I was asking for them all. I'm going to get myself a coffee. Would you like one?'

'Well, if you're going down . . . '

'Milk and sugar?'

I nodded. I didn't take milk or sugar but my tongue seemed to have entered early retirement. Holy shit! What was going on.

I barely thought of anything but James until I arrived at the Courthouse the next day. I had been there a few times before, dropping off the odd file for Julie. I tried not to be intimidated as I fought my way through the throngs of barristers. The pure barrister-ness of them never failed to amaze me. They all looked so prosperous and arrogant in the gowns and wigs that they didn't even take off at lunchtime.

The restaurant was as loud and as noisy as the Law Library had been. Please let James be here. I scanned the room but no sign. I busied myself with choosing a sandwich and pouring myself a mug of coffee, hoping I didn't look as out of place as I felt.

As I poured, I became aware of a large, blond male presence beside me. I looked up and met a very direct, very clear, blue gaze. I was a little taken aback. I looked away quickly. I moved along in the queue. I could feel him looking at me still. I looked back at him again, more challenging this time. He was smiling at me in a blatantly flirtatious way. It made me uncomfortable and not a little annoyed. I snatched up my tray and walked off.

I congratulated myself on finding the last free table in the canteen. Please hurry up, James! Oh no! He was coming towards me. Not James – the blond man. He looked so damned sure of himself.

'Anybody sitting here?' He had already pulled out the chair and was beginning to sit down.

'Actually, I'm waiting for someone.'

'Just one person?'

'Yes.'

'That's okay then, isn't it.' The table sat four. 'I'm Seán.' He spoke in a broad Dublin accent.

I glared at him. As if I cared what his name was!

'Hi, Seán.' I gave him a tight smile.

'And you are . . . ?'

'Waiting for somebody.' I couldn't help myself.

I was shocked at the level of antagonism I felt towards this complete stranger. It was just that he appeared so cock-sure. I needn't have worried about insulting him though. He laughed and began shovelling huge forkfuls of mashed spud into his mouth. I nibbled delicately at my cheese sandwich. It tasted of cardboard.

'Hey, Seán!'

'Mikey, sit down!'

Not another one.

Another man sat himself down across from me. He was dressed in the same dark blue, paint-spattered overalls as his friend.

'What have we got here?' He gestured towards me with his head.

'I don't know. She won't tell me her name.'

God! Would they ever go away?! I pulled a magazine out of my bag and began reading it determinedly.

'I don't think she wants to talk to us, Mikey. Better let her read her magazine.' His voice was more serious now.

They began a discussion, something about a job that they were doing and not having enough paint. I was relieved to be off the hook, but a little ashamed, to tell the truth. They were probably only trying to be friendly. I didn't know why I had been so rude.

'My missus reads those magazines,' said Mikey to Seán in an unnecessarily loud voice. Not off the hook so easily, it seemed. 'There was this story I was reading the other day about this bloke – except he wasn't really a bloke – had his bollix chopped off. Reckoned he always wanted to be a girl. Jaysus – brought tears to me eyes just reading it. Still, great pair of tits on him.'

I glanced up. Seán was looking at me and grinning.

Try as I might, I couldn't stop myself from laughing out loud. I allowed myself to relax for the first time in ages. Suddenly our table felt like a little oasis of normality in a desert of pretension.

'Mind if I borrow this?' Mikey gestured towards my magazine.

'No, go ahead.'

'Where's the problem page? That's my favourite.' He began leafing through the pages.

'So, are you a barrister?' Seán asked me. I nearly choked on my mouthful of coffee.

'No.' I smiled easily at him when I'd recovered.

'A solicitor then?'

'No, I'm a legal secretary.'

'Oh, right. Interesting job?'

'Not really.'

He nodded. As if he understood or something.

I allowed myself to look at him properly for the first time. He really did have the most amazing eyes. Not just the colour. The expression was completely unguarded. He looked at me with what could only be described as undisguised admiration. It was quite a shock to be looked at like that. And he had the most interesting smile. Kind of crooked. Made the corners of his eyes go all crinkly.

'How about you?'

'I'm a painter.'

I nodded, taking in the overalls.

'We're painting the new wing of the Courthouse. Seán's doing me a favour by helping me out this week. We're a bit behind schedule.' Mikey leant back in his chair and patted Seán on the shoulder.

'Fern! So sorry to keep you waiting. The last witness just went on and on.' It was James, looking all important and masterful in his sweeping black gown. He glanced in the direction of Mikey and Seán. 'It's a tad crowded in here. Shall we go somewhere else?' It was more of a statement than a question. I reluctantly pushed aside my half-eaten sandwich and got up to leave.

'You can keep the magazine.'

'Jaysus, thanks!' Mikey seemed genuinely delighted.

'Be seeing you, Fern. Nice name that – unusual.' Seán smiled warmly at me.

'It never really caught on. Bye.'

We left the restaurant.

'Do you know those two?'

'Never laid eyes on them before.'

'They weren't hassling you, were they?'

'No, we were just chatting.'

He frowned and for a fleeting second looked confused.

I felt shy all of a sudden. The last time I'd seen his face it had been inches above mine, contorted and animalistic, filmed with sweat. He was back in control now – the smooth professional James. I realised with a slight chill that I did not know this man – this man who I had allowed inside my body.

'Where are we going?' My voice was quiet and small.

'You'll see.'

He led me purposefully along one of the shiny, sterile corridors of the Courthouse. It reminded me vaguely of a convent I'd visited as a child, except that now my hand was being held by James and not by my mother.

He stopped outside a big, wooden door and looked up and down the corridor in a way that I could only describe as furtive. There was nobody around. He pushed open the door and pulled me inside.

It was an empty courtroom. The atmosphere was stale and forbidding. I felt a prickly sensation at the back of my neck which I later identified as a combination of excitement and fear. I knew what was coming (me, I hoped).

He led me silently up the steps towards the judge's seat.

'Lie down,' he commanded, gesturing towards the space of floor beneath the judge's bench.

'What if somebody . . . ?'

He silenced me with a large forefinger on my lips. By now my heart seemed to have travelled upwards and was keeping up a hollow beat inside my ears. Undoubtedly I was about to fulfil another of James's fantasies.

I lay down. I told myself I wanted to but in reality I just didn't know how to refuse.

I lay stiff as a board as he positioned himself on top of me. He was less generous with the foreplay this time. One kiss on the neck and a tweak of each nipple was all he evidently had time for (push these three buttons to turn her on). I tried to carry myself away on the excitement and danger of the location but I couldn't quite pull it off.

James didn't bother undressing me this time. He just pulled up his gown, whipped out his knob, pulled up my skirt, yanked down my knickers and set to work. I felt a searing mixture of pleasure and pain as he pushed inside me and then – not very much really.

He left his gown on throughout the procedure. It covered my face and surrounded me in heavy black folds at each side of my body. I felt like I was having sex with Dracula.

As James huffed and grunted above me, I wondered idly if we were in contempt of court.

I heard a muffled cry and felt his body shudder. I presumed it was all over. He eventually rolled off me. I hastily adjusted my clothing and he did the same to his. He smiled fondly at me and sighed.

'Nothing like a quickie to set one up for the afternoon.'

I smiled back nervously, unsure of myself. Was he still pleased with me? He seemed happy enough.

'Come on – the Registrar will be along any minute,' he said, looking at his watch and striding towards the door. I scurried after him, brushing the dust off my skirt. Now we could go to lunch.

It was difficult to keep up with him. His strides were a lot longer than mine. We reached an exit door. He turned and kissed me on the cheek.

'Thanks for lunch. I'll be in touch.' He grinned at me.

'But . . . what . . . you mean you're going now?'

'Of course. I'm due back in court in ten minutes.' He looked incredulous.

'Okay . . . Bye.'

I knew that disappointment and hurt were written all over my face.

'Look,' – he seemed to soften – 'we'll do something special together very soon, I promise.'

And then he was gone. I watched his black back retreating, and felt depression and frustration setting in. Back to the office, I supposed.

I'd treat myself to a bar of chocolate along the way. My one solace in a cruel world.

Having chosen the quickest route out through the new wing, I turned a corner and narrowly avoided colliding with a ladder.

'Watch out!' It was Seán, the painter. 'Oh, hello – small world.'

'Hi!' I was embarrassed. I was sure everybody could tell I'd just been having sex. My sense of guilt and shame felt so tangible that I thought it must be visible.

'What have you been up to, then?'

'What do you mean?'

He looked taken aback by the aggressiveness of my response.

'Only asking. Thought you might have gone somewhere nice for lunch.'

'Oh,' – I relaxed – 'we just grabbed a quick bite in chambers.' (A quick bite was right.)

'Is he your boyfriend, then?'

'Yes.' I couldn't suppress the smug grin. Imagine – my boyfriend – a rich, good-looking barrister. Mine!

'You could do a lot better than that upper-class twit.'

'I beg your pardon?' I couldn't believe my ears, consumed as I was with indignation.

'I said, you could . . . '

'I heard what you said the first time, thank you very much. I just didn't believe somebody could be that rude. Who are you to judge him? You don't even know him.'

'I don't have to. I know his type.'

I was morally outraged. 'I don't even know why I'm having this conversation. Good bye.'

He caught me by the arm as I attempted to storm off.

'Don't be like that, Fern.'

Why did he have to know my name? I looked pointedly down at his hand on my arm, and back up into his face. He let go.

'I'm sorry.' To his credit, he actually did look sorry. I was surprised by the gentleness of his expression. 'Let me make it up to you.'

'What do you mean?'

'Let me take you out to dinner.'

'What?' I was hearing things.

'Are you free Friday night?'

'I don't believe this. I just told you I had a boyfriend.'

'And I just told you he isn't right for you.'

'Oh, yes, he is, he's perfect for me. And besides, I don't even know you.'

'We've met twice already.'

'Not out of choice, believe me.'

'Can I have your number then?'

'No! Goodbye!' And this time I really did storm off.

I shook my head in disbelief as I walked away. I knew that he was probably watching me. I had to surpress the urge to sway my hips seductively. But honestly! The nerve of him. To ask out a complete stranger. He probably did it all the time. And to actually presume I'd choose to go out with the likes of him rather than somebody like James! Some men were unbelievable.

O'Connell Street had never looked more lovely – all the trees dancing with white fairy lights. I had to fight my way through the hordes of Christmas shoppers to get back to the office.

I felt vaguely sick at the thought of Christmas. I usually loved it, but this year was going to be different. At least I'd have a boyfriend this Christmas. I thought happily about all the possible presents I could buy for James. Perhaps we could even go shopping together on Grafton Street, like a proper couple. We could drop into Davy Byrne's for a few glasses of Bailey's on ice. I wrapped this warm thought around me to keep out the cold.

It worked. I arrived back at the office in great humour, which was just as well since Julie was in another of her foul moods. I'd heard she'd been constantly suffering from pre-menstrual tension for about ten years. I was relieved when she went off to her meeting at three.

I looked around my office in disgust. What a state! Paper and clutter everywhere. A veritable disaster from a Feng-Shui point of view. Now would be a perfect time to tidy the place up. It would also be a perfect time for going for coffee with Declan.

The apprentices' room was in the basement. It was the worst room in the building. The ancient radiators never seemed to heat up and the cream and brown walls were reminiscent of a school toilet. It was like walking onto the set of *Prisoner Cell Block H*. But that was the best of it. The occupants were even tackier than the décor.

Never before had such a collection of back-stabbers and brown-nosers been put together in the one room. They competed constantly in an attempt to steal points from one another. Even though I considered Declan my friend, he had the capacity to be every bit as bad as the others when the occasion arose. Still, he had the disadvantage of not being a relative of one of the partners, or of one of the bigger clients, so maybe he had no choice.

He was sitting at his desk wearing about four jumpers, dragging fiercely on a cigarette. Luckily Big Tits and the others were out of the room.

'Coming for coffee?'

'Sure. Anything for a break.'

I watched him peel off the different layers of jumpers and put on his jacket, no doubt in case he met one of the partners on the way to the canteen. He also tucked a couple of files under his arm. Just in case.

'So, why are you looking so pleased with yourself? No – don't tell me. You've been out with the caped avenger.'

I swallowed a mouthful of coffee and smiled. 'I met him for lunch.'

'Oh, really? Where did he take you? The Westbury, I suppose, or somewhere equally posh.'

I felt a slight flush move across my face.

'No, we went to the restaurant in the Four Courts.'

He gave a derisory snort. 'That's a bit of a come down, isn't it?' If only he knew! 'You know the best thing about you going out with him?'

'I didn't think you saw anything good about my going out with James.'

'Well – every cloud has a silver lining,' he replied loftily.

I shook my head in despair at him. As usual, my feelings when I was with Declan were a complex mixture of amusement, annoyance and sheer exasperation. Usually the amusement won out. I suppose that's why we stayed friends. I guess he felt the same way about me.

'Go on, then. What's the saving grace in my doomed relationship?'

'You've annoyed the shit out of Big Tits.'

'Really!' I was delighted. I could think of nothing more gratifying than making that cow jealous. It was the highest form of compliment. Declan hated her too. They were both ferociously competitive and got each other's backs up (or front up in the case of Lydia) on an almost daily basis.

'Yeah. The Bitches of Eastwick were giving out about you half the morning. That Big Tits has a major thing for Mr Carver. Been after him for yonks.'

The Bitches of Eastwick – Big Tits, Big Arse and Big Nose – was Declan's collective pet name for the three female apprentices. Imagine, I'd beaten the senior partner's niece, who had massive jugs to boot, to the affections of James! Now I truly knew the meaning of success. Admittedly I didn't like the idea of their saying nasty things about me behind my back, but hey, you couldn't make an omlette without breaking eggs. And James was one hell of an omelette.

'Now, I don't want you to take this the wrong way, Fern, but I've heard something and I think you have the right to know.' Sounded ominous.

'What?'

'Has he ever mentioned a girl called Bronwyn?'

'Yeah – well, I met her.'

'Did you? What's she like?'

'Total cow.'

'Good-looking?'

'If you like that sort of thing.'

'So she is good-looking, then.'

'Shut up!'

'Did you know that she's his ex?'

This I didn't know.

'Of course, he told me so himself.'

'You're such a bad liar, Fern.' Damn! 'Anyway. By the sounds of things she's angling to get him back. So I'd watch her if I were you.'

Hmmmm. This was worrying. How could I possibly compete with all those blonde corkscrew curls? And being a barrister she got to see him practically every day too. No. This was not good news. My euphoria over Lydia's jealousy was overshadowed by this bombshell (blonde).

'Well, obviously he'd still be with her if he wanted to be.'

Declan was not the kind of person to whom you could confess your insecurities.

'Oh, obviously.' His tone was cynical. Annoying bastard.

'Oh! did I mention that I got asked out today?' I'd show him.

'By somebody else?' His eyebrows shot up and disappeared into his hairline.

'Yes, by somebody else, you moron.'

'Who is he?'

'Oh, some guy I met at the Courthouse. Seán is his name.'

'Is he another barrister?'

'No.'

'A solicitor?'

'No.'

'A criminal, then?'

'Ha ha.'

'What then?'

'He's a painter.'

'What, painter as in artist?'

'No. Painter as in painter and decorator.'

'You mean a workman!' He sounded genuinely horrified. Then he started to laugh.

'God, Fern, you're so gullible. You should know what that type are like. You were probably the tenth woman he's asked out this week. I suppose you said yes.'

'No, of course I didn't. What do you take me for?'

'Look, don't get all stroppy with me. I just don't like to think of you being taken advantage of, that's all.'

My annoyance vanished as quickly as it had appeared.

'I know you don't. But, trust me. I know what I'm doing.'

Declan looked unconvinced.

All my good feelings had evaporated. I felt lousy about myself again – as usual. Why did I allow people to do this to me? I was such a wimp.

That evening, at home, after dinner, I shut myself into my room and started painting. For the zillionth time I thanked the stars above that I had my own room. I shuddered to think of the nightmare it would be to share with my sister.

I tried to continue with the landscape that I had been copying from a photograph I had taken on a holiday in Tralee earlier on in the year. It was of a deserted beach I had stumbled across. It was the most tranquil, peaceful place I'd ever seen. I longed to recapture that feeling.

But I couldn't get into it. Maybe I just didn't have peace of mind.

Instead, I painted a picture in lurid colours of a woman with long blonde curly hair and a green face. Her face was contorted with agony and pain. A dagger pierced her heart and blood spurted from the open wound.

I really don't know where I got the inspiration from.

Chapter Seven

Only seven more shopping days until Christmas.

Only seven more presents to buy.

What a nightmare.

And I had a new outfit to buy for my date with James that night. He'd seen all my decent clothes by now. And I really needed to wow him that evening. Bronwyn would be there in all her glory, no doubt, trying to win him back.

I just didn't feel up to it. I was feeling increasingly tired these days. I didn't know what was wrong with me. I was close to tears at times for no apparent reason and I found myself snapping at people who really didn't deserve it. Still, at least I had the thought of being with James to keep me going. He was a godsend really.

We were meeting in the Shelbourne for a drink. I felt uneasy about walking in on my own but I was afraid to suggest to James that we meet up somewhere else first on our own. I didn't want to put him out. It was the birthday party of one of his barrister friends and they would have been drinking for hours by the time I arrived.

I tried to look as if I owned the place as I entered the red, plush, chandeliered lobby. This was no mean feat as I'd never set foot in the place before and had no clue as to where I was going. Follow the noise, James had said. I realised his directions weren't as vague as they'd originally sounded.

The noisiest room in the hotel appeared to be the bar, and slap bang in the middle of the noisiest group in the bar I spotted James and his cronies. He didn't see me arrive. I had to walk right up to him and tap him on the shoulder.

'Fern!' He kissed me enthusiastically and put his arm around my shoulders in a gesture I initially interpreted as protective. I soon realised that he was, in fact, very drunk and was trying to support himself.

We were surrounded by a group of people, of whom I recognised only a few. Zara and Bronwyn were sitting together to my left. They smiled sweetly at me when I came in. I saw Bronwyn say something to Zara when she thought I wasn't looking, causing Zara to snigger.

Phil the joker was holding court to my right. Leonard was there too, laughing his stupid aristocratic head off as usual. Oh, no! Big Tits was standing beside him. We saw each other at almost the same moment.

'Fern, how are you?'

Shit, she was coming over. She was wearing a very expensive-looking dark grey trouser suit with a light-pink lace camisole underneath. She executed a lady-like little skip through the crowd to reach us – a move designed to get the ultimate jiggle out of her boobs. She stood in front of us, tits wobbling like two giant blancmanges.

'Fabulous to see you, Fern,' – even as she spoke she was looking up at James – 'and James. You're looking well.'

'And you look stunning as usual, Lydia.'

She simpered up at him.

It never fails to amaze me how some girls can act so pathetically around men in front of other girls without being embarrassed. Even more amazing is that the men never seem to see it. Or maybe they just like it and don't care.

Their small talk continued for some minutes amidst much giggling, eyelash fluttering and meaningful eye contact. It was a relief when we were joined by the birthday boy and his girlfriend.

'Fern, meet Harry – he's forty today. And this is Elizabeth.'

'Happy birthday, Harry.'

His response was a drunken grin. Evidently all his friends had been buying him birthday drinks. I nodded at the girl with him and then did a double take. It couldn't be! She was looking hard at me too.

'Fern?'

'Lizzie?'

We both laughed.

'What are you doing here?' I had to stop myself from asking her what she was doing out so late on a school night.

'Oh, I've been with Harry for six months now.' She proudly linked her arm through Harry's, smiling broadly. Harry had just spilled a pint of Guinness down his shirt.

'How's your mum?' I knew that this was an inappropriate question to ask but at this point I was blindly groping for conversation.

Lizzie and her family lived on my street. I had babysat her for years. She had been a lovely little thing, cute and blonde. She still was.

'Mum's fine.'

Does she know that you're out with a middle-aged lush, is what I wanted to say. Instead I asked something equally inappropriate. 'How's school?'

Lizzie gave me a strange look.

'Fern, I'm twenty years old.'

Rubbish! I thought to myself. She couldn't possibly be a day over twelve.

Still, totting up the years I realised that she might well be twenty by now. I was nearly twenty-seven after all.

'What are you doing here, anyway?' she asked me, less smiley now. She was probably afraid I'd tell her mother on her.

'I'm here with James.'

'Oh, I thought he was with . . . ' She trailed off, looking confused.

'So,' – James's big hand landed heavily on my shoulder, 'I see you two have already met.'

I really didn't want to get into explanations. I just knew that I had to get away for a few minutes to compose myself.

'Look, I'm going to the bar. Anybody want a drink?'

'Yes, I'll have a pint of the black stuff and one for Harry too.'

'How about you, Lizzie?'

'Vodka and orange, please.' She looked at me defiantly. Coke and crisps is all you're getting, Missy, I felt like saying.

What a relief to get to the bar. Time to gather my thoughts. What did Lizzie mean that she thought James was with someone else? I must quizz her when I went back.

I jostled my way to the front of the bar and half-heartedly attempted to establish eye contact with one of the bar staff. Just this once I couldn't care less if it took me all night to get their attention. Predictably, my order was taken immediately.

'What's a fine filly like you doing in a dump like this?'

I thought I was hearing things. Looking to my right, I found a short, oldish man leering at me. I concentrated hard on the bar ahead of me. Maybe if I ignored him he'd go away.

'Can I buy you a drink?'

'I'm fine, thanks.' Avoid eye contact at all times.

'I know you're fine. I can see that. What I'm asking you is would you like a drink?'

It was with some effort that he uttered these sentences. Some of the words were blurred and ran into each other. There was a touch of drunken aggression in his tone which made me wary.

'I've already got a drink, thanks.' I had paid the barman, picked up the drinks and was turning to go when I felt a hand on my left bum cheek. I got such a shock that I dropped one of the pints. It landed with a loud crash which caused everybody in the near vicinity to stop their conversations and stare.

'Get your fucking hand off me!' I could feel the rage welling up inside.

'What's your problem?'

Taking advantage of my full hands, the drunken oaf decided to fill his own. He slid his other hand around to my other cheek. That was it. I'd had enough. It was as if every bit of hurt and anger that had been building up within me over the last few weeks exploded behind my eyes. I saw red. I slammed the remainder of my drinks down on the bar and landed an almighty slap on the side of his face.

I couldn't even begin to describe his look of surprise. He couldn't believe what had just happened to him. I noted with an immense feeling of satisfaction the red mark of my fingers on the side of his face. He instinctively put his own hand up to it, touching the skin gingerly.

It felt terrific. Girl power! I gathered up my drinks and began the triumphant walk back to my group. They were all looking at me, faces shocked. I didn't care. I was on a high. I could feel the adrenalin coursing through my body. I reached James and held out his drink to him. I noticed that my hand was trembling slightly.

'You shouldn't have done that, Fern.' James's face was deadly serious. He didn't take the drink from me.

'What do you mean? The old codger was touching me up.'

He shook his head and pushed past me.

He went over to the dirty old man who was standing at the bar, looking dazed. He was surrounded by a small gathering of men who seemed to be enquiring after his welfare. James touched him on the arm and started talking to him, his face concerned.

'What the . . . what about me?'

Bronwyn appeared at my side. She looked decidedly gleeful.

'Don't you know who that is?'

'I don't give a shit. He was groping me.'

'My dear, you've just slapped a judge.' Her look was triumphant as she dropped her final bombshell – 'Judge Carver.'

James's father.

Oh, my God.

This couldn't be happening to me.

I had to leave and fast.

I retrieved my coat, my head down, avoiding all the curious, amused glances thrown in my direction.

I had to get out of there.

I chanced looking in James's direction once before I left the bar. He didn't see me leave. He was busy being comforted by Bronwyn and Lydia.

I headed out of the cloying heat of the hotel into the night. The coldness of the air took my breath away. I started to cry. I'm not talking a slight sniffle here. Big, hot tears coursed down my cheeks, and my stomach and chest heaved with misery. I was grateful for the heavy rain which was lashing down, hiding my tears and ensuring that the few passers-by were hurrying to get indoors and barely noticed me.

I'd ruined everything.

My life was a mess.

Things couldn't possibly get any worse.

Yes, they could.

I suddenly remembered that I now had no lift home. Trying to get a taxi in Dublin the week before Christmas was a joke. I might as well start walking the five miles home.

I was overcome. I didn't care about anything any more. Not the rain. Not the danger of walking alone in the semi-deserted streets of the city at night-time. I sat down heavily on a doorstep and cried my heart out. I'm not sure how long I sat there. Could have been half an hour. Could have been five minutes. All I knew was my misery. I didn't even feel the cold.

After a time, a car pulled up to the pavement alongside me. Through the tears I noticed a man staring at me from the driver's seat.

Shit. The last thing I needed was to get attacked. I got up and started walking briskly towards the busier end of town. I hardly dared look around in case he was following. Jesus! He was following me! My misery turned to terror and panic as I tried to stop myself from breaking into a run.

'Fern? Fern, is that you?'

I stopped and turned around. I blinked a couple of times, trying to focus on the man as he walked rapidly towards me. It was Seán – the painter.

'It is you.' He smiled at first and then his face grew serious as he noticed the state I was in. 'Are you okay? Did something happen to you?'

'I'm fine, thanks.' I said ludicrously.

'You don't look fine,' he said, taking in my bedraggled appearance and wet, bloated, purplish face. I stood there feeling ridiculous and thinking how bad I must look with my make-up running in streaks down my face and my hair plastered to my head. 'Do you need a lift anywhere?'

I swallowed my pride. 'I'd love a lift home if you wouldn't mind,' I heard myself saying in a small voice that sounded as if it belonged to a five-year-old.

'Come on, then.' He placed his arm gently around my shoulders and led me to his car where he opened the back door. I allowed myself to be led and climbed into the back of the car like a robot. It didn't dawn on me to be afraid. All my earlier training in never getting into a car with a strange man was forgotten. I'd never felt safer.

We drove in silence for some time. It didn't really occur to me to speak. I stared out of the window listlessly.

'It can't be that bad.' Seán was looking at me carefully in the driver's mirror.

'Yes, it can.'

Nothing else was said for a while.

'Man trouble?'

'You could say that.'

'The barrister?'

I stared out the window.

'You found out about the other girl, then?'

That got my attention. 'What other girl?'

He looked me in the eye for a long second.

'Forget it.'

'What other girl?' I almost shouted at him.

'I'm sorry. I thought that must be why you were crying. I've seen him around the Courthouse with a tall girl, another barrister – long, blonde curly hair.'

Bronwyn!

'But they're just friends.' I sounded whining and pathetic but I couldn't help myself.

'No. It's more than that.' His voice was quiet, definite.

I stared out the window again.

Strangely, I wasn't all that surprised. It all made perfect sense really. The hurt and the shock weren't to kick in until later.

'Why were you crying, then?' he asked me after a while. I wanted to tell him to mind his own business but I felt I owed him some measure of politeness seeing as how he was giving me a lift home.

'James's father groped me so I slapped him in the face.'

'You did what?' He started to laugh.

'It's not funny,' I snapped. 'I didn't know it was his father. And he's a judge.'

'I'm sorry.' He was quiet for a few moments. Then he started to laugh again, harder this time. I started to laugh too, in spite of myself.

'Fair play to you!' We laughed even harder. I was annoyed with myself but I couldn't stop. It was probably hysteria. And then I started to cry again, big noisy sobs. I was so embarrassed, but again, I couldn't stop. His eyes in the mirror widened with alarm.

'Hey, It's okay. There's a toilet roll some-where in the back. Dry your eyes.'

I rooted around on the floor. The car was a mess. There were pads of paper, pencils, crayons, paint brushes large and small littered throughout. And it smelled of dog.

I found the loo-roll and blew my nose disgustingly. I was calming down.

'Better now?'

'Yes, thanks.' I felt like a small child.

He didn't say much else for the rest of the journey, apart from asking me for directions now and again. I was grateful for the silence. My head was buzzing.

He stopped the car. I realised with surprise that I was home.

'Thanks for the lift.' I thought that I should probably invite him in for coffee or something. God knows I wanted to be on my own so that I could sob my heart out but it would have been rude not to. 'Um – would you like to come in for some tea?'

'No, thanks.' The words were out of his mouth before I'd even finished the sentence. I didn't know if I was relieved or insulted.

'Okay then.' I got out of the car, nearly twisting my ankle on all the rubble on the floor of the back seat.

As Seán wound down the window, I noticed what a crap car he had. I stood forlornly on the pavement as he looked up at me from the driver's seat, the perpetual grin on his face. How could someone with such a crap job and a crap car be so damn happy all the time? I mean, it wasn't as if he was a student or something. He must have been pushing thirty.

I kept standing there. He kept sitting there.

'Well?'

'Well, what?'

'Are you going into your house or what?'

'I was waiting for you to leave.'

'Why? Are you only pretending that this is your house?'

'If I was going to lie about where I lived, I wouldn't have picked a dump like this.'

He laughed. 'Maybe you just don't want me to know where you live.'

'I couldn't care less.'

'Charming!'

'Well, are you going or not?'

'I'm waiting for you to get safely inside before I leave.'

'Goodnight.' I rolled my eyes to heaven and headed towards my front door.

In actual fact, I was really touched by his gesture. There was something very protective about it. Something very trustworthy. Once I was inside the front door, I turned towards him. He waved and drove off.

As soon as he'd gone, I remembered how miserable I truly was. Now for my big cry. But funnily enough, I didn't feel like crying any more. Instead I went into the kitchen and made myself drinking chocolate. I took my mug and a handful of chocolate-chip cookies into the TV room. Dad was still up, fast asleep in his chair. His glasses had fallen off his head. He was snoring loudly at the TV.

We sat like this in companionable silence – apart from the snoring – me, Dad and the cat – for a long time. A picture of domestic bliss. Well, it was the closest we could hope to get to it these days. My mother had not called although Sasha had been to see her a few times. I'd call in to see her too – if I wasn't so busy. It looked as if any hopes we might have had for a Christmas reconciliation were going rapidly down the toilet. Not that we had any hopes in the first place. Let's be realistic here. Things had been going badly wrong for a long time. I had no doubt that my parents were better off apart. But still the little child inside me wanted the perfect family Christmas – Mammy and Daddy smiling at each other across the tinsel. Guess my inner child would have to face up yet again to that unpleasant thing called reality.

Dad woke himself with a gigantic snore. He sat up with a start and blinked about the room blindly. He groped for his glasses which were in their customary spot on the floor and put them on. His eyes widened with surprise as he saw me curled up on the sofa.

'You're back early.'

'The party wasn't great.'

'What have you been doing to yourself? You're a mess.' He clocked my dishevelled state.

'Thanks, Dad.'

'Your face is all dirty.'

'My make-up ran, that's all.'

'I don't know why young girls like you have to wear make-up anyway. You don't need it. It just looks tarty.'

'Dad!'

'Your mother never wore make-up when we were courting.' Courting! I love that word. So old-fashioned.

'Yeah, yeah – in the good old days. Everyone wears make-up now, Dad. Where did you used to go, then? For all this "courting"?'

He leaned back in his armchair, his eyes adopting a faraway expression.

'You name it, we went there. The Ierne ballroom. The Metropole. Clery's. The Crystal. Anywhere Dickie Rock and The Miami were playing. Your mother was a big Dickie fan. She was a lovely dancer too. Still is, mind. We won a fair few competitions.'

I nodded at him encouragingly, not wanting him to stop. It was so rare to get my father to open up like this. He probably hadn't woken up properly yet. I didn't want him to.

'I know, I've seen the trophies.' There were several small battered tin cups in the display cabinet in the living room.

'You young people haven't a notion how to dance. All that lepping about like mad and waving your arms in the air. Call that dancing! Times change.' He shook his head slowly, as if weary of it all. 'Where did this chap take you tonight anyway?'

'We went to the Shelbourne.'

'The Shelbourne! It's far from the Shelbourne Hotel you were raised, Missy.'

'Like you said, times change.'

'Did you enjoy yourself?'

'It was okay.'

'When am I going to meet him?'

'I doubt if I'll be seeing him again.'

'Why not?'

'It didn't go too great tonight, Dad.'

He looked at me sympathetically. 'Never mind. We Fennellys have never been lucky in love. I'm going up. Goodnight.'

Now, there was a depressing thought. My disastrous love life was actually genetic and there was nothing I could do about it.

'Oh, and Fern.' Dad stuck his head back around the door.

'What?' I waited expectantly for a nugget of wisdom from my elder.

'Don't forget to let the cat out before you go to bed or she'll shit on the floor, and I'm not cleaning it up again.'

Chapter Eight

The grogginess hadn't lifted by the time I got into work, despite my shower and the ten-minute walk from the train to the office in the bitter cold.

Was it my imagination or was I getting strange looks from people I passed in the corridor? Or was my paranoia totally out of control? It was hard to tell. Fortunately, Julie didn't come barging out of her office as soon as she heard me come in – to admonish me for being one minute late, like she usually did. In fact, she was unusually quiet all morning. She spent most of her time on internal calls and not once did she summon me into her sanctuary.

Later that afternoon, while I was doing my stint on reception, I got a call from Deirdre, Cyril's secretary. She sounded subdued.

'Mr Boland would like a word with you, Fern. Could you pop upstairs for a few minutes? I'll get someone to cover for you.'

'Sure.' I was stunned. Cyril didn't even know my name. He hadn't even recognised me that night at the exhibition. What could he possibly want with the likes of me?

A few minutes later, I was knocking timidly on the senior partner's door.

'Come in.' Cyril looked tiny behind his massive walnut desk. Julie was seated to his left, her legs and arms tightly crossed, her expression blank. She avoided the searching, puzzled expression in my eyes. What was going on?

'Take a seat, Fern.' I wondered again how he knew my name all of a sudden.

'Fern . . . ' His voice was grave. His hands were clasped in front of him on the desk, as if he was praying, and his head was inclined to one side. He was trying his best to look sincere. 'It's come to my attention that your mind hasn't exactly been on your work of late.'

I looked wildly at Julie who was carefully examining her immaculate fingernails.

'Would you agree?'

'I . . . I . . . ' I was speechless.

'Well?'

'I've had a few problems in my personal life lately but everything is fine now.' I could hear the panic in my own voice.

'At Boland, Sharpe & Co. we pride ourselves on being professional and not letting our personal problems impinge on the quality of our work.'

'I . . . I'm sorry, It won't happen again.'

'I'm afraid It's already happened once too often, Fern. We're going to have to let you go.'

His voice was caring and gentle. It was the voice a doctor would use when telling a patient that she had terminal cancer. Julie continued to say nothing very loudly.

'But I've always worked hard, done my best.' I tried desperately.

'I don't doubt that, Fern. But I'm very sorry. You're just not Boland, Sharpe material.'

Not Boland Sharpe material.

Not Boland Sharpe material.

The words swirled around inside my head.

I couldn't speak.

'We'll pay you up to the Christmas holidays, of course. I realise what an expensive time of the year it is. And, of course, you'll be more than welcome to attend the Christmas party.' Was that meant to be some kind of sick joke?

'You're free to leave whenever it suits you.' He stood up and held out his hand.

I'd love to tell you that I read them the riot act. That I told them where they could stick their job. That I threw in a few choice insults and home truths, just for good measure. But I didn't. Instead, I shook his hand mutely and left the room, closing the door quietly behind me. I could feel the tears welling up as I headed for the toilets. I had to make a run for it to reach the cubicle before the dam burst. Luckily no one else was in there.

Not Boland Sharpe material.

I cried my eyes out – again. I was amazed that I had any tears left after last night's flood. I couldn't comprehend what had just happened to me.

Not Boland Sharpe material.

It took over twenty minutes for the crying to stop and for my eyes and nose to lose their purple, bloated appearance. Each time I managed to stop crying I would get an image of the humiliating interview or of last night's débâcle with James and his father, and the tears would start flowing again.

Eventually I emerged. I looked at myself in the mirror. What a mess! I splashed my face with cold water and smoothed down my hair. Slight improvement. Better get it over with then. Fortunately I didn't meet anyone on the way to my office. It didn't take me long to pack up my things – one handbag, one coat and a print of one of my favourite paintings, *Flaming June* by

Leighton. Usually the girl in the painting appeared to me to be sleeping peacefully. Today she looked dead. I had never got around to decorating my office with plants, cartoons and family photographs, as recommended by all the magazines. Perhaps I had always known that I wouldn't be there for the long haul.

Grace the receptionist was the only person I came into contact with on my way out of the building. She barely noticed me leave, so intent was she on her crossword puzzle.

I closed the door of Boland Sharpe & Co. for the last time. I stepped out onto the street full of people going happily about their business as if nothing had happened. The Christmas lights blurred. I willed myself not to start crying again until I was indoors – somewhere quiet and safe and dark.

But I didn't want to go home. It hit me that I had nowhere to go. I'd never felt so alone. I felt as if I existed on a different plane from the rest of the human race. Everybody else went about their business, interacting and communicating with one another. But some invisible force field prevented me from joining in. I longed for a sympathetic listener, someone with whom I could sit down and to whom I could blurt out my whole sorry life story – someone who would listen without criticising or judging me. I needed a best friend but there was no one. How did I get this way? No real friends, no family, no proper home, no money, no job. No life. Just a desperate, hum-drum existence interrupted only by personal crises and disasters. I deeply envied those with normal family backgrounds and a comfortable circle of friends whom they'd known all their lives.

I rang Declan. He picked up the phone to my wet snivellings.

'Who is this?'

'It's me.'

'Me, who?'

'Fern.' There were a few moments of silence.

'Where are you calling from?' He sounded funny.

'I'm in a phone box on O'Connell Street. Meet me under Clery's clock in ten minutes.'

'Fern, I can't just drop everything and leave. I'm in the middle of . . .'

'I don't care what you're in the middle of. I need to see you, now!' I sounded hysterical, even to myself.

'Is that Fern? Put her on to me!' It was Lydia's disemboobed voice in the background.

'If you put that bitch on the phone, I'm hanging up.'

Okay. Jesus! I'll see you in ten minutes.'

I waited impatiently outside the main entrance of Clery's department store. Matronly women glanced curiously at my tear-stained face. Fifteen minutes later, Declan showed up, hands thrust deep within the pockets of his trench coat, nose red and raw against the cold. His manner was furtive. He reminded me of a paedophile or a spy.

'Let's go for coffee.' His voice was muffled into his Doctor Who scarf. I followed him wordlessly to a nearby grotty coffee shop. He ordered two coffees at the counter and I slumped down at a table for two by the window.

'I don't want to sit there.' He was standing above me, bearing two steaming mugs. 'Let's go over here instead.'

I shrugged and followed him over to a table for four in a dark corner.

'Declan, I got fired.'

'I heard.'

'Did you? I suppose It's all around the office by now.'

'Pretty much.'

'Oh, Declan. I feel so humiliated. And now it's probably over with James too.'

He reached over the table and squeezed my hand. It was nice. Comforting.

'What should I do?'

'I don't know. Move on, I suppose. Relax at home for a few days then look for another job.'

'The last place I want to go is home.'

'Well, spend a few nights with me then.' My heart melted a little.

'That's very kind, but won't your parents mind?' Like most apprentices, Declan couldn't afford his own place.

'I meant we could book a hotel room.'

He was staring at me intently. Oh.

'Oh.' Involuntarily I withdrew my hand and placed it safely on my lap. That wasn't the type of comfort I had in mind.

'I don't think so.'

'Fair enough.' Declan drained his coffee cup and replaced it loudly on the table. 'I'd better be off then. See you around.'

'Declan! Don't be like that.'

'I'm not being like anything. I really have to get back to work.'

'Can I at least call you sometime?'

'Whatever.' He got up to leave.

'Please! Stay and talk to me. You took me by surprise, that's all.'

'Just leave it, Fern.'

He wouldn't look at me but I could see his cheeks blazing before he turned and walked out the door.

I got on the bus, gazing vacantly out the window for the entire journey. I got off and started walking until I found myself at Aunt Marjorie's house. My mother answered the door – as if she lived there or something. It felt all wrong. Like I'd called at the wrong house. Sorry to bother you. I thought somebody else lived here.

My mother's face altered slightly. It might have been a smile.

'Come in.'

I followed her through the hall – all worn, patterned carpet and clashing patterned wallpaper. She looked back at me and I saw that the recognition had returned to her eyes.

'Why aren't you in work?'

'I took the day off to do some shopping.' The lie sprang easily to my lips. My mother already knew I was a failure. There was no need to give her further confirmation.

'Did you buy anything nice?'

'Only a few bits.'

My mother proceeded to make tea, as if it was her kitchen, only different.

'So, how are things at home?'

'Okay. You know. Just getting ready for Christmas.'

There was a pause. I wouldn't call it a pregnant pause. More of a twenty-four-hour labour pause.

'What are you doing for Christmas then?'

'I'm spending it here with your Auntie Marjorie and Uncle John.'

This time the baby was born.

'Mam, why don't you come home? It's Christmas.'

She turned to me, her eyes full of sympathy.

'There wouldn't be any point, love. It's over between your Dad and me. Part of me would love to come home for Christmas but it wouldn't be fair to give him false hope.'

'I know you haven't been getting on but surely if you just talked to each other . . . ' My mother was shaking her head sadly but I kept on talking. 'Or maybe if you both went to see a marriage guidance counsellor or something . . .'

'Fern. I'm sorry, love. It's too far gone for that. Being married to and living with your father was making me miserable and that's all there is to it.'

'And what about me and Sasha? Did we make you miserable too?'

'Of course not. But you girls are all grown up now. This separation isn't going to affect you. It's not as if you're little kids any more.' Then why did I still feel like a little kid?

'I just don't get it.' I didn't get it.

'I hope that one day when you're older you'll understand why I had to do this.' She was enigmatic. Like a tragic heroine in a play. I couldn't think of anything else to say.

'Do you want me to call in sometime to give you your present?'

'That would be nice.'

She had lit up a cigarette. She inhaled deeply and stared out the kitchen window onto the rain-sodden garden. That was maybe the one thing I had in common with my mother – my propensity for staring vacantly out of windows, looking for what, I don't know. For the life I wanted perhaps.

I must have been looking out the wrong windows.

There was nothing else for it. I went home.

Chapter Nine

So that was how I entered my twenty-eighth year on this earth. Things were not looking up, to say the least. In fact, it wouldn't be wrong to say that my life was falling apart.

Perhaps you're expecting some great Scarlett O'Hara-esque 'I'll never be hungry again' speech. The reality was a lot less dramatic. When I look back on 'that Christmas' I can't remember all that much. I did my best impression of a Christmas cracker, being pulled in the direction of one side of the family and then the other. I vaguely recall the visitors coming and going. The mince pies, the brandy and ginger. Lots of brandy and ginger.

None of my relations mentioned my parents splitting up, although they all knew about it. Pity – it would have been nice to have talked to someone about it. But they all seemed to identify it as my parents' problem and not mine. I met up with a few friends over the holidays – friends who were home from abroad – people who fortunately had never heard of James Carver. I didn't tell them about my parents either. Or about my job. It seemed selfish to ruin their festive mood.

I rang Declan a couple of times. He didn't return my calls.

My obsession with James had grown to gigantic proportions, now that he was no longer part of my life. He was constantly at the back of my mind. More often at the front. I tried to stop thinking about him but nothing seemed to work. I came perilously close to phoning him several times but I managed to pull myself back from the brink in the nick of time. To be honest, what held me back was fear of what he might say to me, rather than self-respect.

I yo-yo'd wildly between anger towards him and his father – which made my head fit to burst – and a desperate longing to be held and touched by him – which made my heart fit to burst.

I knew it was pathetic, but what could I do? Zilch. I also knew that Old Father Time was a great healer, but I wished he'd bloody well hurry up about it. Typical man – keeping me hanging on.

My other problems were almost a welcome distraction.

What to do about a job?

There was no way I was going back to work in a solicitor's office, or any office. I'd starve first – thereby solving my weight problem and killing two birds with one stone. The trouble was that I wasn't qualified to do anything else. There had to be something out there for me, but when your self-confidence had been reduced to the size of an electron – as mine had been – it was hard to imagine what.

I hit the grey pavements of Dublin on one of those dull January mornings that make you wish that bears weren't the only ones who hibernated in the winter.

I practised the art of positive thinking, as if it was going out of fashion, as I tramped my way from shop to shop, trying not to look and sound as pathetic as I felt.

'Yes, they do need someone like me, yes they would be lucky to have me,' I muttered furiously under my breath, head and shoulders hunched against the rain and wind.

By 11.30 a.m., I had taken more knock-backs than a heavyweight prize fighter. I decided to treat myself to a coffee and Danish. I slipped into a cosy-looking café and seated myself at a table for two, just inside the door, trying to be as inconspicuous as possible. I had never quite got the hang of the art of dining alone, even if it was just morning coffee. I would have bought a magazine but my already overstretched finances had long since lost their elasticity.

I was approached by a friendly-looking blonde girl bearing a notepad and pen.

'You look like someone who could do with a hot drink.' Her voice was loud and cheery. Oh no, I hoped she didn't try to engage me in conversation. I just wasn't up to it. I smiled vaguely up at her, trying to keep my manner polite yet distant.

'A white coffee and a Danish if you have one, please.'

'We certainly do. Is apple and cinnamon okay?'

I nodded.

'Excellent!' She seemed thrilled with my choice as she trotted off to get my order.

I retreated into my rain-soaked shell, mentally counting on one hand the shops that had half-heartedly taken my phone number. She arrived back in what seemed like a minute and a half and plonked the coffee and Danish in front of me.

'Enjoy!' She exclaimed brightly and off she went, exuberantly clearing off a nearby dirty table, singing along tunelessly at the top of her voice to the song on the radio. I noted with irritation that she was getting the words all wrong.

I began to eat the Danish guiltily and self-consciously, all the while expecting a member of the Fat Police to tap me on the shoulder. ('Do you know how many calories that Danish contains, Miss?') I bitterly imagined Bronwyn tucking into her elevenses of celery and carrot sticks.

I noticed with increasing annoyance that the waitress kept looking in my direction and smiling. I concentrated on sending her telepathic signals to go away. It didn't work. To my horror, she sat down opposite me and smiled directly into my face. Feeling slightly panicky, I took a large swig of coffee, almost burning the back of my throat in the process.

'So – doing a spot of job hunting, then?'

My surprise was genuine. 'How did you know?'

'Simple. It's Tuesday morning. You're not in work. You don't have any shopping bags. You're kind of well dressed and you look totally pissed off.'

What did she mean, 'kind of' well dressed? I was wearing my good clothes. Still, I conceded, I probably looked pretty bedraggled at this stage.

'Well, yes, I am job hunting,' I admitted.

'What are you looking for, then?'

I scrutinised her face with its open, kind expression. I felt myself warm towards her.

'Oh, anything to keep the wolf from the door,' I replied miserably.

'Have you ever waitressed before?'

'I did a bit in London.'

'How did you find it?'

'It was okay. Good. In fact, I really liked it,' I amended quickly. Now she had my interest.

'Well this could be your lucky day.' She looked delighted with herself.

'You mean you have a vacancy here? You don't have a sign up.'

'I know. One of our waitresses rang me up half an hour ago to tell me she wouldn't be working here any more.'

'How come?'

'She's been taken into custody for drug smuggling.' She smiled cheerfully at me. 'So her loss is your gain.'

I was a little taken aback but excited just the same.

'So, do I have to do an interview or anything?'

'You just have.' She beamed. 'When can you start?'

'Er . . . tomorrow?' I said doubtfully.

'Perfect. Call in at about ten and I'll show you the ropes.' And with that she went off with herself to serve a couple who had just come in.

I was gobsmacked. Things like that just don't happen to me. I'm simply not a lucky person. Still, I'm not one to look a gift horse in the mouth either. Now at least I didn't have to trudge around for the rest of the day, taking rejection after rejection. It was too good to be true. There had to be a catch. Probably lousy hours and lousy pay. Even so, a job was a job.

My first morning on the job was a nightmare. I managed to send an ice-cube-laden glass of Diet Coke crashing down on the floor right beside an ancient-looking old woman. I could see the headlines flashing in front of my eyes:

'Old dear dies of heart attack at hands of clumsy waitress!'

Cyril would probably handle the case against me.

Luckily she didn't die.

I had trouble remembering the orders. Customers would ask me for something and I would go off into a little daydream only to realise that I'd forgotten what they wanted by the time I got back to the kitchen. I was beginning to form the very definite opinion that I just wasn't cut out for a job that required organisational skills or any significant level of efficiency.

By the end of my shift, I was feeling pretty dejected. When the lunchtime madness was over, I joined Sarah – formerly known as the friendly blonde waitress – in the staffroom. It turned out that she managed the place. I half expected her to give me the sack there and then.

She beamed up at me as I entered the room.

'Well – how was your first day?'

I looked at her doubtfully. 'Okay, I suppose.'

'Well, it was a start, wasn't it? I thought you did great.'

'Really?' I was amazed.

'Yes, I saw the way you handled the customers. You're very good at dealing with people. You're nice to them and they appreciate that. Smoke?'

She offered me a Silk Cut. I took it and accepted a light.

Sarah started telling me about an incident that had happened with a customer over lunch. Something about a batty old woman who came in every Wednesday, nursed a mug of coffee for about an hour and then made a bolt for it after stuffing her handbag full of napkins. I wasn't really listening. I was too busy observing again.

I couldn't recall meeting anyone quite like her. She was a big girl. Not fat. You wouldn't even call her pleasantly plump. Strapping was the word. Her hair was long, straight, silky and golden. She wore it in a simple pony tail tied at the nape of her neck.

Her face didn't look like it belonged to a strapping person. Her features were petite: button nose; small, even teeth; dimples; striking blue eyes. And her expression – she never stopped smiling. Not just her mouth – her whole face – her eyes. She had the kindest eyes. She looked like a big soft angel.

It was weird. She acted as if she wanted to be my friend or something. I was probably flattering myself. She was the type who was just really friendly to everybody. Everybody wanted to be her friend, no doubt. There had to be a catch. I was always looking for the catch.

She sensed that I wasn't listening to her. She stopped talking and smiled.

'Are you doing anything tonight, Fern?'

'No – why?'

'One of the girls who works here – Tamsin – you haven't met her yet – It's her birthday today so we thought we'd go out for a few pints. Are you on for it?'

'Sure, why not?'

I felt almost happy as I got the train back into town that night. Nervous, of course. I always find it difficult to meet a new group of people. Especially when they already know each other.

I walked down the steps of Sinnott's pub, scanning the room for Sarah. It was pretty busy for a Wednesday night. Perhaps people weren't ready to admit that the Christmas party season was over.

'Fern, over here!' I could hear the yell above the loud music. The whole pub probably heard. I turned to see Sarah standing and waving frantically at me. She was surrounded by a group of five or six other girls. She left the group and came over to greet me. 'I'm so glad you could make it. Come and meet everyone.' She squeezed my arm warmly and led me over to where the girls were sitting.

She did the round of introductions. Of course, I didn't have a hope in hell of remembering any of the names. Sarah put me sitting down beside her and went up to the bar to get me a drink. The others were incredibly friendly. They all chatted away like mad, asking me questions about myself and seeming delighted with all my answers. I immediately felt included. It was a heady sensation. I found myself wondering darkly how long it would take them to figure out what a loser I was – but I pushed the thought resolutely aside and decided to enjoy myself for once. It worked too. More than once, I found myself marvelling at the contrast between these friendly, down-to-earth people and those I had hung out with in my previous incarnation as a legal secretary.

I spoke with Sarah a lot of the time. At first she did most of the talking but, as I relaxed, I caught up with her. There seemed so much to say all of a sudden. I got lost in the conversation and forgot to be shy. We laughed a lot too. Silly stuff mainly. When I thought about it the next day, I couldn't remember what we had been laughing at. But it didn't matter.

Several drinks later and the dance floor beckoned seductively. Who cared if it was only the size of a postage stamp and there were forty people dancing on it already? The more the merrier. And it didn't matter if you couldn't dance because nobody had any room to move their arms and legs anyway. Even Michael Flatley would have looked like he was suffering from a severe case of white-boy's-rhythm. It was very intimate too. That's if you didn't mind being squished up against the creature from the black lagoon every now and then. The dance floor was mainly populated with women anyway. The men all stood around the edges balancing their pint glasses on their beer bellies and ogling our wobbly bits (the bits that were meant to wobble, in any case). There was nothing like a good old-fashioned mating ritual.

I felt myself getting out of breath and went to buy myself a fizzy water at the bar. I had the misfortune to position myself beside a man in his mid-fifties – old enough to be my father, as they say. He seemed insistent on telling me his life story. Did he ask me a single question about myself? No. Did he ask me for my opinion on anything other than himself? No. And he was presumably trying to chat me up. Why are men of that generation so bad at talking to women? They can't have a proper conversation. All they do is talk about themselves and try and impress you with their knowledge of useless facts. I felt a pang of sympathy for my mother and all the other Irish women of her generation. They must have been suffering from terminal boredom all these years.

I was transfixed listening to him go on and on about himself. Amazed at the level of self-centredness – almost envying the size of his ego. I could do with a bit of that myself.

'Need any help with the drinks?' It was Sarah. 'I thought you looked as if you needed rescuing,' she whispered out of the corner of her mouth.

I smiled, 'I'm okay. Pete here was just telling me all about himself.'

Sarah offered her hand to Pete and they shook.

'Hi, Pete! God, Fern, that must have been fascinating for you. Anyway, you're needed urgently back on the dance floor. Bye, Pete.' And we ran off, giggling like thirteen-year-olds.

Being a large group of drunken girls, we attracted a lot of male attention that night. Not that any of us took it seriously. It was just good for a laugh and great for the confidence. I couldn't remember the last time I'd had such an enjoyable night. Okay, so I admit I thought about James from time to time and experienced the odd pang of loneliness, but not nearly as much as usual (i.e. all the time).

At the end of the night, I didn't want to go home but I allowed myself to be bundled happily into the back of a taxi. When I got home, I lay on my bed, fully clothed, hugging my new-found happiness into my chest and watching the ceiling spin. I knew that my head would feel like a concrete block and my mouth like the inside of an Arab's sock in the morning but I didn't give a rat's arse. It had been worth it.

Chapter Ten

There was something very liberating about working at a job that didn't require massive amounts of brain power. In the beginning it took a fair bit of concentration to master the art of remembering and doing twenty different things at once, but after several weeks I was beginning to get the hang of it and slipped into autopilot more and more often.

What joy not to have to go home at night and obsess about what Julie was going to say about my work the next day. Not to have to anticipate the angry red biro marks all over the documents that I had typed. Now I just did my work, went home and that was that. The meals I served were over and done with in the one day. There were no red biro marks on the tablecloths when I went in for my next shift.

I began to feel that maybe I wasn't such a bad waitress after all. In fact, I liked working in the café. By day, it was a buzzing, unpretentious spot, frequented mainly by students from the nearby college, and by night the humble café became a trendy bistro. The clientèle were slightly older and more sophisticated.

Of course, the lack of thought my job required had a downside too. I had plenty of time to think about James. I still felt incredibly hurt by the way I had been treated. I tried to turn all the hurt and anger I had inside against him, but I had a hard time convincing myself that I hated him. In fact, I thought about him so much that I barely had time left to dwell on my parents' separation.

At least my painting was coming on well. These days it was becoming less of a therapy and more of an enjoyable past-time. Though I still lacked the courage to show anyone my work.

I didn't take art as a subject in secondary school. My parents considered it frivolous. And, being the obedient daughter, I duly took the typing option instead. It made sense as I obviously lacked the brains to go to college, or – God forbid! – university. No, my sister was the clever one. She had studied commerce and was currently taking the banking world by storm. Yes – we'd both managed to live up – or down – to our parents' expectations.

Sasha was the only person who'd seen my paintings. She barged into my room uninvited so many times that it was unavoidable. After that humiliating experience I hadn't drawn anything in about a year. But I had started up again, slowly but surely. It was something I just felt compelled to do. I had no idea where it came from. Nobody else in my family had any such leanings, as far as I knew.

So there I was, minding my own business – new job, fair attempt at a new life – when my past walked in through the door of the café and ambushed my present.

I was clearing a table at the back of the restaurant. It was busy enough, what with groups of students skipping lectures and worn-out shoppers gratefully downing never-ending cups of coffee. And in walks Seán.

Co-incidental enough, you may say. But there's more.

He goes over to Sarah who's setting a table at the front of the room and taps her on the shoulder. She spins around, squeals with delight and flings her arms around his neck. He in turn lifts her up off the ground and engulfs her in a huge bear hug.

I was aware that she had a boyfriend who had been away for a while but, uncharacteristically, she hadn't talked about him much. Imagine it being Seán! I felt an unpleasant sensation in the pit of my stomach. I vaguely recognised the feeling but couldn't quite place it. I loaded up the dirty plates and turned into the kitchen. For some reason, I didn't want him to see me, didn't want to be introduced – or re-introduced. I was still embarrassed after our last meeting. All that raw hurt and humiliation in the back of his car (not that I wasn't used to being humiliated in the back of men's cars). That probably explained the strange sinking feeling I had experienced when I saw Seán hugging Sarah. Embarrassment. That part of my life was over now. The last thing I wanted was for my promising new life to be infected by memories of my inglorious past. To hell with Seán anyway. He knew too much.

When my shift was over a few minutes later, I snuck out the back door to avoid them. I couldn't help feeling depressed. If I wanted to stay friends with Sarah, I was hardly going to be able to avoid meeting her boyfriend.

I hadn't told them anything about James or the other disasters in my all-too-recent past. It wasn't as if I'd told her lies or anything. I preferred to call it 'glossing over' – filling in the cracks of my life with verbal Polyfilla. I didn't want anyone to know what a mess I'd made of my life so far. I was trying to change. I could do without being dragged down again.

And another thing! It wasn't all that long ago that he had asked me out. He was probably seeing Sarah all along. What a rat!

The next day at work, she greeted me, all smiles.

'Fern, are you doing anything tonight?'

'I'm not sure. Why?'

'My boyfriend's back. I told you he'd been away for a while. I'd love you to meet him. Come out with us.'

'Oh – I don't know, Sarah . . . ' I fished around wildly for an excuse. She looked so disappointed.

'Oh please, you'd really like him.'

'I'm sure I would. It's not that. I'm just very tired today. I was planning an early night.'

'It won't just be the three of us if that's what you're worried about. You won't be playing gooseberry.'

'I don't know . . . '

'Oh come on – it'll be a laugh.' She gazed at me imploringly, her head tilted to one side. 'Oh please,' she coaxed, 'pretty, pretty please – just for me.'

'Oh, go on then.' What the hell. I couldn't stave off the evil day forever. Sarah practically skipped back to the kitchen. I couldn't help smiling. It was nice to be wanted all the same.

My happiness was short-lived, however. I grew more and more deflated as the day progressed. Now they'd all know. The thin layer of mystery I'd managed to wrap around myself would be stripped away and the miserable naked truth would be exposed. Sarah and the others wouldn't want to know me once they found out I'd been dumped, sacked and had no friends. And all because of that cocky, unfaithful bastard. Okay – so he'd been kind to me that one night when he gave me the lift home, but I was willing to put that down to one small island of charity in a sea of badness.

I nearly didn't go. I probably would have chickened out if Sarah hadn't rung me twice to make sure that I was still coming. My lack of enthusiasm that afternoon must have been palpable.

The arrangement was to meet at her place and start the night's proceedings at the local pub. I'd never been to her home before. Her house was the last in a row of red-bricked terraced buildings. The light shining through the stained glass beside the front door lent a warm, cosy air to the place. It beckoned me in from the cruel February night. I longed to be indoors. I rang the doorbell and raised a cacophony of barking dogs. Jesus! I hate dogs. Scared shitless of them, to tell the truth. And it sounded as if they were in the house too. Even worse. So unhygienic!

A blurred figure moved closer in fragments through the coloured-glass window. The door opened to reveal a small, fair, middle-aged woman.

'I'm Fern,' I said stupidly.

'Of course you are. Come in out of the night. You're very welcome, Fern.' She shut the door against the cold. 'Let me have your coat, love.'

It had to be Sarah's mother.

'I'm Sarah's Mam.'

'Pleased to meet you, Mrs Morrissey.'

'Merciful hour, don't call me Mrs Morrissey! There's only one Mrs Morrissey and that's the mother-in-law and I don't want to be mistaken for her.' She threw her eyes up to heaven in mock horror. 'Call me Pam.'

I laughed and felt immediately relaxed.

'Sarah's still upstairs getting ready. Go inside and keep Seán company. Have you met Seán?'

'Kind of.' So much for feeling relaxed.

'I'll bring you in a coffee,' she called back to me as she walked down the hall and into the kitchen. (Come back!) In I went.

Seán was sprawled across the sofa watching *Blind Date*. He was wearing a pair of faded blue jeans. They looked as if they were about one hundred years old. They had that lovely soft-looking quality of genuine, well-worn denim – the quality you can't fake with a pair of new jeans no matter how many times you wash, re-wash and trample all over them. This was genuine vintage denim – a good year by the looks of things. On top he was wearing a plain white T-shirt that had seen better days. It was hardly Persil white. He was slumped on the couch, half-sitting, half-lying down. His long legs were stretched out before him and his hands were clasped behind his head. He looked totally at home.

He glanced up casually as I entered the room and then did a double take. He pulled himself up into a sitting position, the slappers on the TV forgotten.

'Fern! What in the hell are you doing here?' His face was wreathed in smiles. He seemed delighted to see me, even though I say so myself. The two-timing cur! 'Did you leave something in my car?'

Only my dignity, I thought.

'How did you know where to find me?' He looked really confused now, but pleased just the same. He was on his feet at this stage – standing a little too close for comfort if the truth be told. I felt dwarfed. I gazed down at the ugly, brown, patterned carpet, unable to look him in the eye.

'I'm not here to see you. I'm here to see Sarah,' I said curtly. 'We work together.'

By the time I looked up at him again, he had regained his composure.

'What? In the café? But I thought you were a legal secretary.'

'Not any more,' I said shortly. My tone would have left most people in no doubt that I didn't want to talk about it. But Seán wasn't most people.

'Why not?'

'None of your business.' I was taken aback afresh by the level of animosity I felt towards him. He was undeterred.

'It's because you slapped the judge, isn't it.'

I examined the awful carpet again.

'You know, if they sacked you over that, you could take legal action against them.'

I met his blue gaze. His eyes were serious now. He was looking into mine searchingly. I felt my anger dissolve.

'I just want to put it behind me.'

He looked hard at me for a few long seconds and then nodded. 'Anyway, what am I doing? Here – sit down.' He gestured to a nearby armchair – brown to match the carpet. I sat down reluctantly, taking in the whitish dog hairs all over the seat.

'Do you like *Blind Date*?'

'Actually I find it puerile.'

He laughed. 'Yes, I suppose you would.'

He continued to chuckle to himself. There could be no mistake. He wasn't laughing with me. He wasn't even laughing near me. He was laughing at me. He was so rude!

My anger was back, quick as lightning. It wasn't that I was unused to feeling anger. It was just that I was generally able to keep it under wraps – turn it in on myself so that I didn't hurt or offend anyone else. Okay – so I slapped the judge, but that was a one off. But it was as if Seán knew all my triggers. Everything he said seemed to provoke a violent reaction in me.

'So, you've known Sarah a long time, then?' I had to know how long they had been together.

He looked at me strangely. 'You could say that.'

At that moment, Sarah's mother, bearing a tray and accompanied by no fewer than three dogs, entered the room. How she managed not to spill anything I'll never know. Within seconds I was surrounded by a blur of fur, licking tongues and wagging tails. I couldn't suppress a squeal.

'Seán, be a pet and get those dogs away from Fern,' she said as she made ineffectual attempts to whoosh the dogs away from me. Two of the dogs were successfully disposed of. The third, the largest, seemed intent on sticking his snout into my crotch. I was mortified. Seán had to lean over me and yank the dog away by the collar. His face was right down beside mine. He looked right into my eyes and grinned.

'I taught him how to do that.'

I was outraged! Of all the appalling taste. Poor Sarah! Not only was her boyfriend unfaithful. He was also totally uncouth.

I felt something stir inside me and decided to ignore it.

Alone in the room for the first time, I sipped my coffee frenetically. I wanted to go home. I contemplated slipping quietly out into the night before anyone came back into the room. The front door beckoned to me. I had an urge just to run. My eyes darted around the room in a panic. They landed on a picture of Sarah and Seán, sitting on that very same brown couch, smiling and relaxed, looking completely at ease. Judging by the hairstyles, that picture had been taken a few years ago.

Seán came back in and sat on the edge of the couch, his elbows resting against his knees, the perpetual grin on his face. I sat rigidly, legs crossed tightly away from him, my back pressed into the chair, trying to disappear into it.

'I'm sorry if I embarrassed you. It was only a joke – not a very good one, I know.'

'No, it wasn't. A joke is meant to make you laugh.'

'I know – and I'm sorry.' He made an unsuccessful attempt to look chastened.

'So, what did Sarah tell you about me, then? I hope she did me justice.'

'That would be difficult, Seán.' Moral outrage hadn't worked so I decided to try sarcasm.

He laughed loudly, completely unoffended as per usual. 'No – come on – I want to know what she said.'

'Not a lot. Just that she had a boyfriend and he'd been away for a few weeks. She didn't seem to want to talk about you much. Can't say I blame her.'

He seemed to find this hugely entertaining.

I didn't think it was that funny.

I heard the sound of more than one set of footsteps coming down the stairs, and then voices in the hall. The door opened and a radiant Sarah filled the doorway, long golden tresses allowed to flow freely for once. She was wearing a long, blue, gypsy-style skirt and a fitted black top. She looked stunning.

'Hi, Fern – sorry I took so long. There's someone I want you to meet. This is Stephen.'

A good-looking, dark-haired man stepped into the room behind her and nodded at me. He slipped his arm around Sarah's waist and she melted up against him, an expression of pure unadulterated happiness on her face. This was a woman in love.

My brain slowly began to click into gear, trying to fit the pieces of the puzzle together.

Seán was now leaning back into the couch, watching *Blind Date* again and shaking with laughter. Sarah sat down on the arm of the sofa and punched him gently on the shoulder.

'I hope you've been looking after Fern for me.'

'Oh, we've been having a very interesting chat.'

'You'll have to excuse my brother, Fern. He's fine once he keeps taking his medication.'

I knew it a split second before she said it. Omigod! I wanted the brown floral carpet to open wide and swallow me up. Her brother! I didn't know what to think. A curious mixture of emotions fought for precedence – mortification, relief, anger, annoyance. Go back there for a second. Did I say relief? Yes – relief that I didn't have to feel bad for Sarah any more. Her boyfriend didn't have a roving eye after all.

It turned out that Seán and Stephen had been away together for about a month. That explained why Sarah had greeted Seán so enthusiastically yesterday in the café.

'So,' continued Sarah, 'we're off to meet the others in Mahaffey's. Sure you won't change your mind and join us Seán?'

'I'll just get my jacket.' Seán exited the room. We could hear him thundering up the stairs.

'I thought he said he was too tired to go out.' This from Stephen.

'You know Seán – never one to turn down a few pints.' Never one to avoid the chance of giving me a hard time, more like.

On the short walk down to the local pub, I glued myself resolutely to Sarah's side. So what if Stephen wanted to be alone with her? I needed her more right at that moment. Stephen reluctantly moved away from us after a while and walked ahead with Seán. Sarah and I fell behind – just far enough away so that our conversation couldn't be overheard.

'So, how come you were so secretive about Stephen? He's gorgeous.' It was always good manners to rave about a friend's boyfriend's good looks upon first meeting. Fortunately, this time I didn't have to lie.

'I know.' Sarah looked momentarily all dreamy and melty again. Then her face grew more serious. 'It's just that I didn't want to jinx it, you know? I haven't known him for all that long and with him going away for a month and everything, I didn't know how we'd feel about each other when he came back.'

I nodded sympathetically. I understood exactly what she meant. I'd lost count of the men I'd foolishly had such high hopes for at the beginning of a relationship – men I'd offered my body, heart and soul to in vain. Those many hours spent preparing special meals, and all I'd get in return the next morning would be a pile of dirty dishes.

'So, things are going well, then?'

'Oh yes!' Sarah stopped and gripped my arm so hard it almost hurt. She whispered urgently at me. 'Fern – he's asked me to move in with him.'

Her eyes were wide and sparkling as she looked into mine, her expression a mixture of excitement and uncertainty. I felt as if she wanted me to tell her what to do. Me! Of all people! Who was I to give anyone advice? Poor old Princess Di had had more luck with her love life than I had. At least James didn't have jug ears.

To be honest, I felt sick with jealousy. I knew this was wrong – that I should feel deliriously happy for Sarah. But no – selfish to the last – the news made me feel like crying. She had what I wanted – or what I thought I wanted – more than anything else in the world. Imagine, a man as attractive and as nice as Stephen appeared to be wanting to share everything with you.

I pulled her into a hug. This was as much in an effort to hide the tears that were prickling at the back of my eyes as it was to convey my happiness for her. She clung on tightly to me. By the time we separated I had managed to control my emotions and my features sufficiently.

'Well – what are you going to do?'

'I don't know.' Her voice, usually so loud and confident, suddenly sounded small and childlike.

'Well, how long have you known him exactly?'

She looked away shyly. 'About four months.'

My head and my heart began to have a conversation with each other. It went something like this.

Head: That's ridiculous.

Heart: No – It's romantic.

Head: But they barely know one another. How could you possibly get to know a person properly in such a short time?

Heart: But it's a whirlwind romance – full of passion and risk – isn't that what life is all about?

Head: I give them a month of living together. They'll find out they have nothing in common and end up hating each others' guts.

Heart: But they'll never know if they don't give it a try. And if they don't try, they could both end up missing out on the love of their life.

Head: There's no such thing as the love of your life. You can learn to be happy with any number of potential partners.

Heart: But when the right one comes along, you just know.

You just know.

How I longed to just know.

I finally spoke. 'No one can make the decision for you, Sarah. It's your call.' Now! That sounded like sensible-enough advice.

'I know, I know. I just need a second opinion.'

'Well, I only met him a few minutes ago. It's hard to say.'

'But go with your gut feeling, Fern. What does your instinct tell you?' She sounded impatient.

We had stopped walking and stood facing each other on the pavement. Out of the corner of my eye, I saw Seán and Stephen enter a pub doorway across the street. Pedestrians eye-balled us quizzically as they walked by, having to step out onto the road to avoid us.

'How does he make you feel about yourself? I finally asked.

'Like a goddess.' She grinned foolishly.

'Greek or Roman?'

She giggled and pushed me lightly. 'Don't tease me now.'

'And does he treat you with respect?'

She nodded her head vigorously. 'Like a queen.'

'Queen of England or Queen of Denmark?'

'Fern! Stop.'

'Sorry. So he treats you like a goddess and a queen. Does he realise that you're real and you have faults just like everybody else?'

She shrugged. 'I suppose. I mean I've been in a bad mood with him once or twice. And he has seen me first thing in the morning without my make-up.'

I smiled to myself. Sarah's version of a bad mood was to smile a little less than usual. Even then, she still smiled twice as much as the average person. And her colouring was so pretty that she didn't really need any make-up.

No wonder Stephen wanted to live with her. He'd be mad not to.

'It just feels right. Like the perfect fit. He understands me so well and I understand him.'

It made my heart fit to burst to hear her say that.

'Well, if that's the way you feel, go for it.'

She squealed and hugged me again. 'Oh, Fern – thank you.'

'For what? Telling you what you wanted to hear?'

'No,' she said, her face grave. 'Thank you for listening and being such a good friend.'

I felt a lump in my throat. She considered me her friend. It was the nicest thing that had been said to me in the longest time. I felt all warm and glowy inside as we entered the pub.

We were greeted by Seán up at the bar.

'I ordered you a pint.'

'I don't drink pints.'

'You're welcome.'

I looked him in the eye for the first time since discovering he was Sarah's brother. I was on the brink of apologising and thanking him for the drink, but I realised that he was laughing at me again.

There was nothing worse for me than being laughed at.

It made me so angry.

He made me so angry.

'So, what do you think of Sarah's boyfriend then?'

Here we go.

He sipped at his pint casually as if he wasn't really interested in my reply.

'He's a vast improvement on the last one.'

He laughed good-humourdly. It was with some effort that I managed to maintain my disapproving look. I didn't know what it was about Seán but I always felt like I had to assume the role of po-faced maiden aunt when he was around – keeping him firmly in his place yet secretly envying his free ways and lack of regard for the opinions of others.

'Couldn't agree with you more. That last boyfriend she had was a real loser.'

'Yes, very rude. No manners whatsoever.'

'And vulgar,' Seán agreed. 'Don't forget the vulgarity. You could never take him home to meet your mother.'

'And appalling dress sense,' I added, beginning to enjoy myself.

'Hey now – watch it – that's going too far. It took me hours to cultivate this look.'

'And years to cultivate the bacteria growing on your jeans.'

'You get a kick out of insulting me, don't you.'

'Just getting my own back.'

'For what?' Good point. For what exactly?

'For . . . for making fun of me all the time.'

'What!' He was all mock scandalised. 'Would I?'

'And for letting me go on believing you were Sarah's boyfriend.'

'And are you glad I'm not?'

'Yes – for Sarah's sake.'

'And what about for your sake?'

I looked quickly at him but I couldn't tell whether he was joking or not. His tone was still mocking but a strange expression crossed his face fleetingly, momentarily darkening his normally open features.

I decided to change the subject.

'So where did you and Stephen go exactly?'

'We did a kind of round-trip of Europe.'

'Business or pleasure?'

'A bit of both.' He smiled at me. 'The Sistine Chapel needed touching up.'

I laughed in spite of myself. 'Michelangelo will be spinning in his grave.'

'That's better.'

'What?'

'You laughed – for the first time tonight.'

'Did not – I mean, It's not the first time I laughed tonight.'

'Is so.'

'I have been known to laugh the odd time, you know.'

'Since when?'

'Since – forever.'

'Could have fooled me.'

'Are you accusing me of being miserable?'

'No – you just seem sad a lot of the time. It's a shame – that's all.'

'So you pity me?'

'Jesus! You're prickly.'

'Do you blame me? You've just accused me of being a miserable old cow.'

'Fern.' And then he did an incredible thing. He took a step closer to me and placed his hand around the nape of my neck. I was afraid to move. He spoke quietly and seriously. 'I don't think you're miserable. I just think that, for whatever reason, you've been sad for a long time. I'd like to help you to be happy again.'

I barely registered his words. I was too busy concentrating on the rushing sound in my ears.

I eventually came to and shook his hand off my neck.

'What do you think you're doing?'

He looked away and took a gulp of beer out of his pint glass. 'I'm trying to help you.'

'Well, don't! I don't need your help,' I spluttered.

'Fair enough.' He shrugged nonchalantly and took another swig.

I shook my head. I didn't know what to say next. Luckily, Sarah and Stephen chose that moment to make their reappearance.

'Hi guys! Guess what?' The two of them were grinning from ear to ear. 'We're moving in together.' If Sarah had smiled any harder she would have ruptured something. She enthusiastically hugged Seán and myself in turn. I mustered up the cheesiest grin I could and nailed it to my face.

'Congratulations.'

'Yes, congratulations,' said Seán sounding genuinely pleased. He hugged Sarah back and slapped Stephen on the shoulder in a macho show of affection. 'This calls for another round of drinks. Fern, what's yours? Another pint, is it?'

'No thanks,' I replied coldly. He was back to mocking me again. At least it was familiar territory. 'I'm still trying to plough my way through this one.'

He nodded good-naturedly and went on up to the bar.

For the next hour or so we were joined by a selection of Stephen and Sarah's friends. I listened politely for the most part as congratulations were offered, and practised my best false smile whenever it was required of me. It wasn't until much later on, when the crowds had dispersed somewhat, that I had the opportunity – or misfortune – of speaking to Seán alone again. Sarah and Stephen were canoodling right in front of us so I made conversation out of embarrassment as much as anything else.

'So. What do you think of your sister's big news?'

'I think it's great,' he said simply.

'Don't you think they should get to know each other a bit better first?'

'That's why people move in together – to get to know each other.'

'But what if it doesn't work out?'

'Then Sarah can move back home.'

'You make it sound so simple.'

He shrugged. 'It is.'

'Aren't you worried that she might get hurt?'

'Look, Fern' – he was starting to sound impatient – 'Stephen's a great bloke and he's mad about Sarah. Besides, if it doesn't work out, she'll be welcomed back home with open arms.'

His words silenced me. I felt a lump in my throat and had to swallow it back determinedly. Imagine having that kind of family support.

'Do you have any brothers or sisters, Fern?'

'One sister.'

'Yeah? Two-point-four children – just like us.'

No. Not a bit like you at all. An overwhelming wave of sadness washed over me, nearly knocking me off my bar stool. I expected Seán to continue his interrogation but he was silent.

We sat like that for a while. Drinking our drinks. Thinking our thoughts. Our silence was rudely interrupted by the disco starting up next door. The background thud reverberated through the bar. Sarah grabbed both Seán and me by our respective arms.

'Come on. Time to boogie. We've got some serious celebrating to do.'

She rounded up anybody else in the bar that she knew and we were all herded into the disco area.

Sarah's party mood was infectious. In no time she had everyone on the dance floor, myself included. I watched Seán dance with a mixture of curiosity and amusement.

Not a bad dancer – for an Irish man. He just about managed to keep in time with the music. He seemed more interested in chatting than dancing, to be honest. To Tamsin mainly, who was dancing beside him in a style which could only be described as seductive. What was she up to? She was supposed to be going out with Brian!

I watched them closely out of the corner of my left eye, trying not to look too obvious. Yes – a definite case of blatant flirtation if ever I saw one. But was Seán responding? He was acting in a friendly manner, certainly, but then again, he always did. And chatty. Nothing unusual there.

What about body language? I searched for clues. Was he dancing towards her or away from her? What about eye contact? Unnecessary touching? I surveyed Tamsin's pretty features and slim but curvy figure. I compared myself and found that I was wanting.

Enough of this! I left the dance floor and joined the other breathless people at the bar. Just in time. The dance music evaporated into smooch. It was the dreaded 'slow set'. I stiffened. I could scarcely bear to look. After a few long, tortuous seconds I turned around just in time to see Tamsin take Seán by the hand and pull him in towards her for a slow dance.

He didn't pull away.

I was dismayed at how put out I felt. Surely my ego wasn't so fragile as to be threatened every time a man I'd had a conversation with in a pub didn't choose me as his Ginger Rogers at the end of the night. Actually, I didn't particularly want to dwell on it. Instead, I decided to do what I had wanted to do hours previously in Sarah's sitting room: I snuck off home.

Cloakroom.

Back door.

Taxi.

Escape.

Nobody even noticed.

Chapter Eleven

I was horribly hung over the next day. The rattle of the cutlery as I set the table was agonising. Sarah breezed in, looking as fresh as an 'Always' sanitary towel with wings.

'You look well,' I mumbled sulkily.

'That's the most begrudging compliment I ever got,' she said laughing. I could feel her looking at me as she shook off her coat.

'So what happened to you last night? Did you get whisked away by some gorgeous hunk?'

'I had a headache so I went home.'

'Without telling anyone?' I didn't answer. 'Not even me?'

'You were having such a great time. I didn't want to spoil your fun.' Even I could tell that my tone was martyred. Poor Saint Fern.

'Did it not occur to you that I might be worried?'

'You're not my mother, Sarah.'

I was aware that I sounded like an ungrateful brat but I couldn't seem to help myself.

'God! Who rattled your cage this morning?' Sarah flounced off into the back kitchen.

Shit! Now I felt guilty as well as hung over.

I'd already checked the schedule to see if Tamsin was on that morning. She was. That was all I needed.

'Hi, Fern.'

And here she was. Right on cue. All flaming red hair (dyed) and perfect teeth (capped). For fuck's sake! Was I to be forever cursed by good-looking women?

'How's the head this morning?'

'Fine, thanks.' I was cool. Dignified.

'Where did you disappear to last night? We were all looking for you.'

'I'm surprised you noticed,' I snapped. Not so cool. Not so dignified. She looked taken aback.

'Don't mind her.' Sarah came back in, tying on her apron. 'She got out of the wrong side of the bed this morning.'

'Ah yes – the wrong side of whose bed?' Tamsin nudged me suggestively.

'My own. How about you?'

My tone wasn't quite as jovial as hers. I could tell by her confused expression that she wasn't sure whether I was joking or not. She shrugged and walked off.

'That was a bit nasty. What's got into you?' Sarah sounded genuinely shocked.

'Nothing.' I wouldn't look at her. I pretended to concentrate on setting the table, willing her to go away. Uncharacteristically, she did.

I sniffed to myself. She was just like all the rest. Couldn't care less about me. I hated myself for the way I was behaving. And now the girls probably hated me too. I felt tears of self-pity well up in my eyes and I blinked them away, furious with myself and my churlish behaviour. Why was I acting this way?

I continued in this vein for the rest of the morning. I kept myself to myself and went about my duties like R2-D2. I noticed that my tips were smaller than usual. Obviously my grumpiness communicated itself to the customers. I resolved to pull myself together.

By lunchtime the place was buzzing and I hardly had time to think about my foul humour and aching head. Sarah came up to me by the coffee machine as I was frantically attempting to find enough clean mugs to make up my order.

'Gentleman needs serving on Table Eight.'

I rolled my eyes to heaven theatrically. 'Not another one.'

She patted me on the arm. 'Not to worry. It'll all be over by two o'clock.'

I deposited the mugs of coffee and, notepad and pencil in hand, I approached Table Eight. My quick pace slowed to a near halt as I saw who was sitting there.

It was Seán.

He grinned up at me. 'You look surprised to see me.'

'I am. Sarah told me there was a gentleman sitting at Table Eight.'

'I promise – no rude jokes today.'

I angrily flipped back the used pages on my notepad. 'What can I get you?'

'A strong black coffee would be nice. I feel the urgent need for caffeine today. Can't imagine why.' He continued to grin annoyingly.

'Hard night, was it?'

'You should know – you were there.'

'Yeah – and so was Tamsin.'

'What's that supposed to mean?' I noted with satisfaction that the grin had vanished. Without answering, I turned on my heel and walked rapidly back to the coffee station.

As I prepared his drink, my mind was in a whirl. What was he doing here? Why wasn't he sitting in Tamsin's section? Or Sarah's? Perhaps it was the only free table. I glanced around the restaurant. No – there were several free spaces. I told myself to be calm and composed as I brought the coffee back down to him.

'Do you think there's something going on between me and Tamsin?' He was direct. I'd give him that.

'What are you talking about.'

'No – what are you talking about, Fern?' He sounded almost angry.

'She was all over you like a nasty rash last night. Don't tell me you didn't notice.'

'Tamsin's going out with Brian.'

'Exactly.'

'Look – there's nothing between us. I've known Tamsin for years. She's a friend – and so is Brian. She just like's to flirt – especially when she's had a skinful. She doesn't mean anything by it.'

I could tell he was genuine. I was beginning to feel very, very stupid. His expression softened.

'I didn't know you cared.'

'I don't,' I said a little too quickly. 'It's just that I didn't think it was right, with Tamsin being with Brian and everything.'

'Just like you didn't think it was right that I asked you out while I was with Sarah?'

I felt my cheeks redden. I examined my shoes and attempted a sickly smile.

'I'm sorry. I seem to be forever jumping to conclusions where you're concerned. I hope you can forgive me.'

'Well – I don't know. You could try making it up to me.'

My heart began to do a curious little dance in my chest. 'How?' I asked softly.

'Come out with me tomorrow night.'

The dancing in my chest accelerated from a waltz to a highland fling. I scrutinised my footwear again.

'Okay.'

I could feel him peering up at me.

'Was that a yes?'

'I suppose it was. Er . . . can I get you anything else?'

'Just the bill.'

'What about your coffee?'

'I don't feel the need for it any more.' A new flush crept across my cheeks. 'So – do you want to make an arrangement now or will I call you?'

'We can make an arrangement now – if you like,' I said quickly. I was damned if I was going to spend the whole of tomorrow afternoon leaping out of my skin every time the phone rang.

'I'll pick you up at your house at about eight?'

'Okay. I live about ten minutes away from . . . '

'I remember where you live.' He deposited some coins on the table and stood up to leave. 'See you tomorrow night then. What do you want to do?'

'A drink would be fine.' I smiled shyly. He remembered where I lived!

'Tomorrow night then.'

And he was gone.

I felt as if a whirlwind had entered the café and exited just as quickly, leaving me reeling. I didn't know what to think – or where to start thinking. What was I playing at? Why had I said yes? I wasn't even sure if I liked Seán. All we ever seemed to do was argue. And he was Sarah's brother! What if it all went horribly wrong? The last thing I wanted to do was to jeopardise my friendship with her.

I found myself mixing up orders all afternoon. The vegetarian at Table Three ended up with a steak sandwich, medium-rare, and the diabetic at Table Six found herself confronted by 'Death by Chocolate'. I tried to untangle my feelings, but to no avail.

I studiously attempted to avoid Sarah which was impossible as she kept coming over for a 'chat' every time she had a spare minute.

'So,' she said, when she had finally managed to pin me down. 'You seem to be in a better mood. Smiling at the customers, no less.'

My nod was noncommittal.

'How was Seán? I didn't really get a chance to speak with him.'

'Oh, he seemed fine,' I replied casually. 'A bit hung over, perhaps.'

'Aren't we all?' She paused for a few seconds and then resumed her probing. 'He didn't stay long.' It was more of a question than a statement.

'No – he said he had things to do . . . ' I trailed off vaguely. We were both silent for a while. I could tell I was driving her nuts.

'He's nice, isn't he? Seán, I mean.' Now it was her turn to sound casual.

'He seems very pleasant,' I said carefully.

She laughed. 'Pleasant! I can see I'm not going to get any information out of you, am I? Come on. There are tables to be cleared.'

I suppressed a smile as we went our separate ways. She suspected something but she couldn't tell for sure. I wondered if she'd have more luck with Seán.

More to the point, would I?

The next day was my day off. I usually managed to sleep in pretty late but that day I woke at about nine. I tossed and turned for a while but was soon forced to acknowledge that I was wide awake and that all attempts at going back to sleep were futile.

Besides, it was a beautiful day.

Having clambered out from under my floral duvet, I padded over to the window. I drew back my matching floral curtains and surveyed the scene below.

My father was very proud of his garden – and with good reason. I looked down at the rows of green shoots sprouting up around the perfectly square winter lawn. He was out already, pottering around, pulling up real and imaginary weeds. A small congregation of birds fluttered around the bird table in the centre of the garden, competing for peanuts.

I opened the window so that I could hear their twittering. My father heard the sound and looked up. He smiled at me and waved. He was always happy when he was in his garden. He spent more and more time there these days.

The sun was shining and the sky was cloudless and blue. What more can I say? It was definite. Spring was in the air and it felt good.

I hopped into the shower, humming a tune they'd been playing at the disco two nights previously. I carefully observed my pre-date routine – not only washing but buffing, exfoliating and moisturising as I went. It's not even that I was anticipating that the skin on my body would be glimpsed, let alone touched. It was just that I knew I'd feel more confident if I'd carried out the basic groundwork. No skimping allowed.

I eventually floated down to the kitchen, where I actually went to the trouble of making proper coffee, instead of the instant gunk that I usually drink.

My sister was slumped on the couch in her dressing gown, watching *The Big Breakfast*. She should have been at work but she was 'dying' (her description, not mine) with the 'flu' (again, her description). She sniffed piteously to herself and blew her nose repeatedly.

I wandered in and out of the room, humming to myself, straightening and tidying as I went.

'I've made a pot of coffee. Would you like some?'

She looked up at me in amazement, from a pair of red rimmed eyes.

'What – on that old machine! Does it still work?'

'Yes – perfectly – why?'

'It's just that I saw one just like it on *The Antiques Road Show* the other night. This woman's great-grandmother left it to her in her will.'

I laughed happily. Sasha could be quite funny when she wasn't too busy being a nasty cow. Still, she probably didn't have the energy to be mean at the moment. I decided I quite liked her when she was sick. It had a mellowing effect.

I came back into her, bearing a mug of coffee and a plate of hot buttered toast. She eyed me suspiciously.

'What's up with you this morning?'

'What do you mean?'

'You seem different.'

'No, I'm not.'

'You are. You're very . . . ' – she searched around the room for the right word – 'chirpy.'

'Am I not normally in good form first thing in the morning?'

She snorted. 'Do you really want me to answer that?'

I smiled and shook my head. She was right though. I was usually grumpiness personified at this hour of the morning. It was ages since I'd felt this happy.

Of course, I knew it was in anticipation of the night to come. I warned myself not to get too excited. A little black cloud floated across my own personal blue sky as I wondered if I'd feel so happy the following morning – the morning after the date before. I remembered all those other mornings after, when I'd felt so let down and depressed. I decided not to think about it. Better to busy myself for the afternoon. At least I had this much – the anticipation of the date. I decided I might as well enjoy it as it might well turn out to be the best part.

There was one other advantage too. At about 6.30 p.m., I thought about James. Nothing strange about that, I hear you cry. Perhaps not. But the weird thing was that it was the first time that day that I *had* thought about him. That hadn't happened since – well, since I'd met him.

Since the first time I'd seen him in all his dark and arrogant glory, he had resided permanently at the forefront of my brain. It was true what they said. To get over one man, you had to get another one. Perhaps Seán was just the therapy I needed. And when it all went disastrously wrong with Seán, I could obsess about him instead of James. This thought from the little pessimistic person living in my head who had been feeling neglected for all of a few hours.

My current most pressing problem, however, was how to get collected from my house by Seán without my family seeing. By family, I mean my sister. I could do without an interrogation from *that* one, even if her habitual bitchiness had been toned down somewhat by ill health. She still knew how to ask all the wrong questions – or the right ones, depending on your point of view. I didn't want them to meet him.

And I sure as hell didn't want him to meet them. I'd have enough trouble trying to convince Seán that I was normal without his having my family to contend with.

This meant I'd actually have to be ready on time so that I could head him off at the front door. This was no mean feat but I just about made it. At 8.06 p.m. I was in the upstairs bathroom putting the final touches to my tenth layer of make-up. I was just having visions of myself taking it off with a pick and shovel later that night when I heard his car pull up outside. I knew at once that it was his car. I recognised the rattle and wheeze of the engine. I cleared the stairs in record time and flung open the door to the TV room.

'I'm going out. I won't be late. Bye.'

'Where are you . . . ?' The remainder of the sentence was obliterated by the sound of the front door slamming. I'd got the general gist of it.

Seán had made it half way down the garden path. He looked different. Clean, I think it was. Absent was the usual scruffy Bryan Adams-esque approach to fashion. He was wearing light beige chinos with – wait for it – a crease down the front of each leg, a crisp white shirt and a dark brown suede jacket. His hair was slightly less tousled than usual. It made him appear more boyish somehow. I was tempted to ask him if his mother had made him scrub behind his ears.

'Am I not going to be introduced?'

'To whom?'

'Your family of course.'

'What do you want to meet them for?'

He laughed at my defensiveness. 'I was going to ask your father for your hand in marriage – what do you think?'

I was embarrassed. Didn't know where to look.

'Well, you can't,' I mumbled stupidly.

'Pity. We'll have to elope instead. Hop in. I'll take you to Gretna Green.' He was holding the door open for me.

'If you're going to start making fun of me again, I'm going back in.'

He forced the smile off his face. 'Sorry. Won't happen again. Please get in.'

I climbed in. I couldn't help but notice the marked absence of rubble in the car. It wasn't only himself that had undergone a spring-clean. The musty, doggy smell had gone too – masked no doubt by the new-looking Magic Tree air freshener hanging off the rear-view mirror. I was nearly knocked sideways by the whiff of pine. As he clambered in beside me, I noticed another smell intermingling with the pine. It was after-shave! I glanced at the side of his face with surprise. He was actually wearing after-shave – for me! And the clothes, the clean car, everything – it was all because of me. I was overwhelmed. I mentally checked myself. Don't get your hopes up, Fern – or let your defences down. It's early days yet.

'Okay, where do you want to go? Town or local?'

'Town, please.' Less chance of bumping into nosy friends or neighbours.

On the way to the pub, he did most of the talking. I was too busy being shy and self-conscious to join in properly.

We chose a quiet, cosy, little place. Not on one of the major drinking thoroughfares. No loud music blaring. It meant that you could actually have a conversation with the person you were with. I wasn't sure yet whether this was a good thing or not. We claimed for ourselves a secluded snug, and Seán went up to the bar to get the first round in.

God, I felt nervous. I attempted a few deep, cleansing breaths. What was I doing here? This was madness. Who was I trying to fool anyway. Me – trying to go on a normal date and have a functional relationship with a man. I might as well say my farewells and go home now – save us both a lot of grief.

'One large gin and tonic.' He placed the drink in front of me and sat down, easing off his jacket. I tried not to look at his biceps straining against his shirt sleeves. He sat just the right distance away. Not so far that we had to shout at each other and not so close as to invade my personal space. Yes – my boundaries were very precious to me.

'So, are you still working on the Courthouse?' I ventured – oh so politely.

'Oh no. That job was finished weeks ago.'

'Where are you working now, then?'

He paused. 'I'm working on a few different projects at the moment.'

'Such as?'

He shifted around in the seat and began tearing little pieces off his beer mat.

'Well, that decorating job was just a one-off really. I was helping my cousin out. I don't do that sort of job much any more.'

'What do you do, then?'

Now he looked really mortified. He started to rip that poor beer mat to shreds. I was starting to get worried. What could he possibly do for a living that was so shameful? Was he a male stripper? A taxidermist? A chartered accountant? He mumbled something into his pint glass.

'Sorry, I didn't catch that.'

'I'm an artist.'

'An artist.' I was confused. 'Then, why did you tell me you were a painter?'

'Well, I paint, don't I? Artist – painter – what's the difference?' He grinned sheepishly and looked down at his hands. So did I. They didn't fit my image of artist's hands. No fine bones or long, tapering fingers. They were big and brown and rough.

An artist. I felt a knot of excitement in the pit of my stomach. I found that suddenly I had plenty to say for myself. 'What kind of stuff do you paint?'

'Oh, this and that – a lot of landscapes, seascapes – watercolours mainly. But I'm prepared to be flexible right now. Anything to pay the mortgage.'

'Have you sold any, then?'

'A few.'

I was impressed. He didn't know how much.

'I'd love to see some of your work.'

He stole a sideways look at me. He actually looked shy. Imagine Seán looking shy!

'Really?'

'Of course I would.'

He looked pleased. 'You will soon anyway. Sarah's convinced the owner of the café to get me to paint a mural the whole length of one of the walls.

'No way.'

'Yes way.'

This was news to me. I'd never met the café owner. Apparently he was some rich Irishman made good who spent most of his time in the States.

'But why are you embarrassed about it? You get to do what you love most – presumably –

and get paid for it. I mean – what could be better than that?'

'Oh . . . you know – it just sounds a bit precious or something. Pretentious. Most of my mates think it's a bit of a joke.'

I nodded. From what I knew of Seán's family and friends, they didn't strike me as the type of people who spent their time hanging around art galleries and the like. And I wouldn't have guessed in a million years that Seán was the sensitive, artistic type.

It turned out that he had left school at seventeen and had trained as a carpenter. After years of working on the building sites in London, he went to art college as a mature student. I was utterly fascinated. I fired questions at him, hanging on to his every word. And this wasn't your usual 'let-him-talk-about-his-hobbies-and-pretend-you're-interested' trick. This was for real. I totally forgot to be shy.

Some time later, I was in full flight, enthusing about one of my favourite artists, when I caught him staring at me strangely. 'You seem to know an awful lot about art.'

I stopped talking and stood up. 'It's my round. Same again?' I didn't wait for an answer.

I waited to be served at the bar, my head buzzing with a thousand questions and possibilities. I'd never spoken to anybody at any great length about this type of thing before. I'd had to content myself with art programmes on the telly, which my father usually switched off ('Not that bleedin' buck-toothed nun going on about paintings again!') I realised now that they were a poor substitute.

I carefully avoided eye contact when I got back with the drinks.

'Well?' said Seán, after a protracted silence.

'Well, what?'

'Well, you seem to know a lot about painting. How come?'

'I just like it.'

'You just like it.'

'Yes.' I concentrated hard on stirring the lemon around in my drink with the little plastic stick.

'And you don't do it yourself?'

'Do what.'

'Paint.'

200

I chanced looking up at him. His eyes were filled with laughter. Now it was my turn to be embarrassed. 'A bit.'

'How much is a bit?'

'Quite a bit.'

'Ever sold anything?'

I nearly choked on my gin. 'You must be joking. I wouldn't let anyone see it.'

'Why not?'

'It's crap.'

'How do you know if you've never got a second opinion?'

'I did once. My sister's.'

'So, what's your sister – some kind of expert?'

'No. She's some kind of critic though.'

'Why don't you let me see?'

I shook my head vigorously, almost dislodging several of the clips I'd used to put my hair up. It was a 'do' that I'd copied from *Cosmo*.

'Why not?'

'You'd only laugh.'

'No, I wouldn't.' He looked almost hurt.

'Not in a million years.'

'Go on,' – he grinned – 'what have you got to lose?'

'My pride, dignity and self-respect for a start.'

'Is that all?' He was mocking me now.

'Just drop it, Seán.'

He could tell I was serious. 'Fair enough. I won't say another word. It's just that there's nothing worse than a frustrated artist. I should know.'

'Don't worry about me. I won't go chopping my ear off or anything.'

'I hope not. You've got such lovely ears. Really small and neat. I'd love to sketch them some time – and the rest of your face, of course.' I squirmed uncomfortably. 'You know your trouble. You don't know how to take a compliment.'

'You know yours? You never know when to shut up.'

He laughed and held his hands up. 'I do, I do.'

The lights dimmed a couple of times and came back on again. Either we were about to experience a power cut or the management was trying to tell us something. I couldn't believe that the evening was over already. It occurred to me that I really didn't want to go home yet. I glanced sneakily across at Seán who was looking distinctly twitchy. It looked as if another beer mat was about to bite the dust.

'I guess it's time to go,' he said, without looking at me.

'I guess so.' I was crestfallen.

'Unless of course you're hungry.'

'Famished.'

'Really?' He beamed up at me. 'Why didn't you say so before? Is pizza all right?'

'Perfect.'

'I know a great place close by.'

'Let's go.'

I hugged myself with joy as we left the pub. He wanted to spend more time with me. I couldn't be that boring.

The pizza place was nothing fancy. A gingham oilcloth on each table, together with a single carnation in a bud vase and a night light in a simple holder – I liked it. In fact, he probably could have brought me to a barn with a hole in the roof and I would have been happy.

'So,' he said, as we were waiting for the garlic bread to arrive, 'we haven't argued yet.'

'Must be a first.' I smiled shyly.

'In fact, would it be presumptuous to say that we're getting on pretty well?'

I made a great show of considering this.

'Come on. Don't keep me in suspenders.'

'What you choose to wear in your own free time is entirely up to you, Seán.'

He laughed. 'Now you're being cruel.'

'Have you never heard of the "treat them mean, keep them keen" strategy?'

'You don't have to play those mind games with me, Fern.'

'No?'

'Definitely not.' I could tell he was being serious now.

'Well, Seán. I'd say you were pretty okay company.'

'Okay company! Careful now. I might go getting a swelled head.'

'No, seriously, I'd say you're passable company.'

'Well, whatever you think about me, I'd say that you're pretty damned excellent company, Miss Fennelly, and I hope that we can do this again some time.'

'Are you asking me out on another date?'

'Looks like it. What do you say?'

'I'd say that I'll give the matter my most serious consideration.' (Try saying that with a few too many gins inside you.)

'He grinned and poured us both a glass of wine. 'That's very good of you. I'm honoured.'

'You mean, you're plastered. Do you think it's a good idea to mix wine and beer?'

'Probably not.' He cheerfully raised his glass. 'Sláinte.'

I raised mine and tipped it against his. 'Sláinte. What shall we drink to?'

He thought for a moment and then grinned that now-familiar crooked grin. 'To art.'

I smiled happily back at him.

'Yes – to art.'

Chapter Twelve

Sarah was waiting to ambush me the moment I walked into work the next morning.

'Hi, Fern.' She sounded all excited.

'Hi, Sarah.' I ducked out of the way and tried to make my getaway to the kitchen.

'Not so fast.' She caught me by the arm. 'Don't you have any news for me?'

'Um . . . let me see . . . ' I pretended to think for a few seconds. 'That would be a no.'

'Oh, don't be silly. How did you get on last night?'

'What makes you think I got up to anything last night?'

'Oh, come on. I know you were out with Seán. I want to know everything.'

I could tell that any attempt to resist would be pointless. To be honest, I was dying to talk to someone about it.

'Do you two tell each other everything?'

'Well, obviously not everything or I wouldn't have to pump you for information, now would I? Besides, don't you and your sister tell each other everything?'

'Not likely. Everything I said would be taken down and used in evidence against me.'

She looked genuinely concerned for a moment or two, and then the onslaught continued.

'So, tell me all about it.'

'Well, first we went for a drink to D'Arcy's and then we went for a pizza.

'And?'

'And then he dropped me home.'

'Fern! You're useless. I don't want to hear all the boring details – I already know them.'

'What do you want to hear about?' (As if I didn't know.)

'I want to know how you feel?'

'Tired and headachey.'

'God! You're annoying. You know what I mean.'

I took a deep breath. 'Well, I had a really good time and Seán is – great.'

She squealed, hugged me and jumped up and down simultaneously. 'I knew it! I just knew you'd get on.'

'What did you have to ask me for then?' I was laughing with her now.

'Just checking. But seriously, Fern, I have a very good feeling about this. You two are made for each other.'

I felt immediately uneasy. 'Now, hold on a second. We've only been out together once. Don't go jumping the gun.'

'I'm not. Trust me. I know these things.' She tapped her index finger on the side of her nose and gave me a conspiratorial wink. What the conspiracy was, I had no idea.

'So, how about you?' I thought it was high time I changed the subject. 'When are you moving into Stephen's?'

'This weekend. I can't wait. Only problem is that Steve's away with his job the following week so I'll be all on my own in a new place. I'm a bit nervous about it. I don't suppose you fancy coming over to stay with me for one or two of the nights?'

'Yeah – no problem.' I was delighted.

'Brilliant. We can have a sleep-over party.'

'Does that mean that we wear our pyjamas and paint each other's toenails?'

'Yes, and eat cartons of Haagen Dazs and drink too much wine.'

'Excellent!'

'That is, of course, if you have a free night.' Her tone changed to mock serious.

'What are you talking about?'

'Well, you might be out with Seán.'

'That's if he ever rings me again.'

'Oh, he will – you can count on it.'

He did. That very night. Sasha stared at me suspiciously when I came back into the sitting room after I'd finished on the phone. I tried not to look all happy.

'Who was that?'

'Sarah.'

'Is that your new bubbly friend?'

'Piss off!'

'How do you know her anyway?'

'She's a friend of a friend.' Pathetically, I still hadn't told my family about losing my job at Boland, Sharpe & Co. As far as they knew, I was still a legal secretary. In the circumstances, I could hardly tell Sasha that I waitressed with Sarah.

'Which friend?'

What the hell! Perhaps it was time to come clean. 'Sash, if I tell you something, will you promise not to tell Mam or Dad?'

She sat bolt upright in her seat. 'I promise.'

'Brownie's honour.'

'Brownie's honour.' (It's a long story.)

'I don't work in the solicitor's office any more.'

'You never got the sack?' I thought she could have at least tried not to sound so delighted.

'Well, actually . . . '

'I knew it!' She literally clapped her hands together with glee.

'I appreciate the sympathy.'

'What did you do?' She was leaning forward eagerly in her seat, hungry for more.

'Nothing. It just wasn't working out. Anyway, I have a new job now and I like it much better.'

'Doing what?'

'I work in a café in town.'

'You're waitressing! I love it! Mam will go spare!'

'You promised not to tell Mam, remember?'

'Okay, okay. But Jesus! Fern, you're such a disaster.'

'Thanks for the vote of confidence. Now, would you mind changing the subject please?'

Sasha nodded absent-mindedly. She picked up the book that she'd been reading (my book!) and started to read, stopping only to snigger to herself every now and then.

'You were on the phone an awfully long time.' The interrogation continued.

'Only about half an hour.'

'Come off it! More like an hour.'

'Was it?' I looked at my watch, genuinely surprised.

'It's not like you to have so much to say for yourself.'

'Oh, try and be nice for a change, Slasher.'

'I can't. It's not in my nature.'

'You said it.'

'I was expecting a call as a matter of fact.'

'Who from? Your "interesting" boyfriend.' Sasha's boyfriend, Ian the banker, had two topics of conversation: banking and himself. Sasha looked furious.

'Ian is extremely interesting, thank you very much. And at least he didn't dump me after three weeks like every man you've ever gone out with.' That was below the belt! 'Well, at least I'm not stuck in a dead-end relationship, just because I'm too scared that no other man would be stupid enough to go out with me.'

I slammed out of the room before she could respond – all good humour extinguished. She was right though. I did have an incredibly bad track record with men. What made me think that Seán would be any different from all the rest?

For our second date, Seán brought me to an up-market Chinese restaurant. Real chopsticks and those little bowls of warm water for rinsing your fingers with, which my father had once mistaken for bird's nest soup. I asked for a fork instead of chopsticks. As the undisputed holder of the title for messiest woman in the world, I wasn't about to make a show of myself by hurling noodles all down the front of my new dress.

I'd had to buy a new dress, of course. It was mandatory. True, I had the silver-grey kimono number that I had worn that night with James in Pegasus. I'd only worn that the once. But it had bad memories attached to it. In fact, I had stopped wearing any of the clothes that I associated with my time with James. It was a pity really – such a waste. Some of them were brand new too. I wonder if other women do the same thing too.

It's sad to think of all those abandoned party frocks, relegated to the backs of women's wardrobes. We should all get together and sell them off in a giant auction – like Geri Halliwell did with all her Spice Girl gear. Or we could open a chain of shops. Call them 'Dumpees & Divorcees Anonymous', or something equally catchy. The possibilities are tremendous. Not only could we get rid of clothing that is haunted with the ghosts of boyfriends past, but we'd have the opportunity to raise money for the charity of our choice. Not to mention the extra wardrobe space.

Anyway, I digress. Back to the date. Seán was looking very cleanly pressed again. I don't mind telling you that I was secretly disappointed. Call me old-fashioned but I've always found a man more attractive if he looks slightly dishevelled. Builders and mechanics were my personal favourites. James in his pin-stripe was just a one-off. Seán normally looked as though he'd just crawled out of bed, put on the first items of clothing he found strewn on his bedroom floor and run a hand through his hair in place of a comb. Shaving was strictly optional. But tonight he looked as if his Mammy had dressed him.

I decided that a good slagging was in order. 'So, who ironed your shirt for you?'

He looked down at his food. 'I ironed it myself.'

'Liar.'

'Okay – Sarah did it for me.'

'She did? How much did you pay her?'

'Nothing. She insisted. I wanted to wear a sweatshirt but she wouldn't let me. "You can't go out and meet Fern looking like a scruffbag."' He imitated a high-pitched female voice. I laughed involuntarily at his appalling impression of her voice. Not to mention the thought of her bossing him around.

'You know,' I said shyly, 'I really wouldn't have minded if you'd worn a scruffy sweatshirt.'

'Really?' He stared hard at me, trying to fathom whether or not I was for real.

'Yes, really.'

He looked relieved. 'Thank Christ for that! I can't be doing this dressing-up stuff all the time. It's just not me.'

'So promise that the next time we go out you'll be wearing your grottiest clothes.'

'The next time we go out? Are you asking me out, Fern?' I blushed furiously. He let me off the hook. 'The oldest pair of jeans I own and the most frayed and paint spattered T-shirt I can find,' he promised.

'And what about shoes?'

'I have a pair of runners that smell just like finely matured stilton.'

'And I'll bring a bottle of port.'

We both laughed uproariously at this. That probably meant that we were both getting pretty drunk.

Oh dear! I was allowing myself to get drunk again. On a date. With a man. This could have disastrous consequences. I tried to chide myself but found myself pouring out more wine instead. Don't be such a killjoy, Fern. You're just enjoying yourself! I wasn't all that hard to fool.

Untypically, I decided to skip dessert. A hot banana fried in batter isn't really my thing.

'Let's go clubbing!' exclaimed Seán, suddenly throwing down his napkin. I'd barely finished eating at this stage.

'Can I just let my food go down first?'

Okay. We can't have you getting dancer's cramp. You've got two minutes.'

I laughed at him and then stopped, taken aback at the way he was looking at me. 'I'm going to the loo.'

I stood up abruptly, snatched up my handbag and staggered gamely to the Ladies. Once inside, I leaned hard against the sink unit and stared at myself in the mirror.

'O God,' I groaned. I looked like seven shades of shite. Or the wreck of the Hesperes if you prefer. It must be the light in here, I told myself. It seemed to highlight and magnify every spot, line and blemish. I'd looked all right coming out this evening. What on earth had happened to my face in the last few hours? I couldn't have aged that quickly.

I heard the sound of a toilet flush behind me and a woman emerged out of a cubicle. She came and stood beside me and looked at herself in the mirror.

'Oh, holy Jaysus!' she wailed. 'Look at the bleedin' state of me.'

Our eyes met in the mirror and we said almost simultaneously, 'The lighting.'

We fell about the place laughing. There was nothing like a bit of female solidarity to sustain you in times of trouble.

However, even with the support of my new-found sister-in-arms I knew that all was not well in the hair and beauty department. I have enough experience of nights out to know that on your first trip to the Ladies you look respectable enough. On each successive trip you look slightly more dishevelled. Until, by about the fifth visit, you wish you hadn't bothered looking into the mirror at all. I suspect that alcohol probably has a large part to play in this phenomenon. Why can't the drink just make your vision go all blurry so that you have the illusion of getting better-looking as the night wears on?

As I walked back into the restaurant, I silently thanked God for the dim lighting. Seán was sitting bolt upright in his seat, wearing his jacket.

'Going somewhere?'

'I'm hoping you'll come with me.'

We fell out of the restaurant and chattered and giggled all the way to the nightclub. It turned out that Seán had gone to school with one of the bouncers so we got in without any hassle. He seemed to meet people he knew wherever he went. The place was jammers. Wall to wall with sweaty, drunken people. I felt instantly at home. We fought our way to the bar and paid fifteen quid for a bottle of vinegar masquerading as wine. I took a gulp and winced. 'This stuff is such a rip-off.'

'You don't like it?'

'Cop on to yourself – it's vile.'

'Okay, let's dance instead.' He was on his feet and offering me his hand. I took it shyly and allowed myself to be led to the dance floor. We'd only been out there for about thirty seconds when the DJ's voice boomed out over the speakers.

'All right, folks. Time to slow things down. Here's an extra smoochy number for all you young lovers out there.'

And with that, Fat Boy Slim became Marvin Gaye. Or, if you prefer, it was time for the Funk Soul brother to receive some Sexual Healing. It was one of my favourites but I could have done without hearing it at that very moment. I couldn't look at Seán. I didn't have to. His arms encircled my waist as he pulled me close against him. I'd have to admit that this time I didn't give my precious boundaries a second thought.

It felt delicious. He was just the right height for a slow dance. I nestled my head into the sinewy curve where his right shoulder met his neck. Perfect. I was melting. It was as if the outer layer of my skin had been stripped away making my body into one big sensation. I was aware of nothing but the feel of his big, warm, solid arms engulfing me and the broad expanse of chest pressed hard against my nipples.

After a few minutes, just when I thought I couldn't possibly feel any nicer, he began rubbing his thumb gently against the small of my back. Light, tender circles at first. Then, very slowly, he traced his fingers up the curve of my spine. And back down again. And up again. All the while, the same maddeningly slow movement. With his other hand, he caressed my waist delicately. I was sent! Ripples of desire coursed up and down my body.

At this point, I think my feet had forgotten to move. I didn't care. It felt so good! The next time his fingers strayed up my back they travelled to the nape of my neck and entwined in the back of my hair. And then I felt his head turn inevitably towards mine. I slowly lifted my face up and forced myself to look at him. I was taken aback. I didn't recognise the dark expression in his normally candid blue eyes. Then it hit me: pure, naked lust. A strange sound emerged from my throat, which I later identified as a cross between a whimper and a moan. And then his mouth came down on top of mine.

An electric shock couldn't have produced a more violent response in me. My fingers took on a life of their own, clutching and clasping at the hair at the back of his neck, attempting to pull him closer and closer. His kiss seemed to reach the parts that other kisses couldn't reach. I could feel an unmistakable hardness pressing against my stomach. I felt like I was about to spontaneously combust.

I pulled away, gasping for air.

'What's wrong?' His voice sounded husky and unfamiliar.

'Nothing.'

I could feel his gaze bearing down on the top of my head but I couldn't meet it. His hand was caressing my cheek, willing me to look up at him. I pulled further away, escaping the closeness.

'What's wrong, Fern?' His voice sounded more urgent.

'Do you mind if we sit down?'

Barely waiting for his response, I walked quickly back to our seats. I poured myself a glass of wine and took a large swig. It could have been my imagination but there seemed to be considerably less wine in the bottle than when we had left it. You could say that the bottle was now half empty as opposed to half full.

He sat down beside me. I inched away slightly, still avoiding eye contact. He didn't say anything for a while. After a time, he took my hand in his. I had to force myself not to pull away.

'What is it, Fern?'

I shrugged.

The truth was, I didn't know. All I knew was that I was overwhelmed by strange feelings that

I couldn't identify. I didn't know how to handle them. I felt incredibly stupid but I didn't know how else to behave. I was terrified that I was going to burst out crying.

'Can you take me home, please?' I eventually heard myself asking in a small voice.

Seán nodded mutely and we left the nightclub.

We didn't say anything to each other on the interminable walk back to the taxi rank. Seán tried to strike up conversation several times during the ride home but he didn't get very far.

What was wrong with me? Why was I sabotaging everything?

At long last, we pulled up outside my house. I turned towards him nervously.

'Goodnight then.' I began to open the car door.

'Fern, wait for a second. Will you at least tell me what I've done wrong? I deserve that much.'

I shook my head.

'If I came on too strong, then I'm sorry. It's just that . . . ' – he looked away, embarrassed – 'I find you totally irresistible, if you must know.'

'You didn't do anything wrong, Seán. I don't know what's wrong with me. It's just too much, too soon, you know? I just need a bit more space.'

'A bit more space. I've heard that speech before.' He ran his hand through his hair and slumped back in the seat with a sigh. 'Can I at least call you again?'

I nodded, amazed that he'd even want to.

'Tomorrow?'

'Best leave it for a few days.'

'Fair enough.'

'Bye then.'

'See you.'

This time I got out of the cab and practically ran up the driveway, craving desperately to be on my own. I stripped off and climbed into bed, dispensing with the usual bathroom formalities. I lay under the covers, my head in a whirl. I couldn't think about it now. I decided to sleep on it.

Chapter Thirteen

Seán rang me three days later. I pretended not to be in. Didn't know what to say. Didn't know what to do either.

I tried to put it out of my mind as I sat at the top of the double-decker bus on my way to

Sarah's a few evenings later. Of course, things were complicated with her now too. She had been extraordinarily un-nosy and tactful over the last few days, but I knew my chances of getting through the night without a grilling were slim to none.

She flung open the door of the new apartment that she shared with the absent Stephen before I'd even had a chance to ring the doorbell.

'Come in, come in. I'll give you a guided tour.'

The guided tour took approximately twenty seconds. Kitchen, bathroom, sitting room – that was it. Apparently the sofa folded out into a bed. I tried to enthuse about the place, privately thinking that it was a bit of a hovel. Sarah showed me around proudly as if it were Buckingham Palace. It was quite touching really. Evidently the world was a different and altogether nicer place when you were in love. Not that I'd know.

So anyway. Down to business. We settled down in front of the fake-coal fire and I unloaded all my goodies. Let me see: I'd brought crisps (Pringles – sour cream and onion of course), two large tubs of ice-cream (Ben & Jerry – Rocky Road and Cherry Garcia), one packet of double-chocolate-chip cookies and a crunchie bar each. Oh and not forgetting: one large bottle of Diet Coke to wash it all down. It had to be diet of course. That was vital.

Sarah complimented me on my excellent choices.

'Well done, Fern. I'm going to get you to do all my grocery shopping from now on.'

'I wouldn't recommend it. You'd be as big as a house.' Not that she'd care. She was the only person I knew, of the female persuasion, who wasn't obsessed with her weight. Of course, this in itself made her attractive to men. I could see the logic of this approach but I was darned if I knew how to put it into practice.

Anyway, I'd already resigned myself to the fact that I was destined to gain at least ten pounds that night.

'So,' I said, 'let's see what you've got to offer.' Sarah had been put in charge of the wine and video department. She proudly produced two bottles of Jacob's Creek – one red, one white.

'Good choice, Madam. And the videos? Please tell me you got something funny.'

'One sort of sad one and one funny.'

'What's the sad one?'

'*Bed of Roses.*'

'Never heard of it. And the funny one?'

'*When Harry Met Sally.*'

I groaned out loud. 'But isn't that a romantic comedy?'

'So? It's funny, isn't it?'

'I suppose,' I agreed glumly.

I hated watching romantic films when my own love life was going rapidly down the toilet. They were so depressing. Everybody living happily ever after except me.

'Oh, cheer up and have a glass of wine.'

She poured me out a generous helping of red and handed it to me. And when I say generous, we're talking Mother Teresa standards here. The wine glass was massive. More of a tankard really. Still, a glass of wine was a glass of wine and who was I to argue with my hostess? It would have been impolite.

We settled down to *Bed of Roses*, munching and slurping away to our hearts' content.

'So, what's this about anyway?'

'I don't want to spoil it for you.'

'Just give me the general gist.'

'It's about this girl and she's had a really rotten childhood. Then she meets this guy – well she doesn't exactly meet him. He spots her crying in her bedroom window one night and he sends her flowers. He's a florist, you see.'

'Very macho.'

'Shut up. Anyway, he finally convinces her to go out with him and she does and they get on great. Then, after a few months he asked her to marry him, in front of his whole family.'

'The big eejit. What does she say?'

'She says no, because she can't handle it.'

'Can't handle what?'

Sarah was looking at me earnestly now, her eyes glistening with unshed tears, as if she was telling a true story. 'Can't handle the fact that he's in love with her. You see, she has such a low opinion of herself that she can't believe that anyone – let alone a gorgeous, fabulous man – could love her. So, she messes it up in spite of herself.'

'And does it have a happy ending?'

'Watch it and see.'

I did what I was told. At least I had Christian Slater to drool over for a couple of hours. There was a happy ending. We are talking Hollywood after all – not real life. Sarah snivelled beside me.

'It was very moving, wasn't it?'

'It was all right.'

'Did you not find it touching though? Especially when she goes to him at the end?'

'Not particularly.' I was lying.

'You're a terrible liar, Fern.'

She was right. I said nothing.

After a short break for refreshments – not that we hadn't been eating and guzzling throughout the film – Sarah put on *When Harry Met Sally*.

'I can't believe you haven't seen this before, Fern. It's a classic. I've seen it about ten times.'

'Why did you get it out then?'

'Because I thought you'd like it.'

'What's this one about anyhow?'

'It's about this man and woman.'

'Let me guess – Harry and Sally.'

'Don't be smart. When they first meet, she hates him. Thinks he's obnoxious. And then over the years they meet accidentally a few times. Then they become friends. Then they have sex. Then they break up. Then finally they realise that they've loved each other all along and they live happily ever after. So, basically, hate turns into love. Those we dislike most violently in the beginning turn out to be the ones we love the most in the end.'

Call me slow, but I was just starting to catch on. Sarah hadn't mentioned Seán all night but I felt that there was a definite theme emerging through her cunning choice of entertainment.

'Are you trying to tell me something, Sarah?'

She smiled serenely. 'Just watch the film.'

A couple of hours and a couple of bottles of wine later, we were lying side by side on the sofa bed in a food-and-alcohol-induced stupor.

'So,' said Sarah in a drowsy voice, 'tell me all about this barrister.'

I was immediately alert. 'What did Seán tell you?'

'Just that you used to go out with a barrister.'

'And what else?' I was sitting bolt up-right now.

'Nothing else, I swear. You seem pretty touchy about him though, if you don't mind me saying.' I did mind her saying. 'He must have hurt you very badly.'

I said nothing.

'Well, did he?'

'Yes,' I heard myself saying in a stranger's voice.

'What did he do to you?'

I sighed. 'Basically, he used me and then dumped me.'

'And were you in love with him?'

I nodded.

'And you still are.' Her words hung for a few moments in the dark.

And then, to my absolute horror, I started to cry. Great big sobs. 'I'm sorry. I don't know what's wrong with me.'

'It's all right. It's good to let these things out. Tell me everything.'

And I did.

For the first time, I told someone all about me and James. The dashing good looks, the sordid sex, the snobby friends, the beautiful Bronwyn. And what it felt like to be held by him. And the humiliation. And the hurt.

Especially the hurt.

I even told her about slapping his father. And then I decided that I might as well tell her about being fired as well. All about not being Boland, Sharpe material. Oh and what the hell – while I was at it I might as well tell her about my parents' separation. So I did. It all came tumbling out.

I must have talked non-stop for hours – pausing to stop only when the sobs got so hard that I couldn't speak.

Sarah was silent throughout. She just stroked my hair during the really difficult bits. It reminded me of being comforted by my mother as a child. That thought made me cry afresh.

When I had finally stopped talking, she was quiet for a little while. I waited for her to speak, afraid to breathe. I felt so ashamed at my tears and revelations. Finally she spoke.

'Jesus, Fern, you've really been through the mill lately, haven't you?'

I nodded into the half-light.

'Do you know what you need to do now?'

'What?' I was eager for a solution.

'You need to be kind to yourself.'

'What do you mean?' This was an entirely new concept.

'I mean just that. Be kind to yourself, like you're so kind to other people.'

'Am I?' I was surprised.

'Yes. You're one of the sweetest, funniest people I've ever met. Don't you know that about yourself?'

I shook my head.

'Well, you are. But you have to start taking care of yourself or you won't be any good to anybody.'

'What do you suggest?' I wiped my eyes.

'Lots of fun for a start. Enjoy yourself. Buy yourself new clothes, make-up, flowers. Eat what you want, please yourself, go dancing, be silly, take lots of bubble baths – I don't know – whatever it takes.'

'Do you really think that would help?' I asked doubtfully.

'I do. And another thing.'

'What?'

'Let Seán be kind to you too.'

I didn't reply.

'He's nuts about you, you know?'

'That's because he doesn't know me yet. He's just in love with the image of who he thinks I am. Just wait until I fall off my pedestal. It shouldn't take long.'

'I really don't think that's true, Fern. Anyway, never mind what he thinks about you. What do you think about him?'

'I like him.'

'And do you fancy him?'

'Sarah!' I squirmed with embarrassment. 'He's your brother. I can't talk like that about him to you.'

'Don't be daft. Just pretend he's not my brother.'

'But he is.'

'Just do it.'

'Well,' I answered, after battling with my self-consciousness for several seconds, 'I do find him attractive.'

'But . . . '

'But what?'

'I can hear a "but" in there somewhere.'

'What I was going to say was – well – it's not like it was with James.'

'You mean Seán doesn't use you and treat you like dirt?'

'No! It's just that I had very strong feelings for James. It's not the same with Seán.'

'I think you're confusing longing with love.'

'Pardon?'

'You long for James because he's unobtainable, but it's not love. It's just thinking you want something that you can't have.'

'That's not true.'

To tell the truth, I was starting to get a tad irritated. What did she know about James? She'd never even met him and she'd never seen us together.

'Are you sure that's not what it is?' She looked at me doubtfully. I felt myself clamming up, like I always did when I felt threatened in any way. And now she was threatening my memory of James. To me, the memories of the feelings I had had for him were sacred. What I'd had with James had been the real thing. It was just a pity that he hadn't realised it.

Okay. So Seán had his good points. But it just wasn't the same. He paled in comparison beside my image of James.

'Fern . . .' Sarah's tone was cautious.

'What?'

'You know what you said about Seán putting you on a pedestal?'

'Yes.'

'And I said that I thought it wasn't true?'

'What are you getting at?' I almost snapped.

'Well – are you sure that's not what you're doing with James?'

'No, definitely not.'

If Sarah had a point, I certainly wasn't going to admit it. She could probably tell from the tone of my voice that the subject was closed as far as I was concerned.

'All right. I won't say another thing about it. It's your life. Let's just not fall out over it.'

'I agree. Whatever happens with Seán, we shouldn't let it affect us.'

'Deal. Goodnight, Fern.' I caught her smile for a split second before she switched off the lamp.

Chapter Fourteen

It was a few days later and the café was like a morgue. Sarah and I, who had very little to do, were chatting idly when a woman came in and sat alone at a table for two just inside the door.

The very table, in fact, that I'd sat at on that fateful morning a few short months ago while job-hunting.

The words I'd been about to utter froze on the tip of my tongue. Sarah gave me a puzzled look. 'What is it?'

'It's my mother.'

'Do you want me to serve her? You can stay in the back until she leaves.'

I considered the offer. It was tempting.

'No. Let me do it. It's about time she knew that my glittering career as a legal secretary is in tatters.' I forced myself to walk towards her table.

'Hello, Mam. Can I take your order?' Her expression was priceless.

'Fern! What . . . why . . . ?' she looked at her watch in confusion. 'Why aren't you in work?'

'I am in work, Mam.'

'But you work in an office.' She sounded scandalised. My mother's definition of a good job was to work in an office

'Not any more.' Suddenly I felt overcome by a great weariness and I sat down heavily in the chair opposite her. Her expression was dark.

'What happened?'

'I gave it up.'

'Why?'

'I didn't like it.'

'What's "like" got to do with it? You're not meant to like it. You had a good job. That's not something you give up on a whim, you know.' She uttered a harsh tutting sound. 'This is so like you, Fern. You always had a head full of nonsense.'

I felt a surge of anger rise within me. It was with great effort that I managed to halt its progress at my throat and stop the damaging words from coming out.

My mother had spent most of her life working as a cleaner. I knew that it was vital to her that her daughters moved at least a couple of notches up the so-called social ladder. I also knew that waitressing wasn't exactly her idea of social advancement. Change the subject, urged my inner voice.

'So how have you been anyway?'

'Did you get the sack?' There was no stopping her.

'Yes.'

My mother threw her eyes wildly up to the heavens. 'Jesus, Mary and Joseph, Fern! What did you do this time?'

'I didn't do anything.' Oh, make her shut up, please God! And whatever you do, don't let her bring up Sasha.

'I don't know. I brought you two girls up in exactly the same way. You both got the best of everything. How could two sisters turn out so differently?'

Enough!

'Look, do you want to order something or not?'

'Don't use that tone with me, young lady. And yes – I'll have a pot of tea – two bags, mind – don't be bringing me out a pot of maid's water – and a fruit scone.'

'Coming up.' I snapped my notepad shut viciously. A slamming door would have been more of a statement but the notepad was all I had to hand. I walked over to Sarah who was wiping a table nearby, pretending not to listen.

'Will you get it?' I whispered between gritted teeth. 'Tea and a fruit scone.'

'I heard. Two bags.' Sarah grinned.

'And don't forget the rat poison.'

I nearly broke the world record for speed walking on my way back to the staffroom. Luckily, it was empty.

'Fuck!' I shouted at the empty room. 'Fucking, stupid, old bitch!'

I felt better immediately. I snatched up a cigarette, lit it and started puffing furiously, all the while pacing the room. Not for the first time, I wished management had had the foresight to install a punch bag in the staffroom. It would have been an invaluable and effective way of getting rid of the stress caused by difficult customers. And let's face it: they didn't come more difficult than my mother.

After a few minutes, Sarah stuck her head around the door. 'Are you okay?'

'I'm getting there. So, did you get a lecture too?'

'No. She was very pleasant.'

'Huh! Typical. Pity she can't be nice to her own family. What did she say?'

'This and that.'

'Did she say anything about me?'

'She wanted to know how long you'd been working here.'

'What did you tell her?'

'The truth – what else? And she wanted to know why you hadn't brought her order out.'

'What did you say?'

'That you were busy in the kitchen.'

I nodded, continuing to pace up and down the room.

'I'll get you some ice cream.'

'Ice cream?'

'Yes – it'll make you feel better.'

'You think that will solve all my problems, do you?'

'Of course. Did you not know that chocolate ice cream is the answer to all the world's problems?'

'So, if Gerry Adams and Ian Paisley sat down together over a few tubs of Haagan Dazs, we'd have peace in the North?'

'Now you have it! I'll be right back.'

She returned bearing a bowl of chocolate ice cream – half melted, just the way I liked it – and two spoons. We dug in, chatting and laughing about silly stuff. I must admit that I did feel better as we scraped the bottom of the bowl.

'So, are you fit to face the world again?'

'I suppose so. I'd better go out and speak to her before she leaves.'

My mother was looking out at the people walking by on the street.

'Is everything okay?'

'Oh, you're back, are you?'

'Yes. Can I get you anything else?'

'No, thanks. I'm fine.'

'Fair enough.' I turned to go.

'Fern.'

'What?'

'She was looking earnestly at me now, her eyes no longer angry. 'How's your Dad?'

'Not too bad,' I answered cautiously, feeling uncomfortable.

'What's he doing with himself these days?'

'Oh, the usual. Goes to work. Potters around the garden. Doesn't say very much. You know Dad.'

'Unfortunately, yes.'

'Then why are you asking about him?' I snapped.

My mother sighed. 'Sit down, please, Fern.'

I reluctantly sat down opposite her again. I didn't want to but it was as if my bum was drawn to the seat like a magnet. How was it that no matter how old or independent I became, I always felt like a helpless six-year-old when confronted by my mother?

'You know I had to leave, don't you?'

Oh no! I didn't want this. I shrugged. 'I had to, Fern. I was feeling useless. You girls don't need me any more. Neither does your Dad. I had to get away and make a new life for myself while I still had the chance.'

I sat hunched in the chair, wanting to bolt out the door. The funny thing was that I knew that if a perfect stranger had been telling me this, I would have been more than sympathetic. It was different when it was your own mother – telling you that you were the product of an unhappy, loveless union. Her words sounded hollow to my ears. As if she was spouting something that she'd heard on Oprah Winfrey.

She showed signs of getting ready to leave. Thank you, God!

'You will come and see me soon, won't you?'

'Of course,' I lied.

She nodded as she put on her familiar old coat. Not the kind of coat worn by the type of woman who would walk out on her own family. 'You know where I am. Don't be a stranger.'

I watched her leave. I already was.

I barely had time to clear her table before I felt the cool draught of the door opening again. I felt someone standing behind me. I knew it was him before he spoke.

'Hello, Fern.'

Seán.

I turned to face him.

'I've come to see about the mural.' He gestured awkwardly at the notepad and pencils that he was carrying.

'Oh. Will I get Sarah for you?'

'Please.'

I went out to the staffroom. I didn't know how much more excitement I could take in the one day.

'Sarah, Seán's here.'

'For me?' She was looking at me searchingly. I avoided her gaze.

'Yes, for you. He wants to talk to you about the mural.'

'Oh, yeah – come out with me.' She didn't give me much choice as she dragged me out to the front by the arm.

'So – where do you want it, then?' He was businesslike. Brusque even.

'I'm fine, thanks. How are you?'

'Sorry, Sarah. How's it going? Is this the wall over here?'

'Yes. Any ideas?'

'A few. I was talking to Fintan last night. He wants a Celtic theme. Lots of bright colours, that kind of thing. After that, It's up to me.' (Fintan was the café owner in the States.)

'Done any sketches yet?'

'One or two.'

'Let's have a look.'

Seán handed the sketch-pad to Sarah who proceeded to flick through the pages, ooh-ing and aah-ing, until the door pinged, announcing the arrival of another customer. She shoved the pad at me.

'I'll go – it's my turn.'

It wasn't her turn.

'May I?' I said to Seán, as much to fill the awkward silence as anything. He nodded, pretending to inspect the wall.

I slowly turned the pages. They contained rough sketches only but the talent was immediately obvious. After a couple of minutes of me silently page-leafing and Seán silently wall-staring, I handed the notepad back to him.

'They're very good.'

He looked at me, his eyes sharp. 'Do you really think so?'

I was surprised by the note of urgency in his voice. 'Yes, I do. But you don't need the likes of me to tell you that. People pay you good money to do this, for goodness sake. Does that not tell you something?'

He consulted the wall again. I made another attempt.

'What colours did you have in mind?'

It was like flicking a switch. His features leapt into life as he started talking about the mural. I listened mostly. Made the odd comment and suggestion.

I couldn't take my eyes off him as he spoke. I had to admit that the passion and enthusiasm he had for his subject were very appealing.

Eventually, he stopped talking and looked at me, his blue eyes burning. 'Why don't you work on it with me?'

'What?'

'Yes! Why didn't I think of it before?'

'Because it's a ridiculous idea, that's why.'

'No – it's perfect.'

'Listen to yourself. You've not so much as seen one drawing of mine.'

'Well, now's the perfect time to show me.'

'Absolutely not!'

'All right, look, Fern. I don't even have to see. I know by just talking to you that we're on the same wavelength.'

'You're talking shite.'

'You wouldn't even have to do any of the artwork if you didn't want to. I could use a sounding board – someone to bounce ideas off.'

'Really?'

'Yes, really. You'd be doing me a huge favour.'

I admit it. I was flattered. And excited. Why not!

'Okay.'

'You will?'

'Yes.'

Now I understood the expression, 'grinning from ear to ear'. Seán's face was stretched to full capacity. 'When can you start?'

'We're not too busy this morning, so . . . '

So I did. We forgot our mutual embarrassment as we discussed the mural as if it was the answer to all the world's problems. (Sorry, I forgot – that was double-chocolate-chip ice cream.) At one point, I caught him staring deliberately at me and smiling.

'What are you looking at?'

'You know something?'

'Tell me.'

'You're lucky I'm not the type to take no for an answer.'

I said nothing. But I was glad that he wasn't.

He had to leave after a couple of hours. We agreed to meet up that night, after the café had closed.

Chapter Fifteen

I arrived wearing a grotty pair of black leggings and an old blue shirt that had seen better days on my father's back. I had to roll the sleeves up half a dozen times to prevent them from trailing on the ground alongside me.

Seán was already there, in true scruffbag mode. He looked as if someone had taken a large paintbrush, dipped it in paint, splashed it all over him and then repeated the process with all the colours of the rainbow.

'I told you I'd wear my scruffiest clothes next time we went out.'

'I'd hardly call this going out.'

'We're in a bistro – at night time. That's good enough for me.'

'Remember, this is business, not pleasure.'

'I promise that if I start enjoying myself, I'll go straight home.'

'Very funny. Where shall we start?'

'I'd like to start from the centre and work my way out.'

At the centrepiece of the mural were the figures of a Celtic god and goddess. They stood against a backdrop of a wild landscape populated with mythical creatures and fringed with vivid Celtic designs.

It took us a while to work out the scale and proportions. I was surprised at how meticulous Seán was. I'd always had him down as the slapdash type.

He had a miniature of the mural sketched out on a notepad in front of him.

'Is that what you're working from?' I asked, in my innocence.

'Partly. But a real-life model would be more useful.'

It took me a second to catch on. 'Who? Me?'

'There's nobody else around.'

'But I don't look anything like a Celtic goddess.'

'Let me be the judge of that. Anyway, that's not the point. It's the basic female form I'm after.'

'Okay – what do you want me to do?'

Seán took me by the shoulders and gently rearranged me into Celtic goddess pose. 'Just stand there and look beautiful.'

'But I'm not exactly dressed like a Celtic goddess either.' I gestured to my work clothes.

'Don't worry about it . . . I can use my imagination.' He grinned playfully at me. 'I'll dress you with my eyes. Now, will you stay still for a second. I'm trying to work.'

So I stood still and shut up, and Seán worked. We chattered intermittently but most of our time was taken up by comfortable silence. It was almost as if we were communicating anyway, on a slightly different level. There is something intensely intimate about having a man scrutinise you so closely and then follow the curves of your face and body with his paintbrush. It isn't quite like being mentally undressed. More like mentally caressed. Unbidden thoughts about how I'd felt when Seán had kissed me swirled around in my head. I felt myself becoming aroused.

I swallowed and tried to think about something else. Milk! Yes, we were low on milk. I'd have to go shopping. And toilet bleach. Mustn't forget that.

'Take off your blouse.'

'I beg your pardon?'

'Take off your blouse. The Celtic goddess is showing a fair amount of cleavage.'

'Well, it's not my fault the Celtic goddess is a slut. You'll have to use your imagination again because I'm not doing it.'

'Please, Fern. You want the mural to be realistic, don't you?'

'There's nothing realistic about her tits. I didn't know they had Wonderbras in those days.'

He laughed. 'You know that my interest in your breasts is purely professional.' The cheek of him!

'I know no such thing. I've heard about you artistic types. You're not to be trusted.'

'And what about you? I thought you were meant to be the artistic type.' Exactly. And I didn't trust myself either.

'Look. The shirt stays on. You'll have to work around it. Where do you think you are? The film set of *Titanic*?'

'Okay, okay. I get it.'

So I stood there and he stared at my breasts – through my father's shirt – for purely professional reasons.

I was starting to get very hot under the collar that I'd refused to take off the shirt. After a couple of minutes, I'd had enough.

'I need to take a break. Do you want some coffee?'

'No, thanks.'

'I'm having a cup.'

'Go ahead.'

I walked self-consciously over to the coffee station and started fiddling around. Oh! This is ridiculous, I told myself. It was high time I rid myself of my inhibitions. Okay Fern! Pretend you're on that beach in Majorca where you went topless last summer on your holidays. Same difference.

Checking that Seán still had his back turned, I unbuttoned my shirt with slightly trembling fingers, slipped it off my shoulders and unhooked my bra with all the dexterity of a fourteen-year-old boy embarking on his first grope.

I strode back, my heart thudding like crazy. It's only work, I told myself. It means nothing.

Seán still had his back to me, rooting around in a jar of brushes.

'Will this do?'

I stood there defiantly, hands on hips, naked from the waist up, silently willing myself not to fold my arms over my chest. Seán turned around and narrowly avoided dropping the jar of brushes out of his hand. I noticed him swallow.

'Er . . . yeah . . . that should help.'

So we continued working. In total silence now. Not as comfortable as before. After a while, I saw that his lips were curved into a slight smile.

'What?'

'Nothing.'

'No. What's so funny?'

'You.'

'What's wrong with me?' Oh no. Did I have the most hilarious nipples he'd ever seen, or something?

'I just didn't think you'd do it, that's all.'

'Well, I guess you underestimated me, didn't you?'

He stared at my breasts for what seemed like an aeon and then looked directly into my eyes.

'No, I'd never underestimate you, Fern.' His voice was quiet, his tone deadly serious. And he picked up his brushes and started painting again.

I felt my breathing become more shallow and I realised that there were parts of me that were aching to be touched. You know the parts I'm talking about. But I knew that, after the other night, Seán wouldn't make a move.

Without saying a word, I walked slowly towards him and touched him lightly on the arm. Our eyes locked and he let the brush fall out of his hand. I couldn't believe what I was doing. I took one of his large, brown, paint-soiled hands and placed it on my breast. My breathing was laboured as I looked up at him. His expression was unreadable.

'Are you sure you want this?'

I nodded.

'And you promise you won't run away from me again?'

'Promise.'

And with that, he placed both hands around my waist and bent his head. I felt his lips hot and wet on my left nipple and couldn't suppress a moan. I clasped my hands around the back of his head, enjoying the bristly softness of his hair, and pulled his head closer into me. He fell down onto his knees, pulling me tighter towards him and sucking hard at each breast in turn.

Still standing, I looked around unseeingly at the familiar café. I couldn't believe this was happening to me. The surrounding darkness and silence felt so intimate. The most heavenly sensations trickled over and under my skin like a waterfall. I bent towards Seán, wrapping my bare arms tightly around his neck and then lowered myself to my knees.

Seán brought his face back up to mine and concentrated on my face and neck, his kisses ranging from light to feathery to wet to hard and then to light again. I rained kisses back all over his neck and face, marvelling at the smooth tautness of his skin beneath my mouth. Then I slipped my hands up the back of his T-shirt and feasted on his silken back, feeling the muscles move under his skin as he moved his hands all over my body. I reckoned it was time he went topless too. I pulled at his T-shirt until he got the message and tugged it over his head in one smooth movement. Now we were even.

He sat back on his heels and stared at me.

'What is it?' I whispered. I don't know why I whispered.

He smiled a slow, sexy smile that made my heart perform a triple-toe-loop. 'I'm just looking at you.'

I suppose that was all he was doing. It's just that I'd never been looked at like that before. As if I was a masterpiece, or something. It was a pity he wasn't James.

Where did that thought come from? I slapped it back down to the guilty recesses of my mind from whence it had come.

'Seán'

'Yeah.'

'Do you mind if we leave it there tonight?'

'What – you don't want to work on the mural any more?'

'You know what I mean.'

'I know. That's fine. I don't want you to do anything you don't want to do.'

'Liar. You wanted me to take my top off.'

'I was only teasing. I didn't think you'd do it.'

'So you didn't want me to take my top off.'

'Now, did I say that?' He smiled and took both of my hands in his. 'Can I tell you something, Fern?'

'That depends.'

'You have a beautiful body.'

I pulled my hands away and started to get up, fumbling for my discarded clothing.

'Thanks,' I mumbled, almost inaudibly.

'Every little bit of you.'

'Okay, thanks, that's enough now,' I said a little louder. I wished he wouldn't say things that he couldn't possibly mean.

He started to get up himself.

Oddly, I didn't feel the slightest bit awkward about what had just transpired. There was none of the usual mad rush to cover up my boobs. I didn't really know why I'd put a halt to the proceedings when I had. It wasn't as if I didn't want more. Maybe I was just getting a bit of sense in my old age. It was about time.

We didn't get much more work done that night. We kept kissing when we should have been painting.

But it was a start.

Chapter Sixteen

'How long did you say you were in here last night?' Sarah surveyed our handiwork the next day.

'Four or five hours.'

'That long? You didn't get much done, did you?'

'There's a lot of preparation involved in a work like this, you know.'

'Oh, excuse me! I didn't realise I was conversing with such an expert. I just thought you might have got distracted or something.'

I could tell she was merely fishing. You can just go fish, I said to myself. Honestly! Sarah was the best in the world but she was also one of the nosiest. If I hadn't known for sure that she had my best interests at heart, I'd have told her where to get off.

We had arranged to resume work after hours that very night. I couldn't wait. This time I chose my attire with a little more discernment. Gone were the misshapen leggings and masculine shirt, to be replaced by blue Levis and a flowing white blouse. (Very practical. Didn't show the dirt one iota.) I was aiming for the casual-yet-chic look. As for make-up, I had chosen the 'barely there' look. As every woman knows, this takes twice as long to apply.

So, as a result, I was characteristically late. Seán was already stuck in when I arrived – so much so that he didn't hear me come in. I watched his face as I drew closer. His blond hair was sticking up at the front of his head like Tin Tin's and a streak of sky-blue paint emblazoned his cheek-bone. He would have looked comical if it hadn't been for the expression of intense concentration on his face. His brow was furrowed deeply and his lips were pursed together as he blended the colours.

With a shock that wasn't entirely pleasant, I realised just how much I fancied him.

After a few moments, he looked up, evidently sensing my presence. He stood up and smiled candidly at me, wiping his hands with a multi-coloured rag. I smiled back uncertainly. As our eyes met, I had a strange, weakening sensation in my legs. As if they belonged to someone else. As if I couldn't rely on them any more. Something distinctly odd was happening to me and I wasn't sure that I liked it.

I gave myself a shake and walked over to where he was standing.

'Hi! Sorry I'm late.'

He just smiled even harder. 'The late, great Fern.' He bent and kissed me on the cheek. I instantly thought about what we'd been up to on that very spot the previous night and found myself blushing. To take my mind off it, I looked over to what he'd been working on.

'Wow! You've been busy.'

The Celtic goddess was nearly complete. Seán was working on the flowing folds of her sky blue gown.

'She's looking good.'

'I was inspired.'

'Does this mean that I don't have to pose topless for you any more?'

'Only if you really want to.'

I looked up and touched the blue across his cheek. 'Very fetching. Brings out the colour in your eyes.'

He touched his cheek and looked down at his sky blue fingertips. He grinned. 'Promise not to tell the lads that you caught me wearing make-up.'

His grin faded as we had another of those tingly eye-locking moments. I had half a second to register the now-familiar strange sensation in my legs before his mouth was on top of mine and we were kissing ravenously.

Every nerve-ending in my mouth seemed to have a corresponding nerve-ending in each erogenous zone. It was sort of like reflexology of the mouth. I could almost hear my body screaming out to be touched.

He eventually tore his lips away and took a step back, clasping me by the shoulders. Come back!

'Look. If we don't stop now, I'm not going to be in a fit state to do any more work tonight. We'd better do a few hours at least. We're behind schedule as it is.'

I nodded reluctantly, simultaneously envying and resenting him for his self-restraint.

'What do you want me to do?'

'Our Celtic warrior could do with some attention.'

'What? Me do it by myself?'

'Don't panic. I'll be here to guide you every step of the way.'

And that's exactly what he did. For the next few hours. At one stage, he went off to make coffee to keep us alert. I didn't realise he'd gone until he came back.

'See. You're doing it by yourself. You don't need me to help.' With a jolt, I saw that he was right. What a rush!

'Does this mean I'm an artist, then?'

He laughed and gave me a squeeze. 'You always were. Feels good, doesn't it?'

I stood back and surveyed my Celtic warrior. Even I had to admit he looked good. I couldn't stop smiling, as we continued to work.

After a time, Seán turned to me. He looked like an Adam Ant impersonator who had fallen asleep beside a radiator.

'Let's call it a night. We've got loads done.'

'Can we not keep going for another hour or two? I'm flying it.'

'Do you know what time it is?' He showed me his watch. I couldn't believe it. It was the middle of the night. But I didn't want to go home, I was on too much of a high.

Seán seemed to read my thoughts.

'Why don't you come back to mine?'

'Pardon?'

'I mean, just to hang out. I can show you some of my work and we can have a few drinks.

But only if you want to.' His words tumbled out in a rush.

'I'd love to.'

I'm sure we looked like two people competing in a silly grin competition. I think I would have won hands down that night.

Seán's house was a few estates away from his mother's. It was a standard, three-bedroomed semi-d with a small, overgrown front garden.

'The next painting I sell, I'm going to buy a lawn mower,' he said, as he saw me peering into the undergrowth. I half expected a zebra to leap out at me.

The front door opened into a bare-looking hall. Virginal white walls and uncarpeted stairs.

'I didn't realise you'd just moved in.'

'Um . . . I haven't. I've been here over a year now. It's tough keeping up with the mortgage repayments when your income is as irregular as mine. I can only afford to do up one room at a time. See what we struggling artists have to put up with?'

I just nodded. There was no need to explain anything to me. Anybody who could afford to buy their own house in Dublin was loaded as far as I was concerned.

He led me into the kitchen-cum-dining area. This room was done up and *how*. Yellow, white and airy. It looked like something out of an ideal homes magazine.

It was just a pity that there was nothing in the fridge.

'Sorry. Looks like I forgot to go shopping again. But I do have a couple of bottles of duty-free plonk, if you're interested.'

'I've never been known to refuse yet.'

So, we sat up on the counter, sipping Chardonnay and munching on toast from a white sliced pan that Seán had located in the freezer and defrosted in the microwave. For dessert we shared half a bar of dairy milk chocolate which he rescued from underneath the egg compartment in the fridge. I was afraid to look at the use-by date but it tasted all right.

'You really know how to show a girl a good time, Seán Morrissey.'

'I know – smooth or what.'

'007 would be proud of you.'

I looked around at the array of paintings on the kitchen wall.

'Did you do any of these?'

'No. Most of them are by various friends. I wouldn't put up any of my own stuff. I'd feel like I was showing off or something.'

'So, when do I get to see your own stuff?'

'Come with me . . . and bring the wine.'

I followed him up the bare stairs to what was meant to be the master bedroom. He held the door open for me.

'Welcome to what I laughingly call my studio.'

I could see why he had chosen this particular room. It was large and airy with a massive window, curtainless to let in the light. There were several canvasses in the room, all covered with oilcloth. Seán uncovered one of them.

It was a beautiful landscape in subtle blues and greens. I recognised the style immediately.

'You!' Seán was looking away. 'You were one of the artists showing at that exhibition just before Christmas. I went with James.'

'I know. I saw you there.'

I didn't know what to say at first. 'So – the time I met you in the restaurant in the Courthouse . . . '

'I recognised you, yes. Even I'm not normally that forward.'

I shook my head in disbelief. 'Why didn't you say anything before?'

'Don't know really.'

'And did you know that my ex-boss bought your painting?'

'No way! That baldy-headed little fucker was your boss? The one who fired you?'

'The very same. He has your painting up on the boardroom wall. Brags about it to his friends. He fancies himself as a bit of a patron of the arts.'

He roared with laughter at this. 'I can't believe that snobby bollocks was your boss. You're better off not working for the likes of him. Mind you, he does have good taste in paintings. This one is for him too.'

'This one here?'

'Yeah. He commissioned it for his wife's birthday.'

I shook my head again, trying to take it all in.

'You know, Fern, I really think you should consider bringing an action for unfair dismissal against that crowd.'

'No – I couldn't.'

'Why not?'

'It'd just be re-opening old wounds. I couldn't face it. They'd bring up all sorts of stuff about how crap I was at my job. How I wasn't "Boland, Sharpe material".'

'They didn't say that?'

'They did.'

'The bastards!'

I smiled at the feeling in Seán's voice. Then I shuddered as I had a mental image of Julie at the Unfair Dismissals Tribunal, holding up documents that I'd typed, decorated all over with her dreaded red biro. She'd probably kept some of them. I wouldn't put it past her.

'But you can't let people walk all over you like that. It's not good for you.'

'I'll get my own back some day.'

'How?'

'Never you mind . . . I'll think of something. Anyway, I don't want to talk about it now. I'm too happy. Show me the rest.'

I sat down cross-legged on the hard wooden floor, bottle and glass within easy reach, and listened as Seán talked me through his own private exhibition. I was captivated. I couldn't remember feeling so happy and alive. When he had finished, I gave him a round of applause and he came and sat on the floor beside me. He looked pretty happy too.

'What do you think, then?'

'Not bad for a carpenter from the wrong side of town.' He looked even happier. I guessed I must have said the right thing. 'So – do I get a guided tour of the rest of the house, then?'

'Well, there isn't really much point. There's only one other room that I've got around to decorating yet.'

'Which one?'

'My bedroom. I didn't want to seem pre-sumptuous by showing it to you.'

I didn't say anything. We just smiled happily and easily at each other. I knew without a shadow of a doubt that I was about to sleep with him. And I was pretty sure that he knew it too. Funnily enough, I didn't feel in the slightest bit nervous or afraid.

'Are you sleepy, Fern?'

'No.'

'I'd better take you to bed, then.'

I giggled and let him help me to my feet.

His room was warm and dark. He switched on the bedside lamp, sitting down on the bed as he did so. He was looking at me expectantly.

'What would you like to do, Fern?'

Now, there was a question. I thought about this for a few seconds. 'Well . . . '

'Well what?'

'We never got to finish our slow dance that night.' I held out my hand. 'Dance with me.'

He walked over to his stereo and selected a CD. 'Marvin Gaye, wasn't it?'

I nodded happily. He remembered!

We melted into one another as the music began. I found that perfect spot between his shoulder and neck and nuzzled into it, kissing him softly on the throat every now and then. He gathered me up, stroking my hair with one hand and drawing circles on my back with the other.

This time when our mouths met, I didn't pull away. Wild horses couldn't have pulled me away.

Still standing and still dancing, Seán began unbuttoning my blouse. (One-handed with worrying expertise.) I was wearing nothing underneath but a strategically placed white lace bra. A moan escaped Seán's lips as he moulded his hands around my breasts. I was thrilled by the expression of pure absorption on his face.

His fingers reached my nipples and rubbed them gently through the lace. Now it was my turn to moan. My body began to pulsate. I couldn't get my clothes off quickly enough. Seán helped. He was very good like that.

As I stood there, buck naked, I suddenly noticed that he still had all his clothes on. 'Are you going to take your boots off at least?'

'Sorry.' He kicked off his boots and his socks. Some previous girlfriend must have told him how ridiculous men looked in their underwear and socks.

Next came the sweatshirt and T-shirt. He had exactly the right amount of chest hair. Just down the centre, soft, downy and blond, travelling down his belly into a darkening line which disappeared tantalisingly into the top of his jeans. His arms were strong and muscular and covered in the same soft, blond furze. I ran my finger tips lightly over his biceps, closing my eyes at the sensation.

I lay down luxuriantly on the bed and watched him as he took off his jeans and underwear. He had a gorgeous body. Athlete perfect except for a slight, beer-induced belly. I decided to let him away with this imperfection as he seemed inclined to let me away with all of mine.

As I lay on Seán's bed, my body being covered with a thousand kisses and caresses, I allowed myself one final thought of James. It was an image of his straight black back as he walked away from me.

And then, I just stopped thinking.

I won't tell you what happened during the next few hours. Strictly private and confidential. I will tell you that we were still barely conscious several hours later when light began to filter through the curtains.

'Have you ever watched the sunrise?' Seán murmured softly and lazily into my ear.

I shook my head. He rolled away for the first time that night – or was it morning – and stepped out of the bed. Through half-closed eyes I watched him move across the floor and place an armchair beside the window. He drew back the curtains to reveal a pearl-grey sky, streaked with pink and gold. He walked back to the bed and drew back the covers.

'Come with me,' he said, as he lifted me out of the bed as if for all the world I didn't weigh nine and a quarter stone.

He carried me over to the window and sat down on the armchair beside it, drawing me onto his lap and wrapping me in his arms.

'This is one of the best parts of the day. Amazing light.'

I had to agree as the skin on our bodies was bathed in amber-rose light. It felt magical. I felt magical. As if I could do just about anything and everything. So I did everything to Seán, sitting on that very chair, my body golden in the light, feeling closer than close.

Eventually he carried me back to bed and we slept.

When I woke up a few hours later, I thought I'd been dreaming. But he was still there in the bed beside me. That was a novelty in itself. A man who wasn't tripping over himself to vacate the premises before I woke up. (I suppose he did live there, after all.) A thought struck me. Maybe he wanted me to leave. But he wasn't even awake yet. I couldn't see his face as my head was snuggled into his chest and he had his arm wrapped around me. I knew he was asleep because of his deep regular breaths. More of a light snore really.

I slowly wriggled myself free, wanting to look at him, not wanting him to wake up. He didn't. He just snorted gently and shifted position. I propped myself up on one elbow and studied his face in repose. His features were transformed by sleep. In actual fact, I was aware for the first time that I'd never properly looked at his features before. His face was normally so mobile that it was never still enough to look at properly.

I saw that his eyes were deep-set and fringed with heavy, brown lashes. His nose was long and straight, his cheekbones high and his lips full and firm. His skin was lightly tanned and deeply lined in places, giving him the appearance of someone who worked outdoors. His fluffy blond hair stuck up in a tuft on top of his head. He looked for all the world like a weather-beaten Easter chick.

His eyelids began to flicker and he started to come to. I watched the recognition dawn in his eyes as he turned to look at me. Still half asleep, he pulled me towards him and kissed me on the top of my head. Well, it didn't look as if he wanted me to leave just yet. I snuggled down into him again, feeling all glowy, like I'd just eaten two bowls of Ready-Brek.

Perhaps this time it would be different.

Chapter Seventeen

The day of the great unveiling of the mural dawned. The café owner, Fintan, had flown over from Boston especially. It was to celebrate the café's being open for business for two years.

The mural had been a closely guarded secret. Every night when we had finished working on it, we covered it in a massive cloth. Today the cloth had been replaced by an enormous piece of royal purple velvet. I had no idea where Seán had managed to get his hands on it.

Sarah was in charge of decorating the café for the so-called 'unveiling ceremony'. We were officially closed for the evening. Instead, we had invited a selection of our regular customers for a party. Staff were allowed to invite close friends and family.

I had toyed with the idea of inviting my own family members. I soon dismissed it as I actually wanted to enjoy myself. My mother would think the whole thing was a lot of old nonsense and ask me when I was going to stop painting silly pictures and get myself a proper job. My father would rather be at home watching *Gardener's World*. As for Sasha! She had done such a thorough job of humiliating me ever since I'd told her I'd got the sack, that I had vowed never to have anything to do with her ever again. Apart from living in the same house as her. So, I guessed, I wouldn't be inviting anyone. It was their loss. And besides, there'd be more champagne for the rest of us.

I had been on an absolute high all day long. I noticed customers looking at me strangely. They were used to me being pretty quiet and sedate. But today I couldn't shut up. And if I was alone, I couldn't sit still. I would be found pacing up and down, chewing my nails into a pulp or puffing like mad on a cigarette. It was partly excitement and partly nerves. I thought the mural was pretty good, but what if everybody else thought it was load of cobblers? I'd be devastated.

I wore a brand-new outfit for the occasion. I know, any excuse. It was a caramel-coloured, sleeveless, chiffon dress. A floaty little number which I hoped made me look 'artistic' – whatever that was. It would make me cold, that was for sure. I had slapped on plenty of fake tan to focus the attention away from my goose bumps.

I was still waiting for that Hawaiian look to develop when I arrived back at the café that evening. For once in my life, I wasn't late. In fact, I'd had to restrain myself from being too early. Sarah and Stephen were the only ones there, putting the last touches to the decorations. The place looked fantastic – purple and silver as far as the eye could see.

Sarah jumped down off her step-ladder to greet me.

'What do you think?'

'Amazing. You must have been working solidly since we closed.'

'Stephen did most of it.' She threw Stephen an adoring look which he returned threefold. If I didn't like them both so much, I'd have found them completely nauseating. They resided permanently on cloud number nine when they were in each other's presence. The bubble hadn't burst in any case.

Small groups of people began to drift in. I circulated with a tray of champagne, taking generous swigs at indecent intervals. I tried not to glance at the door for Seán every two seconds and distracted myself by talking ninety to the dozen to regulars who looked at me oddly. Probably thought I'd been invaded by a body snatcher. When Seán tapped me on the shoulder, they very nearly ended up wearing the tray of champagne.

'Oh, thank God you're here.'

He gently took the tray away from me and put it down on a nearby table. 'Are you all right?'

'Fine. Fine. I need more champagne though. Get me another glass.'

'Have you eaten anything today?'

'Sure. I had two Weetabix this morning.'

'That's it?'

'That's it.'

'Here, have a . . . one of these things.'

He handed me a tray of vol-au-vents. I waved it away. The very thought of eating anything made my stomach churn like a cement mixer. He shrugged and popped a whole one into his mouth. It was gone in a matter of seconds.

'How can you eat at a time like this? You're a pig, you know that?'

'Thanks.' He grinned, completely unoffended.

We became aware of raised voices and activity at the front door. Seán craned his neck to see what was going on, then beamed.

'It's Fintan and Trish. Come on – I'll introduce you.'

Seán and Fintan had grown up together. Their friendship had stood the test of time, bound as they were by a lifelong devotion to Manchester United and obscure Irish rock bands.

I watched them greet one another, envying their easy warmth and familiarity. I didn't have much opportunity to observe, as Seán nudged me gently forward.

'And this is Fern.'

'Fern! Delighted to meet you. I believe you're the other artist. Seán tells me you're incredibly talented.'

I blushed to the core, warming to Fintan immediately, which was hardly surprising after a compliment like that. He looked like a man who took his image as a successful businessman very seriously. I clocked the dark, expensive-looking suit, the pristine haircut and the manicured nails. His accent, which once must have been broad Dublin Northside had had the corners rubbed off it by a slight American twang. I looked at the two men standing side by side. Talk about the odd couple.

His Bostonian wife, Trish, seemed to want to adopt me as her new best friend. She linked me and drew me to one side companionably. 'I'm so happy to meet Seán's girlfriend. It's about time he found himself someone nice to settle down with.'

I felt my body stiffen. Seán's girlfriend. Is that who I was now? It hadn't been intentional. It kind of sneaked up on me. And what was all this about settling down? First I'd heard of it.

Trish must have felt me tense up. 'Oh, I'm sorry, honey. I didn't mean to be so forward. Just tell me to shut up and mind my own business.'

Yeah, shut up and mind your business, you nosy cow, I thought to myself. But is that what I said? Course not. What I said was, 'Oh no, not at all. I don't think you're being too forward. It's just that I haven't known him all that long.'

Hypocrite!

She smiled at me, all maternal warmth and wall-to-wall teeth. 'But sometimes it doesn't take all that long, does it, sweetie? Sometimes you just know. I knew Fintan was the one for me by the second date.'

I smiled tightly. Jesus! Somebody get me away from this patronising female. Part of me knew she meant well but for some reason she was really getting my back up. I was afraid I might say something I'd regret. (No such luck.)

'You know, between you and me, Fern, I wasn't really a great fan of Melanie. Did you ever meet her?'

Who the fuck was Melanie? 'No, we never met.'

'She wasn't the worst in the world, I suppose. Just not right for Seán. He needs someone more down to earth.'

That was me, down to earth. Fern Fennelly – salt of the earth!

'It was a blessing in disguise when Jil Sander called on her to do the Milan show.'

'Pardon?'

'You know, to model for her.'

'Oh, of course.' And I felt my smile slipping for good this time. A model! A model! Seán's previous girlfriend had been a model and I'd let him see my stumpy little body – naked. Oh my God!

'Seán,' Trish shrieked right in my ear. 'Come over here. I've just been talking to your charming girlfriend.' Seán allowed himself to be dragged over by the arm.

'You know, Fern,' said Trish in a conspiratorial whisper which they probably heard
in Japan, 'Seán was Fintan's best man at our
wedding last year. I'm sure Fintan would be
delighted to return the favour.'

The last thing I saw was Seán's grin as I
mumbled something about people needing more
champagne and made a bolt for the kitchen.

God save us all from loud Americans, I
thought as I gratefully knocked back a swig of
champagne directly from the bottle.

'Did your mother never tell you it's unhygienic to drink straight from the bottle?'

I spluttered and slammed the bottle down. It
was only Sarah.

'You'd better come out. They're about to
start the unveiling.'

I missed the beginning of Fintan's speech.
Everyone was gathered around him in a rough
semi-circle. I stood on my tiptoes at the back
of the crowd, straining to hear. Something
about what a great success the café had been
in the last two years. He proposed a toast to
Sarah, complimenting her on all her hard
work.

'And without further ado, I give you "A Celtic Dream", an original work by Seán Morrissey and our very own Fern Fennelly.'

Before I had time to prepare myself, he pulled the purple velvet aside to reveal the mural. There was a collective gasp from the crowd as the vivid, swirling colours were exposed.

And then a round of applause rippled across the room, gaining momentum and getting louder as it went. And then people started commenting to one another. What were they saying? I strained to hear. I could have sworn I heard my name mentioned a few times. People were actually starting to look around for me and point me out to others. It was Tamsin who solved the mystery.

'I never had you down as a Celtic goddess, Fern.'

'What?'

'The likeness is superb. He's an amazing artist. I think I'll get him to do a portrait of me.'

And then along came Trish. 'Oh, honey. He's captured you to a T. The whole thing is fabulous. Congratulations.' She kissed me warmly on each cheek.

I stared hard at the image of the goddess's face on the wall. It was me! I'd never seen it before. So much for helping him to capture the basic female form. The hair was different, long and cascading, but the features were mine. I hid beneath a mask of embarrassment, but secretly, I was thrilled.

And aside from that, everyone seemed to be raving about the mural. Congratulations and handshakes were offered left, right and centre. Sarah fought her way over and gave me a hug.

'Well done, Fern. It's fantastic. Everyone's mad about it.'

'Do you really think so?'

'I know so. Just look at them. Whose idea was it to use your face on the woman?'

'Not mine. I hadn't realised until now.'

'Her gown is very low cut. I hope you didn't model for it in something so indecent!'

I flashed her an enigmatic smile. 'No, I didn't wear a low-cut dress.'

She looked at me suspiciously. 'Fern Fennelly, if I didn't know you better, I'd swear you posed topless.'

I collapsed into giggles.

'You did not?'

I nodded.

'My God, I hope you were well compensated.'

I nodded again, speechless with laughter.

'No, please. Don't tell me how you were compensated. I don't want to know. He is my brother, remember. And speak of the devil . . . literally!'

'Well done, partner.' Seán held out his hand. I took it in both of mine, looking deep into his smiling blue eyes. After a few seconds, I saw them darken. And then, for all the world to see, I placed my arms around his neck and pulled him into a deep, smoochy kiss. Everyone standing around us started clapping and cheering. We had to stop. We were both laughing too much.

The party went on into the wee hours. I think I talked more that night then I had done in all my previous twenty-seven years. People were just starting to leave when Fintan approached me. 'I've been trying to get you on your own all night. Here – this is for you.'

He handed me a small brown envelope.

'What's this?'

'Payment. For a job well done.'

'But Seán . . . '

'Seán told me that you did half of the work and came up with some ideas.'

'But it's his design.'

Fintan laughed and held up his hands. 'Jesus, I've never known an artist to refuse money before. If you have a problem, take it up with Seán. It was him that told me to give you half the fee.'

'Half?' I was feeling a little dazed. I'd figured Seán would give me something for my contribution but this was far too much. I wouldn't have done so much work on it if I'd known that he was going to give away half his money.

I intended telling him so later on. But first, I'd open the envelope. I chatted politely to Fintan, feigning interest in whatever he was saying, all the while itching to open the envelope and devour the contents.

Eventually, he was coaxed off home by a jet-lagged Trish. Before I could be waylaid by anybody else, I made a bee-line for the loos and locked myself in a cubicle. It was the only way to guarantee complete privacy.

I had no idea what the going rate was for murals. Nor had I any idea of the figure that Fintan and Seán had agreed between themselves. I could hardly contain my excitement as I ripped open the envelope.

Holy fuck! It was lucky the lid was down on the toilet or I might have fallen in and drowned. In the privacy of that cubicle I performed my own little tribal dance of glee. Yes! Yes! Yes! Was this the best night of my life or what?

It wasn't just that I finally had confirmation that I had artistic talent. And it wasn't just the money – although that was damned nice too. It was the fact that my self-confidence had increased three-thousandfold in one night. I felt that I could finally hold my head up high. Fern Fennelly was someone special. She wasn't just a failed secretary, a mediocre waitress, a disappointing daughter or a barely tolerated sister. She was an artist!

In the space of twenty-four hours, a great shift had occurred in my consciousness. So many new possibilities seemed to emerge. Things that I had never thought possible before. For the first time, I was given a glimpse of what

I was capable of and of what kind of future was possible for me. And it was very different and a lot better than anything I had previously visualised.

I emerged from the toilet cubicle like a butterfly out of a chrysalis. A stranger looked back at me from the mirror – a stranger with an unfamiliar glow in her eyes. I felt as if my old self had been abducted by aliens and replaced by a mysterious new creature with special powers. I felt so strange and light-headed. Like I'd found myself in the twilight zone where I wasn't just a pathetic loser. Everything was altered. A parallel universe. The flip side.

I stepped out of the toilets and into this strange new world. The flip side of Seán was waiting for me.

'Excuse me, Ms Fennelly. I'm sorry to disturb you on your big night. I know you must be a very busy woman and I don't want to take up too much of your precious time, but I know someone who's a huge fan of yours. It would mean an awful lot to him if you could find it in your heart to give him your autograph.'

'Oh, all right then. Do you have a pen, young man?'

'No, sorry, Miss.'

I laughed and kissed him on the mouth. 'Now that I've signed for you, you're all mine.'

He placed his arms gently around my waist and stared searchingly into my eyes, as if he was looking for something that he'd lost. 'Is that a promise?'

'It is – if you want it to be.'

'Do you honestly think that anybody could compare to you, Fern?'

I swallowed. 'I don't know. Maybe Melanie could.'

He pulled away from me in a swift reflex reaction. 'Who told you about her?'

'Trish. She assumed that I knew all about her.'

'Oh, right.'

There was a brief silence.

'Well?'

'Well what?'

'Who the fuck is Melanie?'

'An old girlfriend.'

'When did you go out with her?'

'We broke up last summer. We were together about two years.' Two years! That sounded pretty serious to me.

'Why didn't you tell me about her before?'

'Because she's ancient history. Anyway, it's not as if you tell me anything about your past. I know practically nothing about you.'

I was alarmed. 'Does that bother you?'

'No. I figure you'll tell me everything in your own good time. Besides, I know all I need to know.' He hugged me against his chest.

'Seán . . .' My voice was muffled into his shirt. He tilted my face up to his. 'The money. It's too much. I'm giving some of it back.'

'No. It's yours. You earned it.'

'No, it's not fair. What about your mortgage repayments? And the house. You'll never decorate it at this rate.'

'And what about you? Can you not think of a good use for it?'

The words tumbled out of my mouth before I'd even had a chance to examine them. 'It could get me through the first year of art college.'

Seán laughed and pulled me towards him again. 'That's the best idea you've had since you took your shirt off that night.'

I had surprised myself even. Where on earth had that come from? 'Do you really think I could do it?'

'Can't think of one good reason why not. Go for it!'

And there and then, I decided to do it. Told you I was in the Twilight Zone.

Chapter Eighteen

After the unveiling, my life was like a roller-coaster ride with no downward swoops. Things just kept getting better and better.

I set the wheels in motion for enrolling in my first year at art college. Seán helped me to get my portfolio together. I got a raise at work. Tips were higher than ever – customers were seduced by my new-found positive attitude. My social life had never been better either, what with wild nights out with the girls and romantic evenings in with Seán. I'd even gone and got myself a trendy new haircut – short at the back, exposing the nape of my neck, sweeping and floppy at the front, with vibrant red highlights throughout. It was the most expensive haircut I'd ever got in my life – courtesy of Fintan's cheque.

Everyone had raved about my hair. Admittedly they were hardly likely to say it was horrible. Friends don't do that. Dishonesty is the best policy. Lies are always told to protect the innocent stylee. But even my family said they liked it and they certainly had no qualms about telling the truth, no matter how ugly. In fact, Sasha positively revelled in that kind of thing. But the words 'your hair is nice' had actually escaped her lips, probably before she could stop them. I'd say she was kicking herself afterwards.

The only snag about people praising your new haircut to the high heavens is that it makes you suspect that they must have hated your previous style. My own experience has taught me that exclamations such as 'It's much nicer than before' and 'It really is a vast improvement' should be strictly curtailed.

I'd splashed out on a rake of new clothes too. Less conservative than usual. The type of stuff I'd always wanted to wear but never had the nerve to. Well, now I had the nerve. But, most miraculously of all, I seemed to have lost that elusive half stone without any effort.

In short, I barely recognised myself, or my life. My confidence had gone right off the Richter scale – or whatever it is that scientists use to measure confidence.

It was a few weeks after the great unveiling and I was working on the night shift in the bistro. It was pretty quiet so I was out the back with Tamsin having a chat and a smoke. We were getting on famously again, now that I'd got my insecurity under control and accepted that her interest in Seán was purely platonic. (Besides, she was practically engaged to Brian.) She in turn had generously forgiven my previous

coldness, putting it down, I think, to hor-
monally induced paranoia.

The hostess poked her head around the door.
'Fern. You lucky, lucky girl! You've got a
table for two. Wait till you check out the bloke.
Sex on a stick! Pity he's with a girl – otherwise
I'd serve him myself. She looks like ice wouldn't
melt in her knickers.'

I stubbed out my fag and went out front,
looking forward to waiting on this hunk –
anything to make the slow night pass a little
more quickly.

When I saw the back of his head, my stomach
lurched. I turned on my heel and walked back
towards the staffroom. I stood in the corridor
and took a deep breath. Oh my God! Oh my
God! Maybe I should just ask Tamsin to serve
them. I was just about to go and get her when I
stopped in my tracks. I mentally took a hold of
myself and gave myself a good shake. No!
That's what the old Fern Fennelly would have
done. I was stronger now. I wasn't going to be
intimidated by the likes of them any more. I
drew myself up to my full height – five foot five
and a half in stockinged feet (but I was wearing

heels) – and marched back into the restaurant like a soldier advancing onto Normandy beach on D-Day.

'Sir, Madam, would either of you care for a drink before dinner? We have an extensive range of cocktails if I can tempt you.'

James Carver nearly gave himself whiplash when he heard my voice. I wondered if he'd try to sue the café for providing him with such a disturbing waitress. I derived a curious, grim pleasure from the shock and uncertainty in his eyes. Those emotions were short-lived, however. His innate confidence was restored in a matter of seconds.

'Well, well. If it isn't Miss Fennelly. This *is* a surprise.'

I nodded briskly at him. 'James. Bronwyn.' I nodded in her direction. I was quite taken aback by the naked hatred on her face. She caught me catching her expression, which she efficiently replaced with the phoniest smile I had ever seen. It was more of a flash of the teeth really – hadn't the remotest chance of reaching her slanting blue eyes.

We looked each other up and down, as women do. I took in the cascading blonde curls, which I found didn't produce such strong emotions of envy and dismay as they once had. Was it my imagination or was her face a little pudgier than before?

'So, how are you . . . sorry, I can't seem to remember your first name,' she said sweetly.

'Fern.'

Bitch!

'Oh yes. How could I forget such an unusual name? Very . . . unique.' Don't let her get to you! 'So you're working here now?'

'Yes.'

'As a waitress.' It was an accusation rather than a statement. Replace the word 'waitress' with 'child pornographer' and you'll get the general gist. 'How nice. Full-time, is it?'

'Actually, I'm starting college in the autumn. I'll only be working here part-time then.'

I hadn't even been accepted yet but I couldn't let her away with it.

'What is it? Secretarial college? Are you going to be studying advanced typing?' She emitted a strange, high-pitched shriek of laughter.

I just stared at her. There was no need for me to say anything. She was doing such a good job of making a complete show of herself that she didn't require any assistance from me. I glanced at James who was looking at her, his eyebrows raised, a knowing smirk playing about his lips.

'Actually, it's art college,' I said coolly.

'Really?' said James, looking at me with renewed interest. 'I had no idea you were so keen. The best of luck with it.' He actually sounded sincere. I'll admit that I was quite fazed. I hadn't expected him to be nice to me. A cool politeness was the most I had hoped for from him. It made me not a little uncomfortable. In fact, I almost wished he'd be nasty to me. All the better for hating him.

'Have you been working much on your art, Fern?'

'Well, I helped out on that mural.' I gestured at the opposite wall.

'Very impressive. It really is stunning. But isn't that a Seán Morrissey?'

'Yes, it is.' I felt myself swelling with pride. 'He's a . . . friend.' Now why hadn't I said 'boyfriend'?

James bestowed on me a smile that Pierce Brosnan would have been proud of. 'That's marvellous, Fern. Congratulations.'

'Excuse me, can we order now, please?' Bronwyn's tone was distinctly waspish. In fact, she sounded as if she was sitting on a whole nest of wasps.

I quickly took their order and trotted back to the kitchen. It was only when I was safely back in the corridor and out of public view that I allowed myself to breathe normally again. I literally sank against the wall, resting my cheek on its cool whiteness. James Carver! Of all the cafés in all the towns! After all this time.

My emotions were all over the shop. I couldn't for the life of me decipher what I was feeling. I wanted so badly to hate that man, after everything I'd been through with him. Unfortunately I was having a hard time pulling that hatred off. Oh God! Just let me get through this evening with my dignity intact and I swear I'll do anything for you. I'll even start going to mass on Sundays again. I'll listen to Father McCarthy drone on about the evils of working mothers and extra-marital sex until I'm blue in the face. I'll even go to confession. Bless me, Father, it's been fifteen years since my last confession and I can't remember my Act of Contrition. Anything. Just let me hate him God – please, for fuck's sake. I prayed silently and fervently to my creator, choosing to forget that Hate Thy Bastard of an Ex-Boyfriend was not one of the ten commandments. Well, it should have been. I could see an opening there.

The evening took on a dreamlike quality. I shamelessly neglected my other tables. At least two members of staff asked me what was up. Nothing. Nothing was up.

Every time I tended at James and Bronwyn's table it was the same story. James smiled that gorgeous, sexy smile that I remembered so well, having recalled it so many times in the privacy of my room at night. And Bronwyn shot me dagger looks. After a time, she even stopped pretending to be polite as James chatted charmingly to me and studiously ignored her.

Some time between main course and dessert I looked over and saw that they were fighting. I heard it too. Even though I couldn't make out what Bronwyn was saying, her voice was clearly raised and her expression furious. The other diners were looking around at them with amused curiosity. I couldn't help but feel the tiniest bit smug.

After what seemed like centuries, they got up to leave. Even though it was customary for the bill to be paid at the table, James came up to me at the till to pay. Alone. He handed me his platinum credit card. I remembered it well. He had flashed it around copiously enough on our few dates.

'Did you enjoy your meal?' I asked, for want of anything better to say.

'It was acceptable enough but I've had better. At Pegasus, for instance.' He smiled warmly at me. I gulped. He was remembering our first date.

'I'm sorry if the food wasn't satisfactory.'

'Oh I'm not talking about the food. I'm talking about the company.' He stared hard at me, watching for the effect that his words had on my expression. I couldn't say anything. My throat seemed to have seized up. I didn't have to reply. He was gone. Just like that. Taking Miss Frosty Knickers with him.

An air of unreality hung over the café. It was as if I had dreamt up the whole episode. I was never so delighted to see the end of a shift. I wanted to be alone so I could think.

I slept fitfully that night, haunted as I was by a pair of chocolate brown eyes that watched me in the darkness. I woke up once in the small hours with a start. Try as I might, I couldn't remember what I'd been dreaming about. I was just left with a strong sense of being out of control. Maybe it had been one of those falling dreams.

I had planned to go shopping the next day. I would have gone too, if I didn't have procrastination down to such a fine art. Instead, I found myself still curled up in my Dad's armchair at three o'clock. I flicked through the channels, hopping from one dismal talk show to the next. The phone rang at ten past three. I let the answer phone do the talking. It was Seán. He was just ringing to say hello. He asked me to call him back.

At half past three there was a knock on the door. I contemplated ignoring it but the caller was pretty persistent. On the third ring, I padded out to the hall, resplendent in dressing gown, track-suit bottoms and flip-flops. At the door was a very small man, bearing a very large bunch of flowers.

'Sign for these, please.' He sniffed and wiped his moist nose with the back of his hand. Christian Slater in *Bed of Roses* he was not. Poor bastard probably suffered from hay fever.

I signed his forms and relieved him of the flowers. They were orange tiger lilies set against a background of ferns. I opened the card:

'Please forgive me.'

It was signed 'J.C.'

My lips curved into an involuntary smile.

Oh no.

The next day it was yellow tulips. On Wednesday, red roses. Thursday – I don't remember what they were, but they were beautiful.

And each day, a message on the answering machine. From Seán.

It was the Friday-night shift and the first time that week that I'd worked with Sarah.

'So, what's up? You've been keeping a very low profile lately.'

I knew that she was just being friendly but for some reason I found her inquisitiveness incredibly annoying and intrusive. I found that I really didn't want to talk to her.

'I've been busy, that's all. That man on Table Three is trying to get your attention.'

'Oh, right. Talk to you later.'

It wasn't often that a demanding customer came to my rescue.

Later on, that night, there was a call for me. As luck wouldn't have it, Sarah answered the phone.

'Fern – call for you.' The accusation in her tone was wasted on me.

'Hello. Fern speaking.'

'Did you like the flowers?'

My mouth suddenly gave a good impression of the Sahara Desert. The silence grew louder and louder.

'Fern?'

'Hello, James.'

'You didn't answer my question.'

'They're beautiful.'

'Not as beautiful as you.' I would have killed for a glass of water. I was sure he could hear me blushing down the phone. 'So, where would you like to go to dinner?'

'James – I can't . . .'

'There's no such word as can't. I'm begging you, Fern. I've been awful in the past. Let me make it up to you.'

I could scarcely believe what I was hearing. An auditory hallucination, surely. *He* wanted to make it up to *me*! My life really had undergone a radical transformation.

'What about Bronwyn?'

'We'll leave her at home. Three's a crowd.'

'I don't think so . . .'

'Joke. Bronwyn and I are finished.'

'Since when?'

'Since I saw you in the bistro the other night.'

You know when you go out with someone who you're mad about? And then they dump you. (Maybe you don't. Good for you. Me – I was all too familiar with that particular scenario.) And you waste a spectacular amount of time in the following weeks, or even months, wallowing in unhealthy fantasies going something like this:

The dumper has a radical change of heart. Perhaps he sees you out, looking fabulous, with a gorgeous-looking new man dangling on your arm. Or perhaps you have the good fortune to be struck down with a rare, life-threatening illness and he rushes to your bedside and single-handedly nurses you back to good health, vowing never to leave your side again. An alternative to this particular fantasy is that you are, in fact, terminally ill, and he marries you at your hospital bedside. (I had managed to reduce myself to tears at this one.) Or perhaps he just realises in a St-Paul-on-the-Road-to-Damascus kind of a way that you're the only woman for him and that he can't live without you.

But there had always been a common theme to these romantic delusions. I had known that they were delusions. I had just used them to comfort myself in my darkest days. Hence the sense of unreality that this telephone conversation was producing.

'So where shall I take you?'

'The Olive Tree?' It was a new Italian I was dying to try.

'Perfect. Please say you'll meet me tomorrow night.'

I'd never gone out with him on a Saturday night before.

'Okay. See you in the Bailey at seven.'

'I'll be there. I'll be the one wearing the eager expression.'

'See you then.'

'Can't wait. Goodbye, Fern.'

'Bye.'

Click.

I know what you're thinking. There's one born every minute. Couldn't agree more.

Another date, another new dress. At this rate my flexible friend wouldn't be my friend for much longer. This time I chose jade green, long and figure-hugging. It brought out the green in my eyes and the red in my hair. For once in my life, I knew I looked good.

When I saw the expression in James's eyes as I walked towards him in the bar, I allowed myself a small thrill of triumph. This time you're going to beg for it, mate. I'm calling the shots now. Yes, the undisputed crowned queen of fantasy was back with a vengeance.

James was still sporting his dark barrister's three-piece suit and starched white collar. It set off his I've-just-been-away-on a-skiing-trip tan to perfection. If you looked up the word 'devastating' in the dictionary, James's photo would have been beside it.

I'd forgotten what a heady experience it was to be out with such a good-looking man. I hadn't prepared myself for the arrows of pure hatred that were fired from the eyes of the majority of the women we passed by. No sooner had they just feasted their eyes on him, than they spotted me toddling alongside. What has she got that I haven't? I imagined they were thinking. Luckily I was wearing my protective armour of euphoria.

We were shown to the best table in the restaurant, whereupon the waiting staff proceeded to fawn over us as if we were royalty. James exuded wealth and breeding from every pore. He couldn't have been mistaken for anything less than a pure thoroughbred. He even knew the head waiter and chatted casually to him in Italian. I just sat there and smiled, trying not to look as intimidated as I felt. I let James order for me. I had no choice really as the menu was in Italian. I hoped that he hadn't ordered me something messy like spaghetti. I have never quite got the hang of this lark of rolling the pasta around the fork ten-zillion times so that there are no dangly bits. And tomato sauce on the chin has never been a look that has suited me.

I needn't have worried. The meal was delicious, and so easy to eat that my ninety-year-old granny from Limerick could have managed it without her dentures.

James was charm personified. He asked me many considered and thoughtful questions and listened attentively to my replies. I found that I wasn't struck dumb as I once had been and was well capable of responding coherently. And he re-filled my wine glass only at respectable intervals. Gone was the James of the past who had (successfully) tried to make me legless so that he could get his leg over. He was a new man! I wondered if he'd read one of those dating manuals and was following the list of rules at the end of chapter one, which was entitled 'The First Date'. Or maybe he'd got religion. I hoped he wasn't a born-again Christian. That lot wouldn't have sex with you unless you were one of them. I'd be forced to convert. Or was it just sex before marriage they didn't believe in? Well, if I had to . . .

In any case, the net effect of this treatment was to make me feel like a million dollars. And I don't mean all green and wrinkly. I could get used to this, I thought smugly as James dropped me home at the end of the evening in his new BMW. Did he lunge at me? No. He kissed me sedately on the hand and asked when he could see me again.

I restrained myself from suggesting in ten minutes' time. We compromised on Tuesday night. There was a new play on in the Abbey. He'd book the tickets.

Of course he would!

Chapter Nineteen

'Hi, stranger!'

Oh shit. 'Hi, Seán.'

'Everything all right? I was starting to get worried.'

'Everything's fine.'

'I left lots of messages on your machine.'

Silence.

'Are you free tonight?'

'I'm working.'

'Today then?' I sighed in exasperation. I didn't want to see him and face the inevitable unpleasant confrontation. I wanted to be alone so I could spend the day taking out my memory of last night and examining it lovingly. But I supposed he deserved the truth. And it was better to get these things over and done with as quickly as possible.

He called around and, since it was such a nice spring day, we decided to take a walk along Malahide Beach. He chatted animatedly the whole way there, his delight at being with me painfully apparent. I just sat there in the passenger's seat with my arms tightly crossed, staring out my open window and hating myself.

During the walk, he tried to hold my hand but I pulled away. He came to a halt and took me by the shoulders.

'I've had enough of this. What is it, Fern?'

I shrugged his hands off my shoulders. I couldn't bear to have him touch me.

I looked down at my toes burrowing into the sand. Then I looked at the sand dunes, at a seagull flying overhead, at the far-off horizon. Anywhere but into his eyes.

'What have I done wrong?'

'It's not you. It's me.'

'It's not you it's me,' he parroted. 'Next you're going to tell me that it's not that you don't love me, it's just that you're not *in* love with me and that there are plenty more fish in the sea and that we can still be friends. Spare me the clichés, Fern. I'm not stupid.'

I miserably watched the waves crashing against the rocks.

'Can you at least tell me why?'

I hated him for the desperation in his voice. 'I've met someone else.'

I had heard the phrase to be 'gutted' many times before but I had never grasped the true meaning of it until now. Seán looked as if I'd reached into his stomach and tugged out a handful of his entrails. As he struggled to regain his composure, all I could feel was irritation that he was making this so difficult for me.

'Anybody I know?' His voice sounded tight and strange.

'No.'

I felt him peering at me closely.

'You're lying.'

'No, I'm not,' I said, anger gathering inside. Why couldn't he just drop it?

'Sarah told me that a man rang for you at the café the other night.'

I was furious. 'Well Sarah should have kept her trap shut. She's always sticking her nose into other people's business. Especially mine.'

Now it was his turn to be angry. 'Don't you dare talk about Sarah like that. She's been a very good friend to you.'

'Well, I'm sick of her thinking she has a right to run my life. You both seem to think you know what's best for me. Well, you don't.' I was shouting at him now. 'And if you must know, I'm seeing James Carver.'

I watched his face as he tried to work out who James Carver was. I knew he'd worked it out when I saw his expression darken. 'Not that fuckwit.'

'He's not a fuckwit.' I spat, furiously.

'Well, he was the last time.'

'He's changed.'

Seán laughed nastily. 'Well, he'd want to have got a total personality transplant.'

'He wasn't that bad.'

'Fern! Listen to yourself. He was unfaithful. He treated you like something he'd stepped in on the street. He abandoned you when the going got tough. Will I go on?'

'He's apologised.'

'So that makes it all right, does it?' He shook his head in dismay. 'I thought you were smarter than that, Fern.'

'We have unfinished business.'

'What? He didn't treat you badly enough last time so you've gone back for more.'

'Oh, fuck off, Seán.'

'Okay, I will.'

And he did.

I watched him walk away from me across the beach, his head hunched into his shoulders. I sank down in the sand, in the exact spot where I'd been standing. Seemed I'd be getting the bus home.

I dreaded going into work that night and facing Sarah. I knew that she wouldn't be capable of keeping her opinions to herself and I was pretty damned sure that opinion wouldn't swing in my favour.

Typically, she was the first person I met in the café that evening when I went out the back to collect my apron. We faced each other across the room like two gunfighters. The question was, who was going to be the quickest on the draw. I braced myself for the onslaught.

Much to my surprise – and horror – Sarah came over to where I was standing and threw her arms around my neck. No, she wasn't trying to strangle me. She was hugging me.

'I hope you know what you're doing. The best of luck.' I could feel my carefully constructed defences starting to crumble. Keep it together, Fern.

'It's just something I have to do, Sarah . . . '

'I know, I know. Just be careful.' She released me from the hug and looked right at me briefly before she left the room. I saw with shock that her eyes were filled with unshed tears.

I felt momentarily devastated. And then I thought of James and I renewed my resolve. My life had been going from strength to strength of late. James had been the only thing missing from it. I couldn't conceive of turning him away now that I had been given this miraculous second chance with him. I wouldn't allow my feelings for Seán or for Sarah to stand in the way of what I wanted more than anything else in the whole world.

Don't ask me what the play on Tuesday night was about. I could concentrate on nothing but the sensation of James's hand clasping mine in the darkness – and later on, the feeling of his palm resting gently yet firmly on my knee.

A small, sane part of my brain kept whispering something to me but I couldn't quite hear it. My sense of euphoria and the adoration I felt for James drowned everything else out.

The only time he let go of my hand was during the interval when he paid the barman for my drink. After the play we went for yet another posh and expensive meal. It was Pegasus again. James said he wanted to relive the experience of our first date. To me, it was more like returning to the scene of the crime. I wasn't all that sure that I wanted to recall the way things had been before. But James said it would be like starting over.

I plucked up the courage to mention the unmentionable midway through dessert.

'Is your father keeping well, James?'

The forkful of cheesecake which was en route to his mouth froze in mid-air. I didn't take my eyes off him as he let the fork fall back onto the plate with a loud clatter, whereupon he seized my hand in both of his. He proceeded to fix me with a sincere gaze which reminded me of something. (I later realised that it was the expression Cyril had worn on the day that he had fired me.)

'Fern, I must apologise for the behaviour of my father that night in the Shelbourne. It really was unacceptable. And I should have called you afterwards. I know that now. I'm sorry.' His gaze didn't waver throughout. 'Am I forgiven?'

The familiar confident smile lifted up the corners of his mouth and lit up his dark, knowing eyes. I felt my stomach turn to mush.

'Of course you're forgiven, James,' I replied softly. He grinned and lifted my hand to his lips. His kiss was soft and lingering, his lips slightly parted.

I pulled my hand away and averted my gaze back to my banoffi pie. Take it easy, Fern, I chastised myself. Don't give away the goods so easily this time.

I suppressed a fake yawn. It was the only thing I intended faking that night.

'Tired?' James looked and sounded concerned.

I nodded.

'Better get you home, then.'

He asked for the bill. I made a half-hearted attempt to pay it but he waved away my attempts masterfully (or master-card-fully), as I had known he would. It's not that I minded paying my own way. In fact, I usually made a point of it. But it just wasn't James's style to go Dutch. Besides, a meal in Pegasus would have cost me half a week's salary at least, and James was loaded. I was surprised – and not a little ashamed – at how easily I assumed the role of kept woman, and, even worse, how much I liked it.

James's BMW purred up outside my house. I hoped that some of the neighbours were looking out their windows – especially that nosy old bat from number 55. I didn't ask him in. God knows what kind of a state the place was in. My father had probably gone to bed leaving a trail of newspapers and dirty cups behind him.

He kissed me sedately on the cheek and I walked sedately up the path, all the while thinking that what I really felt like doing wasn't sedate in the slightest. I knew in my heart of hearts – and my groin of groins – that I would succumb to James's charms sooner rather than later. But still, once bitten, twice shy. Or in my case, fifty times bitten so it was about time I became a bit shy.

My father was still up – if snoring in front of an obscure Burt Reynolds film counts as being up. I picked his glasses up off the floor and placed them tenderly on the coffee table beside his armchair. Having released my feet from my torturous new shoes and curled up catlike on the sofa, I gingerly retrieved the remote control from beside Dad's foot and flicked through the channels, turning the sound down beforehand so as not to wake him. My ploy failed. Not for the first time, I suspected that he had a telepathic connection with the telly. He woke up with a start.

'Hey, I was watching that!'

'Watching what?'

'That . . . thing that was on.'

He groped around blindly for his glasses and replaced them, looking like his usual self again. I handed over his reason-for-living resignedly.

'Here. I wasn't watching it anyway.' I started to get up.

'Go anywhere nice tonight?'

'The theatre and then for dinner.'

'With that blond lad – Simon isn't it?'

'You mean Seán,' I corrected. 'No, I'm with James now.'

'James, is it? I don't know. I can't keep up with you young ones nowadays.' He shook his head as if it were all too much for him.

Normally he didn't exhibit the remotest interest in my love life. Maybe he felt he should assume the role of nosy parent now that Mam had gone. If she had been here, she would have had James's name, date and serial number long since.

'You should bring him around some time for dinner.' My father said this as if he would be the one doing the cooking and not me.

'Why would I want to do that?'

'So we can have a look at the chap.'

'And find out if his intentions towards me are honourable?'

'Don't be so cheeky, Miss. You're getting on a bit now. It's about time you started getting serious with some young man and stopped your gadding about.'

Gadding about! Getting on a bit! I was only twenty-seven – a mere babe in arms. I thought fathers were meant to think of their daughters as being little girls forever. You'd think he was trying to get rid of me or something.

'Are you trying to get rid of me or something?'

'No. I just think you should give some thought to your future. I'm off up to my bed.'

He got up creakily from his seat. It was difficult to tell which was creaking – my father or the seat.

'I thought you were watching this.'

'I've changed my mind. I'm too tired. Night, night.'

'Night, Dad.' He did look tired. And old, I thought with surprise.

Perhaps I would bring James around to meet the clan. How bad could it be? And besides, Sasha would be dead jealous!

It was about a month later when I finally plucked up the courage to bring him around. I was starting to feel more confident about our relationship. I didn't have the guts to suggest that we all spend the evening together but I thought I could manage a brief introduction on the way out one night.

He called for me on the way to the cinema. This was no ordinary evening viewing – a première, no less. A few of the stars were going to be there. I was dressed up to the nines. I nearly fainted when I opened the door and saw him standing there in his tuxedo. He looked just like James Bond. I was shaken and stirred.

Usually I ran out, slamming the door behind me, like a greyhound out of a trap. Tonight, I opened the door wide and stood back. 'Why don't you come in for a few minutes?'

He raised an eyebrow in surprise and stepped inside the hall that I'd spent half the afternoon cleaning. I watched him nervously as he surveyed his surroundings. I'd thought I'd done a pretty good job at the time but suddenly I saw the hall through James's eyes and became acutely aware of the worn section of carpet travelling up the centre of the stairway and the wallpaper that had seen better days.

To my horror, I noticed that Sasha had seen fit to hang three pairs of tights to dry on the radiator just inside the front door. I placed myself strategically in front of them, just in the nick of time, and smiled winningly to distract him. I opened the door to the TV room and gestured James inside.

Dad was dug into some gardening programme – if you'll pardon the pun. He didn't even hear us come in. Sasha, on the other hand, reacted as if she'd been stung on the ass by a bee. I'd never seen her move so quickly. In one smooth movement, she sprang to her feet, removed her glasses and pulled the scrunchie out from her hair. I had to admire her reflexes.

James was his usual suave self.

'You must be Sasha. Pleased to meet you. I'm James.' He extended his hand in greeting. With wicked satisfaction, I watched the colour deepen in Sasha's cheeks and the eyes fairly pop out of her loathsome head as she shook his hand, as if in a trance. James smiled the smile of a man who was well used to provoking such a reaction in the women he met. I was thrilled. This was just what I had hoped for.

'And what do you do, James?'

'I'm a barrister.'

'Really! You must be the owner of that beautiful new Beamer I've seen pulling up outside the house.'

'That's right.'

Typical Sasha, suss out how much money a man has before you even bother getting to know him. It's not what you are, it's what you have. She was as subtle as Pamela Anderson's chest.

Dad seemed to have snapped out of his impression of one of his beloved plants. He uprooted himself from his chair and went to shake James's hand.

'Pleased to meet you, son. You're very welcome.'

'Thank you, sir.' James returned the handshake gravely.

My father looked astonished. It was probably the first time anybody had ever called him sir in his life.

'So, you're in law, then.'

'I am.'

'What do you make of the O'Leary Tribunal, then?' And they proceeded to make small talk about some tribunal or other that was currently making the news.

There was one thing about my father. He knew his current affairs. Hardly surprising, as he watched or listened to the news on average twelve times a day and read from cover to cover every newspaper he could lay his hands on. Much to his disappointment, neither Sasha nor myself shared his passion for world events. Pure overkill made us both switch off as soon as either of us so much as sensed the imminent approach of a news headline. I just about knew who the current Taoiseach was at any given time. And if I was in any doubt as to who it was, I certainly wouldn't have bothered asking my sister.

I watched the pleasure on Dad's face as he discussed one of his favourite topics with someone who knew what he was talking about. James could be like the son Dad never had, I thought, my eyes filling up with tears of joyful sentimentality. I wondered if James was into gardening . . .

After a few minutes, I decided to intervene in case James was getting bored. There was no stopping Dad when he was in full gallop on one of his hobby horses.

They both accompanied us to the front door. Dad pumped James's hand vigorously on the way out. Sasha just looked as if she'd like to be pumped vigorously by James.

'Don't trip over your tongue, Slasher,' I whispered meanly into her ear. She punched me viciously in the back so that no one could see. Her smile, focused full beam on James, didn't even waver. I was delighted. James had been a smash hit.

Back in the car, James waved enthusiastically back at them and drove off slowly. I glanced excitedly at him.

'Well?'

'Hmmmm?' He looked thoughtful. He was scanning the row of semi-detached houses down our street.

'What are you thinking?' Yes, I know. This is something you should *never* ask a man.

'I was just thinking,' he said vaguely. 'All these people living in boxes, I'd hate that.'

I felt a surge of fury rise within me. 'I beg you're pardon?'

'These houses. They're so box-like.'

'These are people's homes you're talking about. Not everyone can afford to live in Foxrock, you know.' I was really, really angry now. I must have sounded it too because James turned his head and looked at me, genuine surprise in his eyes.

'Hey – I was only saying. I didn't mean to offend you.' He squeezed my knee and smiled his most dazzling smile.

I held steadfast. For about two seconds. Then all of a sudden I felt very stupid. Of course he hadn't meant to offend me. I was just being ridiculously touchy.

We drove in silence for a while. After a time, he began to make small talk. He was very attentive, paying me loads of compliments and hanging on to my every word. By the time we reached the cinema, I was happy again. It was clear that he was trying to make amends. He couldn't help his wealthy and privileged background, poor lamb.

'What did you say your father did for a living?' he asked me as he held open the door to the cinema.

'He's a civil servant.'

James let out a strange sound. It sounded like a suppressed snort of laughter. I looked up at him sharply but his features were composed.

I didn't say anything.

I didn't enjoy the film much.

Chapter Twenty

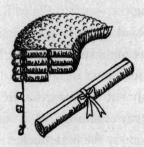

The atmosphere at work had been distinctly chilly of late. In fairness to Sarah, this was mostly down to my sense of guilt.

I had noticed that we were on slightly fewer shifts together these days. As Sarah was in charge of the roster, I could only assume that this was no accident. It saddened me.

Tamsin had been less subtle. She had called me a stupid, disloyal bitch when she heard I had broken it off with Seán. I couldn't find it in my heart to disagree with her. She continued to avoid me as if I was some plague-ridden creature.

Okay. I could see her point of view, but she just didn't understand what James meant to me. He was the man of my dreams and he actually wanted me back. I regretted any injuries I had caused along the way but I felt I had no choice but to go for it. I was considering leaving the café and looking for another job. If things didn't improve soon, I would.

On this particular day, Sarah and I were working together. Tamsin had the day off, thank God. I girded my loins (whatever that means) and went over to talk to her.

She was sitting at a table filling up all the pepper pots, pausing to sneeze every thirty seconds or so.

'Here – take this.' I handed her a tissue.

'Thanks.' She rubbed her nose gratefully.

'Mind if I sit down?'

She shook her head and gestured to the chair opposite her.

'So, how are you?' I ventured.

'Great.' She always was.

'And Stephen?'

'Good. Enjoying his new job.'

This was news to me. 'I didn't know he had a new job. When did he start?'

'Three weeks ago.'

Three weeks ago! I was shocked and embarrassed. Had we grown so far apart that I wasn't even aware of such a major event in her life? Apparently so.

And how's Seán, I thought. 'How's your Mam?'

'Couldn't be better. One of the dogs – you know Sadie – she just had pups. They're so cute. Only a few days old. Their eyes aren't even open yet. So Mam has her hands full with them. You should come out and see them some evening.'

'Yeah, I might just do that.' No thanks. Wriggley little slitty-eyed creatures. Yuck. And how's Seán? 'So – any other news?'

'Not really.' She continued to screw the tops onto the pepper pots. There was a long pause.

'And how's Seán?'

Was that a smile I saw playing about her lips? She didn't look at me as she replied. 'He's fine. Working away like mad.'

'He's busy, then?'

'Yes, very.'

I felt a little crestfallen. Then I gave myself a mental slap across the face. Cop on to yourself, Fern! What right did I have to feel crestfallen? What did I want to hear? That Seán had taken to his bed and was slowly wasting away without me? (Yes.) I should be glad that his work was going so well for him. Fuck it – I was glad!

'Of course, he misses you dreadfully.'

Pardon? What? Really? 'Really?' Yes!

I noticed that Sarah was watching my reaction closely and I attempted to wipe the expression of glee from my face.

'We're all going to Mahaffey's tonight if you'd like to join us.'

'I'd love to. No, wait . . . I can't . . . I have to go to a dinner party.'

Shit! I'd almost forgotten. Or tried to forget. James's friend Phil – he of the plain looks and entertaining personality – had invited us around to his place for dinner. I had been praying to be involved in a minor accident – a broken finger would have been nice – so that I wouldn't have to go.

'That's a pity. I'll tell Seán you were asking for him, will I?'

'Yes – if you like.'

Sarah smiled happily to herself.

I smiled happily to myself.

What was I doing?

I was consumed with a chronic sense of dread as we pulled up outside Phil's Dublin 4 apartment. James told me that his parents had bought it as an investment.

'Who did you say was going to be here tonight?'

'I'm not sure exactly. But don't worry. You'll know a few people. Remember Leonard? He'll probably come along.'

Oh yes, Leonard, the upper-class twit. I couldn't wait.

'And Zara. She should be here. So you'll have some girly company.' Zara – Bronwyn's best friend. Yes, I was sure she'd be delighted to see me.

I girded my loins (I'd been doing a lot of it recently) as James rang the door-bell.

'Bronwyn won't be here, will she?'

'Don't be daft, Fern. Phil may be ugly but he's not stupid. Ah – Phil, old man, how the hell are you? You're looking well.'

James and Phil shook hands as if they hadn't seen each other for six years. It was more like six hours. 'You remember Fern?'

'Yes, of course. Fern, a pleasure to meet you again. You look fantastic.' He shook my hand warmly. I'd say one thing for Phil – he'd always been friendly. Nice person really. Pity he looked so much like a garden gnome.

'Are we the first to arrive?' This from James, who normally was the first to arrive.

'No, Leonard and Declan are here already.' Declan. It couldn't be. A different Declan, surely. 'Fern, have you and Declan met before?'

'Yes. We used to work together.'

'Oh yes, I forgot you used to work at Boland, Sharpe . . . ' Phil trailed off in embarrassment.

Declan was sitting in the corner of the living room. He had taken off his glasses and was polishing them furiously. I remembered how it was a nervous habit of his. He nodded at me curtly and looked down quickly at his glasses again.

'And you remember Leonard.'

'Hi, Leonard.'

Leonard gave me the once over and an idiotic grin which he probably thought was rakish.

'Can I get you a drink, Fern?' asked Phil.

'A gin and tonic would be lovely, thank you.' Make it a triple.

'Coming up. Usual for you, James?' James nodded and handed Phil our jackets, then he launched into an analysis with Leonard of last weekend's rugby international. There was nothing else for it but to make conversation with Fuck-Face in the corner.

I settled down in the chair beside him and prepared to get in a few sly digs.

'Well, Declan, long time no see – or hear.'

'Yes – must be what – six or seven months?'

'Oh, at least.'

'How have you been?'

'Very well actually, not that you'd give a toss.'

He ignored this. 'You look good.'

'Trying to flatter me into submission?'

'No, you do. You know I never say anything nice unless I really mean it.' That was true. 'It's not just the clothes and the hair. There's something else too.' He inclined his head to one side, staring at me as he tried to work out the puzzle. 'The way you carry yourself, I think it is.'

Confidence.

'Well, you seem exactly the same anyway.'

'Thanks.'

'That wasn't a compliment, you two-faced little turd.'

'Fern! You insult me.' He laughed, sounding not in the least bit insulted. I'd forgotten his infuriating habit of being so difficult to insult. Still, that had always been part of his charm too.

'How come you never returned my calls?'

'You know why.'

'No, I don't.'

'Now you're being deliberately obtuse.'

'Don't give me that. I was going through a shit time and you just disappeared off the face of the planet.'

The door-bell rang, saving Declan. I stiffened, fearing the worst.

'Who else is coming, apart from Zara?'

'Big Arse and Big Tits.'

Holy shit! That was all I needed. I could hear Big Tits squealing and gushing in the hall. I sat rigidly in my chair, wishing I could be anywhere else at that moment. (Mahaffey's would have been nice.) I sat, hardly daring to breathe, for what seemed like ages. 'They're taking they're time coming in, aren't they?'

Declan gave a derisory snort. 'Big Arse probably got stuck in the doorway.'

'Or maybe Big Tits tried to come in sideways.'

We laughed heartily and nastily. It was just like old times really.

And then she made her entrance, flinging the door wide open and nearly knocking Leonard off the arm of the chair he was balancing on.

'Hi, guys!' She entered with a flourish. Phil scuttled behind her like some faithful manservant.

'What would you like to drink, Lydia?'

She didn't even hear him. She made a direct beeline for James. 'James! How are you?' She took his hand in hers and kissed him warmly and meaningfully on each cheek – none of her usual air-kissing. This was very definitely skin to lip contact. She was wearing an awful, shocking-pink cocktail dress with an almost embarrassingly tight-fitting top. Lydia certainly didn't believe in hiding her light under a bushel – and her headlights were in full beam that night.

She had almost managed to eclipse the entrance of the quieter Zara and Big Arse, who were still lurking around the doorway. Zara looked exquisite in a simple black trouser suit. Obviously designer. Poor Big Arse looked less resplendent. She was probably relegated to buying her clothes in what Declan referred to as the fat birds' shop.

'You all remember Fern,' said Phil with the innate nervousness of a host who fears that a cat fight just might break out at his party. I was given a dirty look in stereo by Zara and Lydia. It was quite powerful. I felt momentarily pinned down to my chair.

'Oh, hi, Fern.' This from Big Arse, who actually sounded like she was prepared to be civil. At least there'd be one female at the dinner party who didn't want me roasted and eaten for the main course. I only wished I could remember her real name.

After twenty minutes or so of painful small talk we were ushered into the dining room for dinner. I was almost surprised that Phil was actually doing all the cooking. It occurred to me that I had been half expecting a small army of servants to be waiting on us.

'You'll enjoy this. Old Phil is an absolute whizz in the kitchen,' said Leonard, grinning inanely at me. He was seated to my left and James was seated around the corner of the table to my right. It was a boy-girl-boy-girl configuration. Zara was positioned opposite me, which was perfect for her really, as she had the opportunity to glare at me throughout the meal.

The first course was a beautiful-tasting home-made soup, with the texture and colour of cream velvet. It was only after we had finished eating that Phil revealed that it was actually parsnip soup. He really was a gourmet. This would have been a fantastic meal if it hadn't been for the company.

Most of the conversation revolved around the law, everybody there being involved in the legal profession apart from yours truly. I would have been bored silly had it not been for the wealth of body language going on all around me. At times, it was several decibels higher than the actual conversation.

Most vocal was Lydia with her amazing revolving bosoms. She was obviously disappointed that she hadn't been seated beside James and kept throwing longing looks in his direction. I would have felt threatened if James hadn't had his muscular leg practically wrapped around mine under the table, and if he hadn't been stroking my inner thigh rhythmically throughout, as if it was his pet cat.

Tonight was going to be the night. I had put James off for as long as I could. Besides, I was about to explode with frustration myself. He had booked a suite in Jury's Hotel for the occasion. It was a long way from office desks and empty courtrooms.

On Lydia's right sat Phil who gazed at her openly in adoration all night long. Everybody cold see she knew he fancied her but she didn't return the interest. Not that she was above leading him on or using him to make other men jealous. Poor Phil.

Amanda (Big Arse) was quiet throughout. She only really spoke to Leonard, whom she seemed to have a 'thing' for. Leonard, seemingly oblivious, guffawed loudly at the legal anecdotes being bandied back and forth across the table. Mouthfuls of food were no obstacles to his laughter.

As for Zara, she concentrated on sending me hate waves all night. She barely took her eyes off me. If she was trying to make me feel uncomfortable, she was succeeding.

I was suddenly painfully aware of how badly I missed the company of Seán and Sarah and the others. I wondered what they were all talking about in Mahaffey's.

At long last, the main course was finished up (pheasant – I was the only person at the table who had never eaten it before, but you can be sure I didn't admit it.)

'Everyone for dessert? Profiteroles with chocolate sauce?'

Everybody said yes except for Lydia and Zara who both muttered modestly about having to watch their figures, at which point all the men, apart from Declan, said that they were being ridiculous and that the only people who should be watching their figures were men, in admiration, and that if anything, they could both do with a bit of fattening up. At this, both girls giggled coquettishly.

And then Lydia leant across the table and in a whisper that everybody could hear said, 'Amanda, do you really think you should have that dessert, dear? What about your diet?'

'Er . . . none for me either, Phil,' she said miserably.

Suddenly it was all crystal clear. I finally knew the reason why James wanted to be with me. I was probably the only girl he knew who wasn't a complete and utter asshole.

Phil got up and started clearing the table to fill the awkward silence.

'Here, let me help.' I jumped up and started stacking the empty plates from my side of the table. Anything not to feel like a spare fart.

'Not at all. Sit down, Fern. You're a guest.'

'No, let her, Phil.' It was one of the few times Zara had spoken all night. 'After all, she is a professional.'

This time the silence was truly awkward. I filled it by continuing to stack the crockery. As I whipped away Zara's empty plate, a little bit of sauce went flying and landed squarely on the lapel of her jacket. It was an accident, I swear! She leapt up off her chair as if I had scalded her.

'My jacket!' she squealed.

'Don't worry, I'll get a cloth,' said Phil, running towards the kitchen as fast as his legs could carry him.

Red-faced, I followed him out, bearing a stack of dirty dishes. I felt like walking right through the kitchen and straight on out through the back door. Phil was searching frantically for a cloth. I found one and handed it to him.

'Here. I'm sorry, Phil. I didn't do that on purpose.'

'I know. Not that I'd blame you if you had – that little bitch had it coming. Gotta go.' He gestured to the cloth in his hand and legged it back inside.

I forced myself to follow him. A large crowd had assembled around the injured party who looked as if she was enjoying being the main attraction.

'I wouldn't mind but it's a Paul Costelloe,' I heard her wail.

The only two who weren't making a fuss were James and Declan. Declan grinned at me as I sat back down. James looked like he was trying not to laugh. He recommenced stroking my leg under the table.

I was never so glad to be finished a meal. When Phil announced brandy and cigars, I thought for one dreadful moment that he was going to suggest that the women go off together to the drawing room to discuss embroidery and dressage. Fortunately not, and everybody made their way into the living room.

I took a few bowls into the kitchen on the way. Force of habit. I was a professional after all. I became aware that I'd been followed. I turned around smiling, expecting it to be Phil. It was Zara.

'I suppose you think you're very clever, pulling a stunt like that.'

'I'm sorry, Zara. It was an accident.'

'Yeah, right. I've half a mind to send you the dry-cleaning bill, except you probably couldn't afford to pay it on your waitressing salary.'

351

'Don't talk down to me, you snobby cow! It's not my fault that James doesn't want to go out with your friend any more.'

'James is weak. He just can't face up to his responsibilities right now. I don't know how you could do this to another woman, you common little tart! Just wait until the baby is born. He'll go back to her then.' The look on my face must have said it all. 'You didn't even know, did you?' Zara's laugh was a high metallic tinkle.

'Know what?'

'Bronwyn's six months pregnant with James's child. God – he really has been taking you for a ride. You're even thicker than I thought you were.'

I barely heard her insults. I felt like I wanted to throw up. She left the room before I could deck her. The slam of the door reverberated through my whole being.

Six months pregnant! With James's child. It couldn't be true. I had a flashback of Bronwyn in the bistro that night. I recalled her face – cheeks puffier than usual. Not to mention the tigress-like possessiveness she had exhibited towards James.

Perhaps it wasn't his baby. Surely James wouldn't abandon the mother of his own child.

Yes, he would, said the small sane voice inside my head. You know that he's well capable of doing it. You're just lucky that you found out when you did. Get out while you still can.

Without missing another beat, I went out into the hall. I retrieved my coat from the end of the stairs and opened the door into the living room. They were all sitting around, laughing and talking. I walked over to Phil and extended my hand formally. 'I have to go now, Phil. Thank you for inviting me. The meal was gorgeous. It was nice knowing you.'

He looked confused. 'Leaving so soon? But the evening's only starting to get going. Is James going too?'

James heard his name and came over, all smiles. 'Fern, what are you doing with your jacket on? We're not going yet. Sit down.'

'You can stay, but I'm leaving.'

'Do you feel ill?'

No – just sick of you.

'You're not, are you?' asked Phil, sounding really worried. He was probably scared that I'd try and sue him for giving me food poisoning.

'I've felt better.'

'I'll give you a lift home, then.'

'I don't want a lift, James. I'll get a taxi,' I said coldly, shaking his hand off my arm.

'But Fern, what's wrong? You're not going until you tell me.'

I brought my face very close to his. 'How dare you, you bastard,' I practically hissed at him. 'How dare you do this to me – and to Bronwyn. Unless you want one hell of a scene in front of all your so-called friends, I'd advise you to let me go quietly.'

He took a step backwards. I watched his Adam's apple bob up and down as he gulped. I felt I was seeing the true unmasked James for the first time. He was nothing but a gutless coward. He was afraid to stand up to his father, afraid to stick up for me, afraid to stand by his pregnant girlfriend. He was all flash and no character. How come I'd never seen it before?

I left the room, closing the door quietly and firmly after me. I could hear James's angry raised voice behind it. 'Zara, what did you say to her, you interfering fucking bitch?'

I didn't wait to hear Zara's riposte. All I wanted to do was get out of there. I left the building and ran down the steps onto the street, gratefully gulping in big breaths of summer-night air.

Miraculously an empty taxi was driving by at that very moment. I hailed it and jumped in gratefully, thinking that perhaps someone upstairs was watching out for me after all – although he or she had a funny way of showing it sometimes.

'Where are you headed, love?' The taxi-driver peered back at me through his rear-view mirror.

'Mahaffey's Pub, please.'

Chapter Twenty-one

Some of the best conversations of my life have been with Dublin cab-drivers.

I don't know what it is about them. It's a strange relationship. All you get to see is a disembodied pair of eyes until the time you leave the car. That's if you're like me and insist on sitting in the back. You know that you're probably never going to see them again so you can tell them just about everything. Ships that pass in the night. The best kind of one-night stand.

I judged this particular driver to be in his late fifties. He had lovely, smiley, blue eyes that were all crinkly around the corners. He chain-smoked Carrolls throughout. The car looked and smelt like a giant over-flowing ashtray. In fact, it was a kip – sweet wrappers and fag packets all over the floor and seat-belts in the back that didn't work. It reminded me of Seán's car and I felt comforted by that thought. Perhaps it was an omen. I strengthened my resolve to do what I knew I had to do.

'You all right, love?' My friend the taxi-driver looked back at me, concern written all over his face – bless him.

'I don't know.'

'Here. Have a smoke. It'll make you feel better.' He prescribed the cigarette as if for all the world it contained the same amount of vitamin C as a dozen oranges.

I took it eagerly, lighting it with the glowing car lighter and inhaling deeply as if it was the last cigarette on earth.

'So, what's wrong?'

Bless me father for I have sinned. 'I've just found out that my boyfriend's ex is having his kid.'

'When?'

'In about three months' time.'

'Hmmm. That must have come as a bit of a shock all right.'

'You could say that.'

'I take it he knows.'

'Oh, yes.'

'And did he know about it when he took up with you?'

'I think so.'

'But you're not sure?'

'No.'

'So, you haven't talked it out with him then?'

'No.'

He was quiet for a while, a faraway expression in his eyes. He looked as if he was digesting the information I'd just given him and formulating his diagnosis. It was a pity he needed his hands to drive or he could have taken notes.

'If I were you, love, I'd talk it out with him before I did anything hasty. You know, give him the benefit of the doubt. But between you and me, yer man sounds like a bit of a bollix.'

'He is. I only just copped on to it a few minutes ago.'

He nodded sagely. 'You know what they say – love is blind.'

'And deaf, dumb and stupid.'

'That too.'

We drove in companionable silence for a while. 'You don't seem all that upset, if you don't mind me saying.'

'No, I'm not,' I replied, realising with a surprise that I was, in fact, okay. I suppose it must have been the relief to know that I didn't want him any more. I smiled to myself. I knew exactly what I wanted.

'Here we are. Mahaffey's Pub.'

'How much is that?'

'That'll be nine euro fifty.' That'll be three Hail Marys and an Our Father.

I paid him. It seemed very good value. The counselling session must have been thrown in for free.

'Bye now, love. Good luck to you whatever you do.'

'Thanks – the same to you.'

I tipped him generously. I felt that a hug would be going a bit too far.

I entered the pub, feverish with excitement. It was Thursday, pay-day, and even though the bar had finished serving, the place was hopping. The loud, upbeat music was almost drowned out by the roar of a hundred different conversations being conducted at once. The atmosphere was hot and stuffy. I took off my coat as I moved through the crowd, rubber-necking like mad.

My heart soared as I spotted Seán propped up in his favourite place at the bar. He was chatting to Stephen and Tamsin's boyfriend, Brian. There was no sign of Sarah. I searched around wildly. Where the hell was she? I needed her. I took a deep breath and began to fight my way through the drunken throng towards Seán.

When I was nearly there, I lost my nerve and ducked into the Ladies.

To my relief, a familiar big, blonde angel was just inside the door applying a coat of mascara to her heavenly lashes.

'Sarah! Am I pleased to see you!'

'Fern!' The expression on her face was unreadable. It was a new one on me anyway. 'What happened to your dinner party?'

'It was a disaster. I'm finished with James.'

She raised her eyebrows. 'Really?'

'Yes, really. And this time it's for good. You were right about him all along. I don't know how I could have been so stupid.'

She continued to look at me, silently. This wasn't the enthusiastic reaction I had anticipated.

'I thought you'd be pleased.' My high spirits were sinking a little.

'Oh, I am. I'm delighted you've come to your senses.' I smiled happily at her. 'I'm going out to talk to Seán.'

Again, the unintelligible expression. 'Perhaps now is not a good time.'

'Why not?' I was starting to get ever so slightly worried.

The toilet flushed and out of the cubicle emerged a very tall, very slim, striking brunette.

'Fern, meet Melanie.'

Like the big eejit I was, I smiled warmly at her. 'Hi there, Melanie! Nice to meet you.'

Sarah was looking at me uncertainly. 'She's just flown in from Milan.'

And it was only then that my whole world came crashing down around my ears.

The model ex-girlfriend.

This wasn't happening.

I tried to smile at Melanie but I couldn't seem to get my mouth to work.

'Fern, are you okay?' I was vaguely aware of the note of alarm in Sarah's voice. It seemed to be coming at me from a long way off. 'I don't think she's very well. Too much to drink,' I heard her say in the distance. 'I'd better take her outside.'

I allowed myself to be dragged out through the bar. It was so hot. Too hot. I imagined I could see droplets of human sweat trickling down the walls. And then we were out into the blessed night air. Its coolness acted like a slap across my face, or a bucket of iced water, bringing me back to my senses.

'Here, sit down.' Sarah tugged me down beside her to the step outside the front door of the pub. The bouncer approached her.

'Sorry, ladies, you can't sit here.'

'Fuck off, Derek! This is an emergency.'

'Sorry,' Derek mumbled, suitably chastened. He retreated and left us to it.

'Why did you come here tonight?'

'To see you.'

'And?'

'To talk to Seán.'

'About what?' I squirmed uncomfortably on the cold, hard step. 'Come on, Fern. What were you going to say to Seán?' I continued to squirm. 'You were going to ask him to take you back, weren't you?'

'No. Well – yes. Maybe. Look, I don't know.'

'I agree, you don't know. You haven't given this much thought, have you?' I shrugged sulkily. 'What did you think? That he'd just welcome you back with open arms after the way you treated him?'

I still said nothing.

I didn't much like the way this conversation was going. I thought Sarah had brought me out here to comfort me, not to give out. She actually sounded a bit angry, which was the equivalent of a normal person being very angry indeed. I was starting to feel a little scared. My behaviour must have been even worse than I had thought.

'I just wanted to explain things to him.'

'Explain why you dropped him like a hot brick as soon as James crooked his little finger?'

This silenced me again. I knew she was right and it was killing me. This conversation wasn't going at all in the direction I wanted it to go.

'Anyway, it wouldn't have made any difference now that that skinny bitch is back.'

'Melanie happens to be a very nice girl!'

I turned and looked at Sarah in surprise. Whose side was she on? Pathetic tears of shock at her relative nastiness and self-pity at my dire situation began to well up in my eyes. She looked at me and her expression changed. She put her arm around my shoulder and gave me a small squeeze. 'Not as nice as you, of course.'

That was better.

I rested my head against her shoulder and allowed myself the luxury of a little cry. Sarah made small soothing voices.

'What happened tonight with James, anyway?'

I told her everything.

'No way! Oh, Fern, you poor thing.'

That was more like it.

We sat like that for a few minutes. Derek the bouncer was beginning to hover again.

'All right, all right,' said Sarah, sounding scary again. 'We're going. Fern, you can come back with me tonight. I don't want you being on your own.' I nodded obediently.

Twenty minutes later, She was tucking me into the sofa bed with a hot water bottle and a hot whiskey.

'But where will Stephen sleep?' I asked her drowsily, as she crawled in beside me.

'On the floor. It'll be good enough for him. He always snores when he's been out drinking.' Was cloud number nine starting to lose some of its fluffiness?

She turned off the lamp and I lay for a while, staring into the darkness.

'Sarah.'

'Mmmmm?'

'Is Seán going out with Melanie again?

'I don't know. She only got back today – just turned up out of the blue.'

'Does he like her?'

'I don't know.'

'Does she like him?'

A pause. 'She seems pretty keen.'

I said nothing for a while as I absorbed this information.

'Sarah.'

'What?' She was beginning to sound impatient.

'Am I really nicer than Melanie?'

She laughed. 'Yes, you are. Now, will you please let me sleep?'

'Okay. Sorry.'

'Okay. Goodnight.'

'Goodnight . . . Sarah?'

'Yes?'

'I really am sorry. For everything.'

'I know. Night, Fern.'

'Night.'

I didn't know where I was when I woke the next morning. I could hear a male and female voice whispering somewhere behind me. I remembered where I was and pretended to be asleep.

'Six months pregnant! Jesus, that's a bit of a bummer, isn't it?'

'Keep your voice down, Steve. You'll wake her up.'

'Sorry. How many sausages do you think she'd like?'

If the voices hadn't woken me, the smells would have. A fry up! The best hangover cure in the world. Not that I had a hangover that morning. That was one blessing. At least I had my health.

And friends, I thought gratefully. Although it was tempting to fake slumber, I made movements and noises to indicate that I was awake. I was immediately handed a mug of tea by Sarah. I sat up in bed, slurping it gratefully. She jumped in beside me, curling up into a ball.

'I don't want to go into work today,' she groaned. 'Make it go away, Steve.'

'Breakfast in bed is the best I can do, I'm afraid.' He handed her a plate. 'And for you, Fern.'

We sat side by side, milling into the food and getting crumbs all over the sheets.

'You lucky cow, you've got today off haven't you?'

I nodded. 'You should know – you gave it to me.'

'What are you going to do?'

'Catch up on some much-needed sleep.'

'Sounds like heaven. That's what I'd do if I had the day off.'

In truth, I would have welcomed something constructive to do. I didn't relish having time on my hands to think about my predicament. Perhaps I'd paint. I'd been neglecting my painting a lot of late. Too many distractions. It was about time I re-focused. I had a strong sense of needing to take stock of my life.

I reluctantly left the warmth and cosiness of Sarah and Stephen's apartment to make my way home. She saw me to the door.

'Are you going to be all right today?'

'I think so – yes.'

'I'll give you a ring at home this afternoon, see how you're doing.'

'I'd love that. Thanks for everything, Sarah.'
I gave her a hug, feeling very emotional all of a sudden.

'And Sarah . . . '

'What?'

'You won't say anything to Seán, about me being in the pub last night?'

She didn't answer.

'Promise me.'

'I promise.'

'And Stephen.'

'Steve will keep his mouth shut. I'll make sure of it.'

'Thanks. There's only so much humiliation one person can take.'

She smiled sympathetically. 'Bye, Fern.'

I went straight to bed when I got home. I just wanted to escape from reality for a few hours – take a break from the mess that I jokingly called my life. I couldn't possibly think coherently right now. My feelings for James and my feelings for Seán were all jumbled up inside my head.

My sleep was light and troubled by strange and vivid dreams. I didn't dream about my current problems – just tangled images that didn't make any sense. I woke with a start, with the phrase 'I dreamt I was vague among puddles of footsteps' revolving in my head. As always, when I went to sleep during the daytime, I didn't know what day it was when I woke up. I was startled by the sound of the door-bell ringing. That must have been what had woken me. I searched around for my watch in the dimly lit room. 2.21 p.m. Who could it be? Perhaps they'd go away.

They didn't. The door-bell rang again. And again. And again. This bugger wasn't giving up. Cursing under my breath, I angrily pulled on my dressing gown and slippers and went down to open the front door.

'Fern . . . I went to the café and they told me you had the day off. I took a gamble that you'd be home.'

I looked at him. I looked down at myself. I was wearing an old pink dressing-gown that my mother had left behind. It had that attractive, quilted, seventies-bedspread effect. Two of the buttons were missing and there was an egg-stain slopped down the front. I looked further down at my bunny rabbit slippers. They had been a Christmas present from Sasha, the last of the big spenders. I couldn't see my head but I had a rough idea of what I looked like. Last night's make-up still caked in and my hair sticking up in a north-easterly direction.

And I discovered that I didn't mind him seeing me like this. That's when I really knew that I didn't want him any more.

'You'd better come in.'

James entered my house for the second and last time. I showed him into the TV room. He sat on one end of the couch. I sat on the other. I didn't offer him tea or coffee. Nor did I make small talk to put him at ease. I wasn't going to bother trying to make this easier for him.

'I'm sorry. I should have told you.'

'Damn right, you should.'

'It's just that I was afraid that you wouldn't give me the time of day if you knew.'

'Do you not think that was my choice to make?'

He didn't reply to this. He just inched a little bit closer to me on the couch and smiled his most winning smile. When I didn't respond, it faded a little. Uncertainty clouded his features. I wondered if this was the first time that his smile hadn't had the desired effect. I felt a delicious surge of power.

'Tell me. How long have you known?'

'Known what?'

'That you were going to be a Daddy.'

He winced at the word. 'A while now.'

'Since before you asked me out?'

'Yes. But there's no guarantee that it's mine,' he added quickly.

'Do you have any good reason to think it's not yours?'

'She told me she was on the pill.'

'So it's all her responsibility, is it?'

'She trapped me,' he said bitterly. 'You have no idea what she's like, Fern. She's a manipulative little bitch with her eye on the main chance. She can sod off if she thinks I'm going to pay for her brat.'

'Get out.'

'What?'

'Get out of my house and don't come back.'

He stood up and looked down at me angrily, his mouth twisted into an unfamiliar cruel line.

This was James stripped of his charming, urbane veneer. A chill rippled through my body. It could have been me. I could have been the one left holding the baby.

I stood and drew myself up to my full height, determined not to look intimidated. 'Are you leaving or do I have to throw you out?'

'Oh, I'm going all right. This is the last time I'll be setting foot in this dump. You're a very stupid girl, Fern. Go back to your struggling artist. See if I care.' And he slammed out of my house and out of my life.

I felt myself physically crumple and I sank back down into the couch. I'd go back to the struggling artist in a flash, I thought, if he'd have me.

The phone rang. What now!

'Hello.'

'Is that Fern?'

'Declan?'

'The very same. I'm glad I caught you.' There was a long silence. 'Fern – are you still there?'

'I'm still here.' He sounded funny. I didn't have the energy for this. 'What do you want, Declan?'

'I was just wondering, if you're not too busy that is, if you'd like to meet up some evening this week?'

'For what? Old times' sake?'

'No. For what I believe the young people these days refer to as "a date".'

You've got to be kidding! 'You and me Declan? Come off it now!'

'Why not? You know you've always been my Number One.'

'Goodbye, Declan.'

Chapter Twenty-two

July and August are usually my favourite months. This year they dragged by. I went about my business robot-like. I got up – went to work, went to bed, got up – and did the same thing all over again the next day. Not that I was complaining. I welcomed the dull routine. I needed it to give myself time to recover. It had been some year so far.

I got very depressed at times. I put this down to my love life, or lack thereof. I was sitting with Sarah one day while we were on our break.

'You've been very quiet lately. You seem down.'

'I suppose I am. I think the James thing took a lot out of me.'

'Are you sure that's all it is?'

'What do you mean?'

'Well, your parents got separated only eight months ago. Your whole family has disintegrated. You never see your mother. You barely speak to your sister. No one in your family speaks to each other, as far as I can tell. And you never ever talk about it.'

I was shocked. I'd never really given it much thought. There'd been so much else going on. But she was right. The revelation didn't bring much comfort.

She didn't mention it again and neither did I. But it gave me something to think about.

As for Seán, I hadn't seen him. But Melanie had, as far as I could tell. I didn't dare ask Sarah for details in case she told me something that I couldn't stand hearing. I'd been keeping a very low profile, afraid to socialise with Sarah and the others in case I was confronted by the happy couple. Seán hadn't darkened the door of the café either. I didn't even know if Sarah had told him about my split with James, but knowing her, I figured she had.

To my credit, that wasn't the only thing on my mind these days. The college placements would be out shortly and I was pretty nervous about the whole thing. I spent most nights up in my room, painting and sketching ferociously, wondering fearfully what I'd do if I didn't get in and wondering even more fearfully what I'd do if I did get in. I felt like such a fraud at times. How could I fool these people that I had any artistic talent to speak of? I longed to talk to Seán about it. I knew he'd be the one to understand and reassure me. I didn't have the nerve to ring him. What if Melanie answered?

I was upstairs getting ready for work one morning when I heard the letter box clatter and a familiar thud on the hall carpet. I flew out of the bathroom and down the stairs. Sasha had got there before me. She was flicking through a handful of post.

'Anything for me?' I stood behind her, looking eagerly over her shoulder.

'Why? Are you expecting something? A letter from James perhaps, telling you he's made a terrible mistake?'

I snatched the post from her. Sasha had no idea what had transpired between me and James. All she knew was that he was no longer on the scene and, of course, she assumed that I'd been dumped.

Yes! There was a letter for me. An official-looking one in a white envelope. I handed the remainder of the junk mail back to her and walked into the kitchen, closing the door quietly behind me. I looked at the envelope and muttered a silent prayer. Come on, God – don't let me down this time. I ripped open the letter and read the contents. I didn't get much further than the first line. Feeling a little faint, I pulled out a chair and sat at the kitchen table.

Sasha had come in behind me.

'You know, Fern, you can be an ignorant sow. Who do you think you are snatching like that . . . ?' She trailed off as she looked at me. I was sitting statue-like, my face in my hands, tears trickling down my cheeks.

'What is it? Is it bad news? Are you all right?'

'I've just been accepted into art college.'

'You what?'

'You heard.'

There was a long silence.

'I didn't know you'd applied.'

'Well, I had.'

'But you can't draw.'

'I guess the National College of Art doesn't share your opinion.' I looked at her triumphantly. Her face had gone very pale and her expression was grim.

'Why didn't you tell anyone?'

'I did.'

'But you didn't tell me, or Mam or Dad.'

'Because I guessed what your reaction would be and you've just proved me right.' She started to leave the room. 'Aren't you going to congratulate me, then?'

She turned and gave me a look that turned all the dairy products in the kitchen sour. 'Congratulations.'

I sat, reading and re-reading the letter for about fifteen minutes, thoughts whirling around in my head and making me dizzy. What would it be like? Would I be good enough? Would I be the oldest in my class? Where would I live? Would I stay at home or move closer to college? Would I keep my job at the café? Would I start dressing like the art students who hung out at the café? Get tattoos and body piercing?

I stretched and wiped the tears of happiness away. I got up and turned on the radio, skipping through the stations with slow music, commercials or DJs talking shite. Then I found what I wanted. Perfect! 'I will survive' by Gloria Gaynor. Not even caring if Sasha walked in and caught me, I sang along at the top of my voice, dancing and jumping around the kitchen like a mad woman. I would have kept it up longer too, if I hadn't noticed the time. Shit! Better go to work.

I floated through the door of the café only ten minutes late, which I thought wasn't bad, considering. I went straight over to Sarah who was in the process of fixing the temperamental cappuccino machine.

'Guess what?'

She smiled at my excited face. 'You've won the lotto.'

'No.'

'You've just heard that James has broken his neck in a freak ski-ing accident.'

I giggled. 'No. Even better than that.'

I watched her face grow serious and her eyes widen and I knew that she had guessed right. 'You got accepted.'

I grinned idiotically and nodded. She squealed and ran around the counter. We hugged and jumped up and down like a couple of deranged lunatics. The customers sitting close by stared at us in consternation.

'I knew you could do it. You should call Seán and let him know. He'll be thrilled.'

I felt my face clouding over. 'Do you think that's such a good idea?'

'Yes, I do. He was only asking about you the other day.'

'What did he say about me?' I knew I sounded overly eager but I couldn't disguise it today. My emotions were too highly charged. Sarah was looking at me carefully.

'Just that he hoped you weren't neglecting your painting,' she said, equally carefully.

Oh. Was that all?

'Anyway,' she changed the subject, 'let's go out tonight and celebrate. This is definitely an occasion worth celebrating – not that we ever need an excuse – but that's not the point.'

'I'd love that, Sarah. Let's do the whole shebang – pub crawl, late-night bar, nightclub, Leeson Street, greasy spoon, early house . . .'

She laughed. 'Some of us have to work tomorrow, you know. We don't all have the day off.'

'Take the day off. What's the point in being the boss if you can't take a day off in an emergency?'

'This is an emergency, is it?'

'Yes – an emergency celebration.'

'Okay, I'll see if I can do a swap.'

'Great.'

'Now, go and try to do some work – not that you'll be any good to anyone today. Just try not to break too many plates or spill any scalding drinks on the customers.'

'Sarah, can I stay on here part-time when I start college?'

'Of course you can. We don't want to lose one of our star waitresses, especially now that you're going to be a famous artist one day. Hey – maybe I should get you to autograph a few serviettes. We can hang them on the walls. Now go. The place is starting to fill up.'

I glided through the particularly hectic lunchtime shift as if it was the easiest task in the world. Wouldn't it be great to feel so elated all of the time? Life would be a cinch.

After a couple of hours, the worst of it was over and I was clearing up the debris. Tamsin came over and nudged me.

'Someone to see you, Fern.'

I looked around and just about managed not to drop the dishes I was carrying.

'Seán!'

He walked slowly over to me, his face unsure. 'How are you doing, Fern?'

'Great, thanks. How are things with you?' I felt myself swallow.

'Fine. I just heard that the college placements are out. Did you get in?'

I couldn't get over the concern in his eyes. And he had come to the café especially to ask me. I toyed with the idea of pretending I hadn't got in, just to test his reaction, but it wasn't possible to disguise the kind of happiness that I was experiencing. 'I'm in.'

I wished I had a camcorder to record the transformation of his features. It was as if somebody had turned a light on from within. His blue, blue eyes literally sparked to life and the grin that I knew so well sprang into action. It took every ounce of willpower I had not to fling myself into his arms.

'That's brilliant, Fern. I'm really delighted for you.'

I couldn't say a word. I was trying not to burst out crying again. For one incredible second I thought that he was going to hug me, but instead he patted me on the arm as if I was one of his soccer buddies.

'Well done,' he mumbled.

We looked at each other for a few seconds. Neither of us could think of anything to say. I was appalled by the awkward silence. I had never felt that with Seán before. I understood that I was the one who had made it this way and the thought sickened me.

'Well, I just had to know. Satisfy my curiosity – you know how it is?' He smiled tentatively and turned to leave, evidently feeling as uncomfortable as I did.

'Seán! Wait.' Oh God. What was I doing? He turned back and looked at me expectantly. 'I'm going out tonight to celebrate. Why don't you come along?' I blurted out, before I had a chance to think about what was emerging from my mouth.

He didn't say anything. Oh, no – he was going to make up some cock-and-bull story about why he couldn't go. I'd just gone and embarrassed both of us for nothing.

'I mean, you can bring Melanie – if you want to, that is – I mean it won't only be the two of us. Sarah, Stephen, Tamsin – everybody will be there.'

He nodded grimly. 'I know what you mean, Fern. I'll try and make it. See you.'

I watched in despair as he left the café. I'll try and make it. What the hell did that mean? It was hardly a commitment to show up. The bastard! (I conveniently forgot that I was the bitch in this particular scenario.)

As I had expected her to, Sarah casually sidled up to me a few minutes later.

'Was that Seán I saw in here just now?'

'You should know. He *is* your brother.'

'Smart arse! What did he want?'

'He wanted to know if I got the place.' She wiped the table beside me. 'Sarah.'

'Yes?'

'I've already wiped that table. It's spotless.' I was ignored.

'If you like, I'll ask Seán if he fancies coming along tonight.'

'I already have.'

'Really?' She looked delighted.

'Yes – I asked Melanie too.'

'You did?' She laughed. I looked at her quickly. 'What's so funny?'

'Nothing. You just surprise me sometimes, that's all. Are they coming?'

'I don't know.' I started to set the table angrily, slamming down the cutlery. 'He said he'd try and make it.' I turned to Sarah, pointing at her with a knife. 'And don't you go trying to convince him to come. I don't want him doing me any favours.'

'I won't, I promise. Just stop pointing the knife at me.'

'Sorry.' I put the knife down.

Fuck it anyway. I'd been in a good mood until Seán had shown up. Sometimes I just hated men.

I finished setting the table thoughtfully.

'Sarah, can you do without me for a few minutes? I want to make a call.'

'Fire away.'

I went out to the white, empty corridor and made my call. My Auntie Marjorie answered.

'Who's that?'

'It's Fern.'

'Fern! It's been such a long time I barely recognised your voice.' Her sarcasm wasn't squandered on me.

'Is Mam there?'

'Hold on – I'll get her for you. Helen – phone,' Marjorie shrieked and put the receiver down.

It took my mother a little time to come to the phone so I was left listening to all the disembodied household sounds. I could hear the music to *Knots Landing* blaring in the background. Uncle John was as deaf as a post so he always turned the telly up as far as it could go. I could also hear Marjorie's pet dog yapping away like mad. Disgusting little ankle-biter with a ridiculous pony-tail on its head. She was always blathering on about its pedigree. It was a wonder Mam could stand living there.

'Hello?' Mam's voice was softer and quieter than Marjorie's.

'Mam, it's me.'

'Fern . . . how are you?' The equal measures of surprise and pleasure in her voice made me cringe with shame.

'I'm fine, Mam. How are you?'

'Oh . . . good. Tipping along, you know how it is. Is everything all right?' She sounded alarmed. It was a fine state of affairs when my own mother thought that I'd only ring her if I was in trouble.

'Everything's just fine. In fact, I have some good news.'

'What is it?'

'I've been accepted into art college.'

I waited with bated breath for her response. I felt so proud. And it wasn't often that I got the chance to give my parents the opportunity to feel proud of me.

'Art college?' She sounded shocked.

'Isn't it great?' I prompted hopefully.

'Well . . . yes . . . I suppose it is. Why didn't you tell me you were applying?'

'I hardly told anyone. I was afraid I wouldn't get in.'

'Did you tell your father?' Her tone was icy.

'No.'

'Oh. Are you sure you can afford it?'

'Yes, Mam. I've got that covered.' Be happy for me, for pity's sake! There was a void of silence which I felt compelled to fill with words. 'I thought you'd be pleased.'

'Oh, I am pleased, Fern. It's just that . . . art college . . . it's not very practical, is it? I suppose that at least you've got your typing to fall back on if it doesn't work out.'

Sometimes I wondered why I bothered.

We started out that night in O'Neill's on Suffolk Street. I felt drunk before I even arrived.

It had taken some doing to get out of my house. My father had heard the news from Sasha by the time I got home and he had taken it upon himself to buy a pineapple Tea-Time Express cake for the occasion. I found the gesture oddly touching. Mam had always been the master of family celebration ceremonies in the past. There had always been a special tea to celebrate birthdays, exam results (Sasha's usually) and general rites of passage. Dad must have recalled that a cake had always figured prominently in these proceedings (Mam had always baked). He seemed to have forgotten the rest of the meal though.

I cobbled together a hum-drum, everyday dinner as quickly as possible – eager to be out – and we sat around the TV eating it.

'Imagine,' said Dad, tucking into his southern fried chicken steak with gusto, 'all that time you spent messing about with paints and crayons up in your room. Your mother and me always thought you were a bit of a dreamer. And now this. We have an artist in the family. I don't know where you get it from. Nobody in this family ever had any talent in that direction. Not on your mother's side either. Mind you, your Gran's father, my grandfather, was a dab hand at carving little animals out of wood.'

I smiled at Dad's speech. He appeared to be quite pleased, in a vague sort of way. Meanwhile, my sister glowered in the corner, saying very little. This suited me fine. I'd always liked it when she sulked. It gave me a bit of peace and quiet.

Finally, the cake was eaten, the tea was drunk and I was able to make my getaway. As I said before, I felt drunk before I'd even had my first whiff of alcohol in O'Neill's. I was high on excitement and happiness.

The one blip on my horizon was the Seán question. I couldn't work out whether I wanted him there or not. If he didn't come, I'd spend the entire night watching the door and feeling disappointed every time it wasn't him. On the other hand, if he did come and he brought Melanie with him – well – seeing your ex slobbering over his model girlfriend is enough to put any normal person off their celebratory night out. On the third hand, if he came on his own . . . now that was a different kettle of fish altogether. Perhaps Melanie was strutting down a catwalk in some exotic location at this very moment. Wouldn't that be the best for everyone concerned?

No such luck. They arrived together. I'd already been drinking for two hours. Everybody had been buying me drinks and my feet were barely touching the ground. I had managed to smash two glasses already. The alcohol seemed to lose its magic powers when I saw her walk in beside him.

She certainly was a head-turner, if only because she was a foot taller than everyone else in the pub. My inner bitch instinctively took control as I dissected Melanie's face and figure, examining her for flaws. Sadly, I found few faults to comfort myself with. I'd have to focus on her personality instead. I hoped she was thick or annoying or both.

I got the opportunity to test her out just a few minutes later. Seán hadn't come near me so far. He had just glanced over and nodded in my direction before joining Stephen and Brian at the bar. I was a little hurt but I couldn't blame him.

Melanie fought her way over to Sarah and me. I braced myself.

'Hi, Sarah! Hi, Fern! Do you remember me? I met you briefly in Mahaffey's a couple of months back. You weren't feeling all that well.'

'Yes, I remember. Melanie, isn't it?' As if her name wasn't engraved on my brain.

'That's right. Well done for getting into art college. I know the competition's very stiff. You must be good.' Her smile was friendly and open, her tone of voice revealing no underlying sarcasm. I mumbled something humble and looked away uncomfortably.

'Can I buy you both a drink – I'm going up to the bar?'

'I'll have a vodka and orange and Fern is drinking G&Ts,' Sarah said quickly.

As soon as Melanie had gone, Sarah turned to me. 'Are you all right?'

I nodded miserably.

'Come on. Don't let it get to you. Remember, this is your big night. You can't let anything spoil it. You've just achieved something really amazing and you're about to start a whole new life. Just think of all those gorgeous arty men you're going to meet when term starts.'

'But they'll all be about eighteen,' I moaned pathetically.

'Well then, you'll have no choice but to have an affair with one of your lecturers.'

'No, thanks. I don't want anything to do with some dirty-minded old codger who still wears a leather jacket and rolls his own.'

Sarah shook her head. 'I don't know where you get your ideas from. I suppose you want someone of around – oh, I don't know – Seán's age?'

'Oh, belt up.'

'Oh, cheer up! You'd think somebody had just died. We'll finish these drinks and go somewhere livelier – get you back in the party mood.'

So we did. I worked on the premise that if I acted happy I'd start to feel happy. It worked up to a point. At least, I think I managed to fool everybody except myself. I didn't dare approach Seán. I barely looked at him. But having said that, I knew exactly where he was at any given moment, who he was talking to and how many feet he was away from the lovely Melanie.

I tried very hard to hate her but I found that I couldn't. Sarah talked to her a lot, which annoyed me nearly as much as Seán talking to her. Honestly – she could do with a few lessons in loyalty, that one! Of course, I couldn't exactly claim to be the one fit to teach her.

We were in our fourth licensed premises of the evening and I had gone up to the bar at the far end of the pub, away from where everybody I knew was congregated. I could feel my happy mask starting to slip so I thought I could benefit from a few moments alone.

'Hi!'

Seán was standing right behind me. Startled, I turned quickly and my lips brushed against the side of his neck. Our eyes met for a split second and then fell again as I backed away a few inches.

'Are you trying to get served too? It's crazy in here, isn't it? I've been waiting nearly five minutes . . . ' I babbled. Fortunately, he cut me off before I could say something really stupid.

'No, I just wanted to talk to you.' He wanted to talk to me.

'About what?'

'About why you've been avoiding me all night.'

'Me avoiding you?' I was drunkenly indignant. 'I think you'll find, Seán Morrissey, that it's you who's been avoiding me.'

'Have not.'

'Have so.'

'Fern, when I arrived tonight, you just looked right through me. I was about to come over and say hello but I thought better of it.'

'I did not look through you.'

'Did so.'

'Did not. Besides, you had Melanie with you. I didn't want to cramp your style – not that you ever had any style in the first place.' Shut up, Fern!

He was smirking now. 'But, Fern, you invited her.'

'Did not.'

'Did so.'

'Did not . . . ' Hold on. I did, didn't I? I made a sulky verbal retreat. He was laughing openly at me now, the bastard! 'Well, I hope Melanie's enjoying her night out.'

'Oh, she's having a great time.'

'Good for her.'

I fumed inwardly and outwardly, groping around in my brain for a suitable retort. Unfortunately, I had already killed most of that night's quota of brain cells with gin. Luckily for me, Seán changed the subject.

'So, you must be looking forward to starting college?'

I relaxed and returned his smile. 'I am. A bit nervous though. Any tips for me – as an old pro?'

'Yes,' – his expression grew serious – 'remember how brilliant you are, don't take any crap off anyone and never forget you deserve to be there as much as everybody else, if not more.'

I stared at him for a couple of seconds and then looked away quickly as I felt unexpected tears prickle at the back of my eyes for the umpteenth time that day.

'That's a very nice thing to say, Seán – thank you. I know it's more than I deserve from you in the circumstances.'

'It's the truth.' His voice was low and husky. I chanced looking up at him again. Was it my imagination or did his eyes darken a little? I felt my breathing quicken. 'Besides,' he continued, his voice still soft. I nearly stopped breathing completely as he moved his mouth closer to my ear. 'If it doesn't work out for you, I predict you have a great future in topless modelling.'

Our eyes locked for a moment and then we both started to laugh, the tension broken.

'Yes,' I continued, 'if a life-drawing class isn't going well for me, I can just strip off and they can sketch me instead.'

'Hi, guys. What's so funny?' It was Melanie. Seán stopped laughing long enough to answer her.

'Nothing. We were just discussing alternative career plans for Fern.' Seán and I grinned at each other.

Melanie looked uncertainly from me to Seán and back again.

'Actually, Seán, I'm feeling a bit tired. Will you take me home?'

Was it wishful thinking on my part or did Seán look disappointed?

'Sure, Mel. Whenever you're ready.'

'I'm ready now.'

'Oh . . . okay. I'll get my jacket. See you, Fern.'

'Bye, Fern.' Melanie gave me a strange look and they turned to leave.

I miserably watched them saying their goodbyes. I turned back to the bar and to the two drinks that had just materialised. Gin for me and vodka for Sarah.

'That'll be six euro twenty please.' The barman held his hand out for the money. Without answering, and without bothering with the mixers, I downed each short in one go. I winced at the sharp taste and wiped my mouth with the back of my hand.

'Same again, please.'

The barman didn't bat an eyelid. He just turned on his heel and got me two more drinks. I had to admire his professionalism. No doubt he was well used to lushes like me.

I finally paid the poor man and stumbled back to Sarah. She smiled brightly. 'We're all going back to ours for a party – what do you think?'

I shrugged. I really didn't care about anything any more. 'I'm feeling the worse for wear, Sarah. I think I'll go home.' Her face fell ten storeys. 'Oh no, you can't.'

'Why can't I?'

'Because it's your big night out. What about your plans for finishing up in an early house?'

'That was this morning. I've had enough excitement for one day. I think I'll call it a night.'

'Now, Fern,' – her tone was stern – 'I went and took tomorrow off just so that I could come out tonight and celebrate with you. You can't wimp out on me now.'

'Oh, okay. You win,' I agreed huffily. I might as well get totally hammered. I was well on the way already.

So we all went back to Sarah and Stephen's flat. Thirty or so people squished into an area that was barely big enough for two people to live in. You could say it was cosy.

I ensconced myself into a corner of the kitchen, beside the drinks stash, taking large swigs from a flagon of gin that I'd brought with me from the pub in a brown paper bag, like a wino.

I stood morosely in the corner, watching everybody else enjoying themselves, feeling increasingly alone in my little universe. When they started doing the dance to 'The Birdie Song', I decided that enough was enough and I screwed the top back onto my flagon and put it back into its brown bag. (I wasn't leaving it there.) I resolved to look for my jacket which I had carelessly discarded in some unknown spot in the so-called living room.

'Leaving so soon?' I heard a deep, male voice behind me. I swung around to find a dark, attractive-looking male. I recognised him as a well-known lothario who had briefly dated one of the waitresses some time ago, carelessly dumping her as soon as he knew he had her hooked. I couldn't remember his name.

'I'm Rob. Fern, isn't it?'

Ah yes. Rob. I remembered his name now, although it was usually prefixed by 'That prick'.

He extended his hand and I shook it limply. As he grinned at me and sidled dangerously close, I looked him up and down. He wasn't half bad-looking. That quiet little sensible voice inside my head told me that he hadn't looked so good without the benefit of sixteen gins and dim lighting, but, in time-honoured tradition, I chose to ignore it. He was male and the proud owner of two arms, two legs and a head. What more could a girl like me ask for?

'So,' he continued, sliding a slick arm along the counter behind me, 'are you on your own?'

'Looks like it.' I found this simple phrase alarmingly hard to utter. There were just too many Ls' in the one sentence.

'That's a shame. Pretty girl like you.'

I laughed drunkenly. Did he really think I was dumb enough to be taken in by such a line?

'Can I get you a drink?'

'I'm grand, thanks.' I gestured to the crumpled paper package that I was clutching possessively against my chest.

'Oh, come on! I can do better than that. I'll make you a cocktail.'

Without waiting for my yea or nay, he began banging about in the general area of the food mixer, chopping up a banana and slopping around with ice cream and fruit juice. I watched him as he poured in overgenerous helpings from various bottles of booze. My gaze travelled to his bum encased in a pair of black levis. Not bad.

He grinned toothsomely at me as he poured us both a helping of the gloopy-looking concoction and handed me a glassful.

'Cheers!' he said, banging his glass into the side of mine and downing a mouthful of the stuff. I sniffed at my glass gingerly and recoiled. It smelt uncannily like diesel. I grimaced at him.

'What did you say you put in this?'

'I didn't. It's a secret recipe. Try it. I call it Lethal Weapon 4.'

I giggled foolishly. To hell, I thought, as I knocked back a large mouthful. In fact, it wasn't half bad. I drank some more. Rob didn't take his eyes off me once, obviously calculating the best moment to pounce.

'You know, you really are a babe,' he whispered into my ear. His words tickled. I giggled again, feeling flattered even though I knew in my heart of hearts that the situation was ludicrous and that I should take to my heels. Against my better judgement, of which I had none in my present state, I stayed put.

After further perfunctory conversation, which consisted mainly of Rob making suggestive comments and me making giggly, half-coherent replies, he put down his glass and took the half-empty one out of my hand and placed it on the counter. He smiled wolfishly at me. Then he placed one hand at the back of my neck and brought his mouth hungrily down on mine.

I returned his kiss half-heartedly, thinking vaguely to myself that his lips felt like a wet hoover with bad suction. Unbidden, a vision of Seán kissing Melanie flashed into my mind. I kissed Rob harder, trying to block out this disturbing image, trying not to think about what they were more than likely doing together at this very moment.

We snogged like this for a while. I felt that my lips belonged to someone else and that I was looking down from somewhere close to the ceiling at the two of us standing in the kitchen.

I felt that it was time to pull away when I felt his saliva beginning to dribble down my chin. I laid my head heavily on his shoulder, allowing him to pull my body closer against his. With some effort, I managed to raise my bloodshot eyes and scan the room, hoping that nobody had seen what I had just done.

Unfortunately they had. The last thing I remembered was Seán staring at me in disgust and then slamming the door of the flat behind him without a backward glance.

Oh, fuck!

Chapter Twenty-three

Over the next few days, I was plunged into despair. I didn't feel like doing anything. I didn't want to go to work, I didn't want to make preparations for the start of college and I certainly didn't want to go on any nights out. I had proved it to myself time and time again that I wasn't to be trusted. I was much better off staying home with a packet of crisps and watching *Hetty Wainthrop Investigates*.

It turned out that Sarah had made a point of telling Seán about the party and had told him to make sure that he came back to it alone. Why did I always have to mess everything up?

Just when I thought that things couldn't possibly get worse, that's precisely what they did. I was dragging my way through a lunch-time shift later that week when Tamsin told me that there was a phone call for me. Her voice was full of concern. 'I think it's your mother. She sounds upset.'

Alarm bells automatically went off in my head. My mother had never rung me at work before. In fact, she barely rang me at all. There must be something wrong. I fought my way through the busy café, trying not to break into a run. Out in the corridor, I made a dash for the phone and brought the receiver up against my temple so hard that I nearly brained myself.

'Hello?'

There was a crackle and then a woman's voice sounding far off and afraid. 'Fern – is that you?'

'Mam?'

'Oh, thank God!' Her voice sounded unfamiliar. I realised that she was crying. I felt the adrenalin course through my body as I prepared myself for whatever it was that she was about to tell me.

'What's wrong?'

'It's Sasha – she's been in an accident – oh, God . . . ' She broke off into hysterical sobs. Now I was really scared. If there was one thing my mother was not, it was a hysterical woman.

'What kind of accident?' It was as if I was hearing someone else speak. I was surprised at how calm I sounded.

'She was pulling out of the driveway. Joy-riders. They ploughed right into her.'

'Is she . . . where is she now?'

'They've taken her to the hospital. Your Uncle John is bringing me there now. I'm on his mobile.'

'Is she . . . bad?'

'Oh, Fern! She's all smashed up . . . her poor little face . . . ' She broke off into sobs again. I could feel my stomach churning with fear.

'I'll be right there. I'm leaving now.'

'Will you call your Dad first? I couldn't get through to him.' I nodded and then realised that she couldn't see me.

'Yes. But, Mam. Is she going to be okay?'

My only answer was a loud crackling noise and then the phone went dead.

I muttered incoherent prayers under my breath as I walked swiftly up the driveway to the hospital. I hate hospitals with a vengeance. Even the smell of them. I could never understand why anybody would want to be a doctor or a nurse. To be surrounded by sick and dying people when you don't have to be. I gave Sasha's name at reception and to my horror was told that she'd been rushed to the operating theatre. I carried out a demented search for my mother, eventually finding her pacing up and down a corridor close by the operating room.

When she saw me, she erupted into a fresh bout of loud sobbing and pulled me into a fierce hug. I stood stiff as a board, my hands straight down at my sides, not knowing how to respond. This was unfamiliar territory.

'Thank God you're here, Fern.'

'Have you heard anything?' I gently attempted to extricate myself from her vice-like grip.

'No, they won't tell me anything,' she wailed. I found her lack of self-control frightening. I hated myself for wondering if she would have been this upset if I was the one being operated on. I banished the thought immediately.

'What happened anyway?'

It turned out that Sasha had been visiting with my mother and Aunt Marjorie. As she pulled out of the driveway, a car being driven through the estate by two young joyriders, at eighty miles per hour, had ploughed into her. The driver of the stolen car was dead. My sister was lucky to be alive.

We heard rapid footsteps echo on the corridor behind us and turned quickly, thinking it might be a doctor with some news. It was only Dad. He looked as if he'd aged twenty years. His skin was ghostly pale and his white hair, usually so neatly parted, stood up in a messy tuft on the crown of his head.

He bypassed me and went straight to Mam, clasping both of her hands in his. This provoked a fresh batch of sobbing on her part. His eyes were dry but red-rimmed.

'It's okay, Helen. She's going to be fine. C'mon. Sit down now.' He placed an arm tenderly around her heaving shoulders and led her to some plastic chairs at the side of the corridor, for all the world as if the last nine months had never happened. I looked away. I felt like I was intruding.

After a vigil that extended into the early hours of the next morning, the nurse on duty finally convinced us to leave the vicinity of the Intensive Care Unit and go down to the cafeteria. Actually, she practically shoved us into the elevator.

It was everything you could possibly hope for in a hospital canteen and more. Coffee in non-biodegradable polystyrene cups, sandwiches made of three-day-old bread and square Danishes in little plastic bags. The icing stuck to the plastic when you took it out of the bag, leaving you with a naked piece of confectionery.

Animal, mineral or vegetable was the question that most frequently came to mind.

We collectively munched our food in silence, all staring at our own individual pieces of space. My father bought *The Irish Times* and turned the pages methodically. You could tell he wasn't reading a word. Still, I understood his need for comforting ritual. It was the same with the endless cups of tea and coffee we drank although we really didn't want any.

'Do you remember the last time we were here with Sasha, Bill?' Mam spoke suddenly. Her eyes were wide and bright and slightly manic looking. She looked like somebody on the brink of losing control. There was a contradictory smile playing about her lips. My father smiled fondly at her.

'The chimney pot.'

When she was about four years of age, Sasha had managed to stick her head into a loose chimney pot. It had remained stuck and she had had to have it removed in casualty. I had heard the story dozens of times before. Mam's features relaxed as she smiled back at him.

412

'She thought it was great fun. She laughed all the way to hospital in the car.'

'And the doctors gave her sweets when her head came free,' I joined in, even though I had only been six months old at the time.

'She kept asking if she could go back to see the doctors and nurses for weeks afterwards,' Dad finished.

We all laughed, as if hearing the story for the first time. Then we had the time that I got kicked in the mouth by a little girl on a swing. I'd had to have three of my baby teeth removed in hospital. The little purple pinafore I'd been wearing had been ruined with all the blood.

Then we had the time Sasha had gone for a walk in the woods, only to end up face down in the mud, her wellies standing bolt upright beside her.

I watched my parents recount the well-worn tales to each other. Today was the first time they had spoken since Mam had left home. It was as if the past months had been obliterated in a few horrific hours. Talk about putting things into perspective. My own personal worries were put

413

firmly in their place. I couldn't believe I had wasted so much time worrying about so little.

And that wasn't all. I felt a connection with my parents that I hadn't felt since I was about twelve years of age. My eyes filled with tears as I thought of Sasha lying upstairs, wired up to all those machines. What would I do without her? True, I could probably find someone else to insult me from a great height on a daily basis but nobody could do it quite like Sasha. She had turned tongue-lashing into an Olympic sport.

But things were going to be different from now on. As soon as she was better, we'd behave like proper sisters. We'd go clothes shopping together on Saturdays; do each other's hair; give each other sound advice and support when it came to make-up and men. We'd become best friends. I'd make sure if it. All I needed was a second chance.

Ian – Sasha's long-suffering boyfriend – had arrived. None of us knew what to do with him. We looked on, mortified, as he sat snivelling beside her bed, his face buried deep into his hands. I have to admit to being a little shocked.

I had always thought that their relationship was a superficial one, conducted mainly by E-mail and cellular phone. I guess he loved her after all.

When Mam and Dad were out of the room, I tipped him gently on the shoulder. He looked up at me, blinking as if he didn't know where he was.

'Er . . . would you like a cup of tea, Ian?' I asked lamely.

He gave me an incredulous look, as if it would be sacrilegious to drink tea at a time like this.

'Why did it have to happen to Sasha of all people?' he wailed up at me. I was taken back by the raw emotion in his voice. I patted his shoulder awkwardly. I hardly knew him really.

'I don't know, Ian. It doesn't make any sense.'

'But Sasha of all people. She's such a sweet person.'

I looked at him and he looked at me. Even through the intense fog of his grief, he knew that he couldn't get away with that one. 'Okay, she's a bitch. But she's *my* bitch,' he sobbed.

Sasha was going to be all right. It was official. The doctor had told us. I decided there and then that I was going to marry him, even if he did look more like Deputy Dawg than Doctor Doug.

The sense of relief was like nothing I'd ever experienced. We stood in the corridor and clung to each other – the entire Fennelly family, who never showed emotion in public.

Sasha was still unconscious for the most part. We were allowed to visit her two by two. I went in first with Mam. We sat on either side of the bed, my mother clutching Sasha's hand as if she was never going to let go of it again. I stared at my sister's face, marvelling at how young and innocent she looked without make-up and with her hair scraped back.

'When do you start college?' Mam asked me, without taking her eyes off Sasha's face. The question took me by surprise.

'Er . . . not till October.'

'You must be looking forward to it.'

I eyed her suspiciously. Was this a trap? 'Yes – I suppose I am.'

There was a long pause before she spoke again. 'You know, I've started taking art classes at night.'

I'm sure the expression on my face was priceless. 'You!' I spluttered.

My mother tore her eyes away from Sasha. 'Yes, me!' Her voice was indignant. 'You didn't think you got it from the wind, did you?'

'I didn't mean . . . I mean . . . you never said anything before.'

Mam held her head up proudly. 'Oh, yes. I was quite an artist as a young girl. I still have a lot of my old drawings up in the attic.'

'Have you?'

'Oh, yes. I've been threatening to throw them out for years but I never got around to it.'

Another pause.

'I'd love to see them sometime.'

'Would you?' Mam looked shyly at me across the bed.

'Yes. I'd really love that.'

She beamed at me and I smiled back cheerfully.

I was silent for a while, taking it all in.

'What I don't understand is why you never told me. I mean, I was always up in my room painting and sketching.'

'I didn't want to encourage you.'

'Why not?'

'You always had your head up in the clouds, Fern. You don't get anywhere in this life by being a dreamer. I was always trying to bring out your practical side.' She looked at the expression on my face. 'It was for your own good, Fern.'

'So why are you taking it up again now?'

'Oh, I don't know. When I heard about you going to art college, it brought it all back. I decided to give it another go – just as a hobby, mind.'

'Why did you stop in the first place?'

Her eyes took on their familiar far-away look. 'My father didn't approve. He said that art was a waste of time. Especially for a girl. He was right too.'

I looked searchingly into her face, as if seeing her for the first time.

'But I think it's great that you're going to college all the same, even art college. Qualifications are very important, you know.'

'I know, Mam.'

'And if doesn't work out, you still have your secretarial.'

Chapter Twenty-four

Sasha's recovery was nothing short of miraculous – everyone said so. Even the doctors. Aunt Marjorie put it down to the candle that she'd asked her neighbour to light in Lourdes. Either that or the novenas. But one or the other was definitely responsible for Sasha's return to health.

Within the week, she was sitting up in bed, chatting to visitors. I was alone with her for the first time on Thursday afternoon. I watched her drift in and out of sleep and felt my own eyes grow heavy. I woke with a jump as I felt my head fall backwards. I looked around in confusion and saw that Sasha was now awake. She was smiling at me – not her usual cynical smirk but a sweet, open smile.

'Tired?'

'A bit.' I could hardly see, I was so exhausted.

'Mam says you've been here the whole time.'

I shrugged.

'Thanks.' Again the smile. I'd forgotten how pretty she looked when she smiled properly.

'That's okay,' I mumbled, feeling embarrassed. I wasn't accustomed to this – Sasha being nice. I didn't know how to respond.

'So, when does college start?'

'October.'

'You must be thrilled with yourself.'

'I suppose I am.'

'I'm sorry about the way I was before. It was mean of me. I think it's brilliant.'

'You do?'

'Yes. You deserve it. You're very talented.'

Was I hearing things? 'But you told me that my drawings weren't fit to hang in a dog kennel.'

'Did I?'

'Yes, you did!'

'I'm sorry if I said that. I don't remember saying it.' Incredible! An insult that I'd planned taking to my grave and she didn't even remember saying it.

'It's just . . . ' she started and then trailed off, looking uncomfortable.

'Just what?'

'Well, it's just that you've always been the good-looking one. I couldn't stomach you being the talented one too.'

Now I really was gobsmacked.

'But you're forever telling me not to go out of the house without my make-up in case I frighten small children.'

She laughed guiltily. 'I did say that, didn't I?'

'Yes, you bloody well did – several times.'

'Well, I didn't really mean it. Just put it down to good old-fashioned jealousy and be flattered by it.'

I shook my head and then we both started laughing.

It was amazing all the same, what a massive blow to the head could do for your personality.

When Sasha finally fell into a deep sleep – I think she was worn out from all the laughing – I decided to join the sick people outside the front door of the hospital for a fag. I got a light off a man in a wheelchair who was attached to one of those portable drips.

I was taking long, luxuriant puffs and stretching out my cramped limbs when I saw a familiar figure waddle past. It couldn't be. I did a double-take.

'Fern!'

'Hello, Bronwyn.'

'What are you doing here?'

'Visiting my sister. You?' As if I needed to ask.

'I'm having my final scan,' she said proudly. She was ever so slightly out of breath and a film of sweat glistened on her temples and upper lip. She looked about thirteen months pregnant. 'Did you hear my news?'

'No.'

'Look.' She shoved her fist towards my face. For a fleeting second I thought that she was going to punch me. Instead, she nearly took my eye out with a massive, sparkling engagement ring.

'It's gorgeous.'

She drew her hand back and smiled smugly.

'Do you want to try it on?'

'No, it's all right.'

'It's from James. We're getting married at Christmas.'

'Congratulations,' I said blandly. I could only assume that James had caved in to family pressure and popped the question.

My reaction – or lack of reaction – seemed to irritate her.

'Oh – I'm sure you're very happy for us,' she goaded.

'Bronwyn, I think you were made for each other.' I could tell she didn't know how to respond to this. She looked as if she was searching for something horrible to say.

'So, it didn't last long, did it?'

'What?'

'What do you think? Your sordid little affair with James,' she almost hissed.

I shrugged my shoulders at her. 'It was long enough.' I wasn't interested in getting involved in this discussion.

'I knew he'd drop you like a hot potato sooner or later and come back to me.'

I kept my peace. James must have told her that he had ended things with me and not the other way around. I wasn't going to disillusion her. Neither was I going to ask her why James hadn't accompanied her to the hospital. I was mildly surprised at how little the sight of my ex's heavily pregnant fiancée bothered me. All I could feel for Bronwyn was pity. Her problems were only just beginning.

I took in her white, angry face – far too white – and her swollen ankles.

'How are you getting home?'

'My father is picking me up. Here he is now.'

She trundled off in the direction of the car park without saying goodbye. I watched her slow progress, assuming that she was headed for the dark green Merc which was parked at the bottom of the driveway. Much to my amazement, a stocky, middle-aged man in overalls jumped out of the Hiace van parked beside the Merc and opened the van door for her, tenderly helping her in.

Wonders would never cease.

As I got the lift back up, I reflected on the strange day that I was having.

Outside Sasha's room I heard the newly familiar sound of her laughter ring out. She must have visitors.

Seán and Sarah were sitting beside her bed, one on either side. Sasha was sitting propped up on her pillows like a queen, with a huge bouquet and a selection of brown paper bags before her.

'Fern' – she beamed up at me – 'look what your friends have brought me.' She held the flowers out for inspection.

We were joined by Mam, Dad, Aunt Marjorie and Uncle John. For a few minutes, we were the noisiest corner of the ward. I didn't say much. Neither did Seán. We were too busy pretending not to look at each other. Eventually, the sour-looking matron came over and 'suggested' that some of us leave as we were disturbing the other patients.

'Her face would disturb some of the patients, all right,' Dad muttered under his breath.

Seán and Sarah said their farewells and I went to see them out.

'So, how are you doing?' asked Sarah.

'Good. I'll be back to work in a day or two.'

'I didn't mean it like that. Take your time coming back to work. It's just that you look as if you've lost a lot of weight.'

'Really?' I said hopefully.

'I didn't mean it as a compliment, you big eejit. You look run down – doesn't she, Seán?'

He mumbled something to the effect that I looked a bit pale all right, all the while addressing his shoes.

Sarah glanced from me to Seán and back again.

'Anyway, I'd better get back to work. I left Tamsin in charge.' She leant over and kissed me warmly on the cheek. 'Look after yourself, Fern. Are you coming with me, Seán?' Her tone was faintly mocking.

'No. I think I'll stay here for a while.' He addressed his shoes again.

'Right so. Be seeing you both soon, no doubt.'

And off she went down the corridor, humming to herself. She looked back at me once and winked.

I turned to Seán. I decided to chance looking him in the eye. He returned my gaze, his expression grave.

'Do you fancy a walk?' he asked me.

No. I fancy you. 'Okay.'

In contrast to the stark, ugly interior, the hospital grounds were beautiful. The lawns were lush and the well-tended flower beds were bursting with colour. Every so often, an ancient tree offered shade against the hot afternoon sun. Copper beeches were intermingled with oaks and silver birches. The air was heavy with the fragrance of late-summer flowers and the scent of freshly mown grass. We strolled in a silence that was punctuated only by birdsong.

I was almost breathless with anticipation. It was evident that Seán had something on his mind. But he wasn't saying anything for the time being. I stole a sly glance at him. He was looking straight ahead, his features set and serious. I couldn't stand it any longer. I had to say something.

'So, how have you been?' I struggled.

'All right.'

'Sold any paintings lately?'

'A few.'

'That's good. Look – do you want to sit down?' I beckoned to a sun-kissed patch of grass directly ahead. He shrugged and eased himself onto the ground, where he sat, resting his elbows on his knees. I sat cross-legged beside him, careful to keep a respectable distance between us.

I looked across at him again as he sat in silence. The sunlight highlighted his blond tousled hair and his eyes matched the sky above his head. He was wearing his oldest, faded-blue Wranglers and a loose white T-shirt. I tried not to notice the way the sun brought out the downy blond hairs on his tanned, muscular forearms and the intoxicating way that the denim strained at his thighs. He caught me looking at him and I tore my eyes away, my cheeks burning.

'How's Rob?'

The question took me unawares and for a few seconds I genuinely didn't know what he was talking about. And then the sickening recognition. The slurpy one from the party. It felt like several centuries had passed since then.

'I haven't a clue. I barely know him.'

'You looked like you were getting to know him pretty well that night.'

Ouch! Two could play at that game. 'What's that got to do with you? I'm single. I can do what I want. What do you expect me to do, Seán? Act like a nun while you're bonking Melanie.'

He laughed coldly and without humour. 'You! Act like a nun! Give me a break.'

Now that *really* stung. I could feel myself starting to get upset. This wasn't the warm, easy-going Seán I used to know. His voice and eyes were reaching sub-zero temperatures.

'So, you just came here to have a go at me, did you? Well you didn't pick a very good time. This hasn't exactly been the best week of my life, you know.' To my horror, I heard my voice start to crack. Blinking back hot tears, I scrambled to my feet, absently brushing the grass off my clothes.

In an instant, Seán sprang to his feet and took me in his arms. I shook with silent sobs, my face crushed against his chest. He stroked my hair rhythmically. With some effort, I managed to pull away.

'Let me go.'

'No.' He pulled me back against him. I could feel his breath hot against my neck as he spoke. 'I'm never letting you go again.' His voice was thick with emotion. I hardly dared believe my ears.

'What about Melanie?'

'It's over.'

'Since when?'

'Since the night of the party.'

'What happened?'

'She wanted me to tell her that I didn't love you any more.'

'And?'

'I couldn't.'

I looked up into his smiling blue eyes. I had a feeling that this time it was going to be all right. I just knew.

We stood like that for a while. Wrapped around each other, bathed in the sun. After a while, Seán spoke.

'Hey, Fern.'

'Yes?'

'Fancy a game of Doctors and Nurses.'

Epilogue
Five years later

Seán pulled the car up outside the offices of Boland, Sharpe & Co. He turned to me and smiled.

'Are you sure you don't want me to come in with you?'

'No, thanks. I want to do this by myself. Wish me luck.'

'Good luck.'

I kissed him and stepped out onto the pavement.

I rang the buzzer on the familiar old Georgian door. The door looked smaller now. Less imposing. It could have done with a lick of paint too.

I was buzzed into reception. Grace, the receptionist who had been there in my day, had been replaced. There had always been a high turnover of staff in Boland, Sharpe & Co. Solicitors.

'Mr Boland will see you now, Ms Fennelly.' The altogether cheerier replacement smiled at me and gave me directions to Cyril Boland's office. There was no need. I still remembered every step.

I walked slowly up the elegant flight of stairs, examining each painting that adorned the wall. Some I remembered. Others were new. I smiled as I passed one of Seán's.

I couldn't resist taking a detour on the way. I stopped off at the second floor. As I reached the door to my old office, a young girl flew out and narrowly avoided colliding with me. She sprang back. 'Oh, I'm very sorry.'

I looked into her huge frightened eyes before she scurried away. It was like seeing a ghost.

Glancing furtively up and down the corridor, I quickly opened the door of my old office and stuck my head inside. The place was virtually unrecognisable, it was so neat. Julie's new secretary was evidently tidier and more efficient than I had ever been. It was just as well.

I closed the door gently and moved to the door to the next office. I read the gold-plated inscription:

'Julie Benson – Associate.'

So they still hadn't made her a partner. I resisted the temptation to open the door. I had seen what I had come here to see.

By the time I reached the fourth floor, my heart was racing. He was already standing in his doorway, waiting for me.

'Ah, Ms Fennelly, I presume. You're most welcome. Do come in.'

I was gestured inside Cyril's immaculate office. He showed me to a leather-bound chair and buzzed his secretary, demanding coffee and chocolate biscuits for two.

We made polite small talk while we waited for the refreshments to arrive. I remembered how I and the other secretaries used to pilfer the good chocolate biscuits that were meant to be exclusively for the clients, when we'd get fed up with our own plain Mariettas.

Cyril's secretary arrived. She was also new. She placed the cups and plate subserviently on the desk and exited the room, head down.

'I must say,' began Cyril, through mouthfuls of coffee and biscuit, 'it's a rare treat to meet the artist of a painting that I want to buy.'

I smiled encouragingly at him.

'I've been following your work for some time now and I'm most impressed.'

'Why, thank you, Mr Boland. You're very kind.'

'Please – call me Cyril.'

'Thank you, Cyril.'

There was a pause where I suppose he expected me to invite him to call me Fern. When it didn't happen, he continued.

'You know, you look very familiar to me. Have we met before?'

'Actually, we have.'

'I thought as much. Was it at the opening of that new gallery on George's Street?'

'No. I didn't go along to that.'

'Where then?'

'Here.'

'Here?' His smile faded a little.

'Yes. I worked as Julie Benson's secretary about six years ago.'

I could almost hear him trying to work out who I was. I looked on impassive, noting how his head was now even more highly polished than his massive walnut desk.

When I saw the expression in his eyes alter, I knew that the penny had dropped. His demeanour and body language became less open, more guarded, and he shifted on his seat as if it had suddenly become uncomfortable.

'Well, anyway. Let's get down to business. Did you have a particular figure in mind?'

'Not really.'

'So you'd like me to make you an offer?'

'No.'

This really stumped him. I decided to put him out of his misery. 'The painting isn't for sale, Cyril.'

'Why not?'

'It just isn't Boland, Sharpe material.'

JUDI CURTIN

Sorry, Walter

PAN BOOKS

Cork school teacher, Maeve, is stuck in a rut. When she's not trying to keep six-year-olds from killing each other, her colleagues are boring her with tales of domestic bliss and the finer points of football. The only thing getting Maeve's love and attention is her garden.

All washed up at the age of thirty-four? Not our Maeve. Taking a giant leap of faith, she leaves her yellow wellies behind and heads across the pond to Canada. Under the clear blue skies of Vancouver, she realizes what it's like to live a little on the wild side. There's the edible Wes, with his blond hair and toothpaste smile, and there's someone else . . .

Sarah Webb

Something to Talk About

PAN BOOKS

Can men and women ever really be friends?

Lucy and Max have been best friends for ever. Lucy, a bored beautician with a Jamie Oliver obsession, is determined to find a girlfriend for kite-maker Max. Someone who will live up to her own high standards . . .

In the name of true love and with the help of Jamie's *Naked Chef*, Lucy decides to hold a meet Max dinner in order to find the right woman for him. And when Max seems to hit it off with her gorgeous friend Jenny, Lucy is convinced she's done just that. It seems food, wine and romance do go hand in hand after all.

But it's not long before easy-going Max is running scared of man-eater Jenny. He decides he'd much prefer to be out flying his power kites than falling into the dating pit again. However, fate works in mysterious ways . . .

A delightfully wicked romantic comedy – if you're a *When Harry Met Sally* fan, you'll love this book!

OTHER BOOKS

AVAILABLE FROM PAN MACMILLAN

JUDI CURTIN
SORRY WALTER
0 330 42635 4
£6.99

SARAH WEBB
SOMETHING TO TALK ABOUT
0 330 49328 0
£6.99

SHANE WATSON
THE ONE TO WATCH
0 330 41928 5
£6.99

MORAG PRUNTY
POISON ARROWS
0 330 42031 3
£6.99

All Pan Macmillan titles can be ordered from our website,
www.panmacmillan.com, or from your local bookshop
and are also available by post from:

Bookpost, PO Box 29, Douglas, Isle of Man IM99 1BQ
Credit cards accepted. For details:
Telephone: 01624 677237
Fax: 01624 670923
E-mail: bookshop@enterprise.net
www.bookpost.co.uk

Free postage and packing in the United Kingdom

Prices shown above were correct at the time of going to press.
Pan Macmillan reserve the right to show new retail prices on covers
which may differ from those previously advertised in the text
or elsewhere.